BODY BY THE DOCKS

Detectives investigate a baffling mystery

DIANE M. DICKSON

THE
BOOK
FOLKS

Published by The Book Folks

London, 2021

© Diane Dickson

ISBN 978-1-913516-83-3

www.thebookfolks.com

Body By The Docks is the second DI Jordan Carr murder mystery.
A list of all the author's titles can be found at the end of this book.

Prologue

The baby had been crying for over an hour. He was teething. His cheeks were bright red and every time Molly thought she'd soothed him, and his eyes began to close, something would disturb him. A door slamming nearby, noise in the street outside, cars or people just under the window, and off he'd go again. She was worn out, hadn't had a decent sleep for over a week. That lad next door was going to get a piece of her mind. Just when Jakey began to feel heavy in her arms, just as his little fingers started to uncurl and his breathing deepened and slowed, stupid Mike revved up the bloody bike and Jakey began screaming again.

Molly pulled the Thomas the Tank Engine curtains to one side and looked out of the window. It was still daylight and it was still warm. She smiled a little and shook her head. It wasn't fair to blame Mike. What would a teenager know about teething babies? Ha! She did though. She was probably less than a year older than him herself, but there, she'd made her bed and she would lie in it.

She jiggled her son gently in her arms. He was hot and sweaty. She took him down the narrow stairs and through the hall, intending to stand outside and maybe cool him down. The living room door was closed. "Mam, I'm going to stand in the front a bit. Mam. Mam."

There was no answer. She didn't go into the room. There would be a huff and a tut and the look that said she was failing.

Molly sighed. Her mother had been complaining about the baby. She'd been sulking a bit. "I've been through this already, four times. I brought you lot up and I didn't think to be doing it again." But Molly knew she didn't mean anything, she was happy having her and little Jakey staying there. She hadn't been well, that's what it was. Her heart trouble was playing up and they were all worrying about the diabetes. There was always something niggling away, making her worry.

She called through the door. "I'm sorry, Mam. I'll take him out in the pram for a bit, give you a break."

Mam's bag was on the hook by the door, she wouldn't have gone anywhere without it. The kitchen was tidy, the worktops wiped, all the pots put away and Jakey's high chair pushed back into the corner. "Mam," she called out again but there was still no response. Oh well, she'd pour her a glass of sherry later and they'd have a bit of a laugh.

Molly walked for an hour. Back and forth through the streets, there wasn't much to pass for countryside in this part of Liverpool. It didn't bother her, it was what she was used to, and she enjoyed it. There were still children playing out, people coming home from work and life to look at. Jakey lay back in his pram drooling over his plastic teething toy. Poor little thing. She'd put some gel on his gums when she got back and hope for the best. Maybe if he was still as bad next week she'd go and stay with their Sandra, give Mam a bit of peace. She had the appointment at the hospital on Monday, but Sandra was going with her, no point taking Jakey there.

The lights were still out when she arrived back at their house. There was a small shiver of unease inside. She hadn't checked her mother's bedroom before she went out. What if she was ill, what if… *no – she wouldn't think that.* By the time she had trundled the buggy into the silent hallway she felt a little panicked. Leaving the baby in the pram she ran up the stairs, stopped outside the bedroom door and took a breath. *It was okay, it was all okay.* She knocked once and walked in.

The room was tidy, everything as it should be. The flowered dressing gown was thrown across the bed, her nightie folded on the pillow. Molly snorted out a little laugh. She was a daft cow. She pulled the door closed behind her and went back downstairs. Jakey had fallen asleep now. She'd leave him where he was. They could have a little drink and watch the TV for a bit.

The television wasn't on, the lights were out, and the room was empty.

Chapter 1

Detective Inspector Jordan Carr stood up and flexed his legs. He'd been crouching over the grim remains too long. He rubbed at his thighs to ease the tension, pulled off the blue nitrile gloves and tucked them into his pocket and walked back along the safe route which had been marked out with stepping plates. The paper scene suit rustled as he moved, it'd be good to get it off. "That's nasty." He half turned to address Terry Denn who was following, and struggling to remove his own protective clothing.

"Very grim, boss. Going to be a horrible job trying to identify it."

"Yeah. That's probably the whole point of the burning. Well, part of the reason. I think plenty of people now believe it'll destroy evidence – prints obviously but DNA as well."

"That's a shame, given how much we rely on it."

"I don't think it's true though. From what I've read it can still be detected even after exposure to heat. Anyway, Phil Grant'll be able to tell us and you can bet if there's something there she'll find it."

They turned to look behind them to where the slender shape of the medical examiner could be seen as a moving shadow on the plastic walls of the crime scene tent.

"We know it was a woman," Jordan said, "from the unburned parts, I'd say she wasn't young. They weren't a young woman's shoes. The skirt was dark-coloured as well, what was left of it. It was long and pleated and just not fashionable."

"Unless it was someone cross-dressing or transgender," Terry muttered.

"It's always possible I suppose, and as with everything else we must keep it in mind. Okay, let's just say the unburned parts of the legs appeared to be a woman." Jordan stopped speaking and looked around at the backs of the houses and the debris scattered across the abandoned building site. "No point speculating too much right now, anyway. We'll find out when Dr Grant gets her back to the mortuary. For now, we'll just get on with the door knocking and have a word with the youngsters who found her."

"Two boys and a girl," Terry told him, "I reckon they were probably out here for a smoke. It's well known they use the old shed." He pointed to a dilapidated hut that was somehow managing to stay upright despite the loss of one wall and part of the roof. "The patrol guys said it's been a problem ever since the building company went bust. Why are kids always drawn to such grotty places?"

"Well, weren't you? I know I was. It's precisely because they're horrible – they assume no adults will come near. They're probably right most of the time. I don't reckon she's been here too long though. Maybe just today at the most, it's term time so the kids would be in school, college, whatever."

"Aye, the ones who weren't skiving off," Terry said.

"True. They're old enough for us to speak to them without an adult, unless things start looking dodgy. If there's any reason to suspect the witnesses didn't just come across the poor thing by chance, then we back off and go through the motions. Take them back to the station, contact the parents or a responsible adult and what have you. Where are they now?"

"They've taken them away, to wait outside the gates. Did try and persuade them into a car but they weren't having it, full of nonsense about being carted off."

"So, they're not too broken up about finding a part burned body, at night, in the middle of a field?" Jordan said.

"Apparently not, just a bit excited. They'd been taking pictures and the uniforms had a hell of a time stopping them uploading to social media. Might not have stopped them in time, to be honest, though they say not. Christ, fancy scrolling through TikTok or Twitter and seeing a picture of your mother or sister in that state."

Chapter 2

DCI Richard Cross had a polystyrene box on his desk. As Jordan stood across from him the stink of curry was nauseating; that and the smear of orange sauce across the senior detective's chin.

"I can come back later, sir," Jordan said.

"No, you're fine. I've been in meetings all day. All I've had are sandwiches and biscuits. Don't know when I'm supposed to get something proper to eat."

Jordan looked at the uniform jacket straining across his boss's belly and wondered if a couple of missed meals would actually be such a bad thing.

"So, what have you got?" Cross asked through a mouthful of chicken and rice.

"A part burned body. Found on an abandoned building site. Female, not young we don't think. No cause of death yet and no ID. We're going through the Misper list at the moment. She wasn't a kid so that might help to narrow it down a bit. It was fairly grim, the hair mostly gone, the eyes and lips. Upper torso, arms, hands pretty much destroyed – just blackened remains really. Cinders."

With a groan the DCI closed the top of the curry box and wiped his mouth with a little paper napkin.

"Bloody hell, Carr. I didn't need that right now."

"Sorry, sir." It was a struggle, but he managed to keep the grin at bay. "It's a suspicious death obviously. I've got DC Denn organising things. Operation Roedeer. We're sorting an incident room. I'd like some officers on the ground to do the house-to-house. It's quite a densely populated area so there's a chance someone will have seen something. The prospect they'll talk to us is less, but you never know. The crime scene itself is a small piece of land. Used to be part of a farm but it was sold off some years ago. Building was started and then the builders went bust."

"I'll see what I can do about troops for you. I can't promise much but we've got a couple of new recruits with us, it'll be a good exercise," said Cross.

"No experienced officers?"

"Probably not. You know the situation we're in. The government may have promised us more bobbies, but they can't be produced by magic. Anyway, it'll be good for you as well to take the new lads by the hand and show 'em how it's done."

"Yes, sir. Thank you, sir."

As he walked back down the corridor it was a fight to keep the frustration at bay. A suspicious death, a poor burned woman and he was offered new recruits doing on-the-job training. He knew they all had to start somewhere, and it was true it was throwing them in at the deep end, which was great. But just once he'd like to feel as though he wasn't being fobbed off by the boss. It was stupid, he had to convince himself it was nothing to do with him being an outsider, originally from London.

He had reached the incident room and swung in through the open door. A small dark-haired woman turned to greet him. "Hiya, boss."

"Rosalind. Brilliant, are you with me?"

"Seems so, if you want me."

"Yes, I want you. Of course, I want you. Are you fully fit now?"

"As a flea, sir, passed my medical last week."

And suddenly the world was a better place. Rosalind had been new earlier in the year, coming to him as an untried detective and when push had come to shove she had put her body on the line and together they'd triumphed. So, okay he had newcomers, but at least they weren't jaundiced and bitter. They'd be keen and fresh. He could work with that.

Terry Denn finished the notes he was entering on the whiteboards and joined them. "I wouldn't be too happy if I was you, Ros. You do know the weekend's a write-off. I was going to the match, have to sell the ticket now, I suppose. Were you planning anything, boss? Do you go? To Anfield?"

"No, never been. I'm not really into football," Jordan said. "I know you probably find that odd, but we just didn't. My dad used to take us to the cricket though. He loved his cricket. Anyway, it's a shame about the weekend. My grandmother, Nana Gloria, is coming up from London. She wants to see the house and spend a bit of time with Harry. She hasn't seen him for ages. Penny's been cleaning and scrubbing and all that, but it was supposed to be down to me to do the cooking."

"You do that?" Terry said. "I can manage to heat up a tin of soup and that's about it."

"Well, yes, it's something I do, and she'll be expecting it. Tomorrow is okay, I'm doing Jamaican oxtail stew. But that's been all day already, in the slow cooker."

"Bloody hell – hidden talents or what?"

"I learned to cook after my dad died. Mum taught me recipes from home, didn't want us eating junk anymore. It was nice to have some of her attention all to myself to be honest. With two sisters and two brothers we had to fight for our rights." He laughed. "Okay it wasn't quite like that but one-on-one time with her in the kitchen was better than knocking about in the street or arguing with the others about what crap to watch on the TV. I'll cook you something one of these days. I know – when your sergeant's promotion comes through. We'll have a get-together with some of the others. Would you be up for that DC Searle?

"Yeah, you're on. Shame about your weekend though," Rosalind Searle said.

"It is. I miss the family and Nana Gloria sort of saved me from myself when I was a kid. I was going off-piste a bit, running with the wrong crowd, and she sorted me out, brought me back onto the straight and narrow. Her and my mum. We don't get back very often these days, but I guess it can't be helped and this poor woman's family will never be able to spend time with her again so, we should just count our blessings and prioritise this. We've got more weekends to look forward to, she hasn't."

Chapter 3

By now everyone in the area was fully aware of what was going on. Children on bikes, gangs of youths, phone cameras flashing, and a few old men leaning on the creaky fence in the fading light watching the action. Not that they could see much, everything was hidden by the plastic tent. But the word was out, and nobody wanted to miss the departure of the coroner's van.

Jordan was surrounded by a small group of uniformed policemen. It was true most of them were young. There were a couple of PCSOs but there were also a couple of older officers hovering around the edges of the group, hoping to avoid being singled out for anything too strenuous. A bit of overtime was welcome, especially if the other option was an empty house or a stool at the pub staring into your glass and wondering where the time had gone.

"I've printed out a list of questions for those of you who haven't done this before. You can either use it as a guide or, if it's easier, just hand it over and ask them to read it. You might not always get it back though, so I've done a couple for each of you. We need to know if anybody saw this woman, alone or with someone else. Any odd activity on the field, any strange vehicles parked up. It's all in there. Make notes with names and addresses and so on."

They left the troops to get on with it. It was late and they felt not much would be accomplished but Jordan needed to know everything was set up ready for an early start the following day, plus they would at least catch the residents who were usually out at work. In the incident room, the desks were already equipped with electronics and landlines. There was a whiteboard for images and notes, and a screen. They would have some clerical assistants allocated in due course. It was frustrating when he just wanted to get going but he had done all he could for the time being.

He had his coffee machine. Terry had grinned and given him a thumbs up when he saw it. The other option, a machine in the corridor, dispensed brown liquid that nobody was able to name no matter which buttons were pressed, except for the soup because it had lumps in it. "I'm getting one of them for home. Your fault – I didn't mind the stuff out of the machine or instant until you brought that thing in."

"Oh well, there's hope for you yet." Jordan grinned. "We'll start as we mean to go on this time. Before you go, put a call in to the mortuary will you, ask them to make sure we're informed when they schedule the examination. I'll go with Rosalind. You can handle things here, yeah?"

"No probs, boss. We've had nothing show up on the missing persons list yet. We're not going to be able to do much in the way of appeals or anything with this one. Not with her all crispy like that."

Jordan winced, but he didn't correct the black humour. It was the way some people handled the grimmer side of the job. Terry was a bit free with his mouth and he had to learn to curb his thoughtless comments but now wasn't the time to get into that.

"Surely if your mother or your gran went missing, you'd have the alarm sounded pretty quickly. It's possible she's wandered off from a care home or hospital so that's something we need to double-check. Get in touch with the missing persons section first thing. Of course, we have to keep in mind she could have been on her own somewhere. You know, some poor old soul with nobody to miss her. Then there's the burning, there has to be a reason for that, surely not just some random act."

"I hope not but it's not impossible. A mugging gone wrong and someone trying to cover their tracks. Jesus, that's grim," Terry said.

"Talking about muggings, how is your mum now, after her run-in with a thug?"

"Ah she's fine. Just shrugged it off really. She doesn't even talk about it now, just something that happened. I've bought her a personal alarm. She's supposed to wear it around her neck. She was less than pleased, accused me of treating her like a kid or some old one. She did take it with her, mind, last time she went out on her own at night, so that's something."

"Well, you can only do your best. Anyway, early start tomorrow, get the team organised and so on."

"Boss, we won't have that Beverly woman this time, will we?" Terry screwed up his face remembering one of the clerical team from their last big case. "I mean, she was okay but talk about obsessive. Do you remember?"

"I do. Colour-coding all the files, notice board with a legend, oh and flags. Yeah, different coloured flags on the emails. Well, I hope not, I don't think we parted the best of friends, did we?"

"No, she was pretty, erm – sensitive, wasn't she?" Jordan dragged his jacket from the back of the chair. "Right, that's it I reckon. "

"Have you got time for a quick one, boss?" Terry Denn asked.

"No, I think it's best I get off home. We could be in for some long days and I want to see Harry before he goes to bed. See you in the morning, unless anything happens before then, of course."

Chapter 4

Molly ran down the stairs. The hammering on the door would wake little Jakey and she'd just got him off. As she passed the hook on the wall she reached out and touched the handbag. It had quickly become a habit. It was turning into some sort of religious observance. While it was there she knew her mother would be coming back. It was just waiting for her, her bus pass, her purse, and her rain hood inside, all just ready to carry on as normal. Tears started to her eyes as she looked at the brown leather, the rubbed part of the handles worn away by constant use. It was still hard to believe she'd gone anywhere without it. She must have been really upset. She was missing her, she needed her there telling her what to do, helping. They usually got on well and this was horrible.

She dragged open the door.

"Cut the noise, Gary, what the hell are you doing? The baby's in bed." As she shouted at her brother, she pulled her long hair back and secured it with an elastic scrunchy.

Gary made no attempt to come into the house. His face was flushed, sweat had popped out on his forehead and he gasped as he tried to speak. "I need to speak to

Mam, is she okay? I want to talk to her. I know I'm being daft, but I just want to see her."

"But is she not with you? I thought she was at yours. She was in a strop and I reckoned she was staying with you. I was miffed with her because it's not my fault. He's teething. She knows what it's like."

"There's a woman. They said it's a woman. Up on the spare ground, the building site."

Already Molly was reaching for her coat. "Is it Mam? Is she alright? Why is she up on the building site? Just a minute, let me get the baby."

Before her brother had time to respond she had turned and was thundering up the stairs grabbing Jakey's snow suit as she went.

When she came out of the bedroom Gary was on the landing. "Hang on, I don't think you should go. Just wait," he said.

"Get out of the way, Gary, of course we have to go. Don't be stupid. Come on. Is she sick, did they say? Maybe she's confused. Christ, she could have that Alzheimer's or maybe she's had a stroke." She tried to push past her brother, jiggle the fractious baby against her hip, and slide her arms into her own jacket. "Shit. Here." She thrust the baby at Gary, but he pulled away.

"No, wait. Chrissake, listen. It's a body."

For an endless moment there was a lull, the clock in Mam's bedroom, the old one that had been in the Irish farmhouse all those years ago, was loud in their ears. Even the baby had quieted. It didn't last long.

"What are you saying?" Molly spoke softly, just above a whisper, shock and fear suppressing her voice. She stepped backwards and Gary had to reach out and grab at her jacket to save her and the baby from the stairs.

"It's a body. A woman they're saying. Dead."

"Aw, Jesus. No, Gary, don't." A floodgate opened. Tears flowed down Molly's cheeks. "Aw no. Did you see, Gary, did you see? Maybe it was just some other old woman, maybe it wasn't a woman at all. It could be a dummy, or a scarecrow or, or…"

"I don't know, Molls. All I know is there are bizzies everywhere and a crowd of people and one of them tent things. I asked Davo and he said Chip and Kelly had found a body."

She was shaking her head now. "It's not Mam, I'm sure it's not. If it had been Mam I'd have known already. She always said I had the sight. You know I do. I see things. No, if it had been Mam I'd have known. We should go though. I've got the baby up now and we should find out what's going on."

"I don't think you should. What if you're wrong? What if it is her? We can't be there if it is."

"Well, why did you come then? Why did you come here getting me all upset? Course we have to go. Come on." She thundered down the stairs and out of the front door, flicking open the stroller as she staggered down the short path and out into the street.

Chapter 5

Jordan couldn't sleep; the things he had to do in the morning were churning in his brain. He'd started his book but there was so little to put into it. In the end he slid out from under the duvet and dressed in the bathroom. He went into Harry's room and stood for a moment, watching his son sleeping.

Was it really possible this woman had been so alone that nobody had missed her? With youngsters it happened, they ran away, it had always been that way. But surely a mature woman had someone to miss her. If she'd been a bag lady, a street sleeper, then that would be one thing, but it wasn't the way the evidence pointed. What was left of her after the burning had been the body of an ordinary woman. The shoes weren't worn and tatty, they fitted her feet. More importantly there had been a ring, a simple gold ring on the remains of the woman's wedding finger. No way would a rough sleeper wear jewellery so obviously, in the unlikely event they had any in the first place.

He thought of his own granny. Nana Gloria. She was surrounded by people who loved her. His big extended family down in London never left her alone. If she had so much as a cold, they swarmed around her making sure she was taken care of. So, why were the police not aware of a missing elderly lady. Even if she was from outside the area it would have been in the national reports. He went into the kitchen and switched on the kettle. While the water heated, he booted up his laptop and went through the notices for the last couple of days. No alert about a missing woman in the Liverpool area. He checked the force Facebook pages, nothing. He typed in '*missing woman – Merseyside*'. There were reports. There were a couple of older pleas. *Help me find my mum. My granny is confused and we haven't seen her for three hours* – all that sort of thing but they were old. Mostly they had been solved, one way or the other. It was odd. The other option was that she hadn't been missed yet. They would need to put something on the system. The front desk officers had to be alerted because they couldn't send concerned relatives away telling them to wait a while longer. Those manning the phones had to take details and pass them on. They couldn't miss this, if they did there'd be hell to pay. The newspapers would tear them to pieces and the internet would be unforgiving.

He drove out to Wavertree, down dark streets. It was drizzling with rain and his headlights reflected in the wet tarmac. There was just the swish of his tyres through the standing water. He parked beside the deserted building site. The hubbub of earlier had dispersed now and there were just two uniformed constables trying to find some shelter under a feeble, struggling tree. The tent was still in the field but there was no light inside, no movement. He flashed his warrant card. "Has the body been moved?"

"Yes, sir. About two hours ago. Crime scene manager reckons there's no point trying to do any more now, the SOCO team'll be back in the morning, early doors."

"Nothing unusual going on? Nobody loitering, no cars hanging about?" Jordan asked.

The officer shook his head. "Nah. Once the body had been moved everyone lost interest. A few punters hung about a while jangling, but they'd gone by the time it got properly dark."

"Were you here then?"

"Aye, me and my mucker." He pointed to the other man who made a casual salute and then went back to studying his feet, keeping the rain out of his eyes.

It was a miserable shift and Jordan felt sorry for them, but it was part of the job and there was nothing to be done about it.

"Nothing seemed off to you? Nobody asking questions?" he said.

"Nothing particular. Some people were more upset about it than others. Especially the older ones. Some of the youngsters were a bit – inappropriate, shall we say. We had a job stopping them taking pictures. But otherwise, no. They just hung about and then drifted away when the excitement was over."

"They get my goat." This from the other bobby who had wandered over to join them. "I mean, they bring their kids, they stand around for ages. What are they hoping to see? They can't do anything, it's just sick really. Like public hangings – that's what it feels like. Then they pretend to get all upset. One of them skriking and carrying on, had to be taken away by her fella. Stupid bint. If it's so upsetting, she should have stayed at home."

"Human nature, I guess. You don't know who it was, I don't suppose? She didn't speak to you?" Jordan said.

"No, just some rubbernecker with a kid in a pram."

"Okay. Anyway, thanks, guys. I know this isn't a nice job but if anything seems off, you will be sure to let us know, won't you?"

"For sure. I could do with a couple of extra hours, sir. Any chance I could help with the house-to-house later?"

"Yeah, have a word with the sergeant, tell him I'll clear it. Constable…?"

"Howarth, sir."

"Get your name on the rota, Constable."

The dashboard clock was showing half past four. Jordan headed for the office. There might not be much he could do but just being at his desk would make him feel better.

He'd only been there a short while when he heard footsteps outside. Terry Denn swung in through the door. He'd brought milk and a couple of sausage rolls, still warm, from the supermarket down the road. The day had started.

Chapter 6

Terry didn't say anything when Beverly Powell walked into the incident room along with two other civilian assistants. But Jordan caught the raised eyebrows and the way he closed his eyes for a couple of seconds and covered his face with his hands. He knew he'd been meant to see but didn't acknowledge the overreaction. Yes, she was what Terry called '*tightarsed*'. She was finicky and obsessive, but she got the job done. The bigger problem as far as he was concerned was she found it hard to work as part of a team. It had become a bit of a joke last time that she had a crush on him. She was rather prone to appearing at his desk with a slice of cake she'd brought in from home, a bag of mixed nuts, when she found out that was his favourite snack, a cup of coffee as soon as he came back into the office. Teacher's pet, Terry called her, and it made Jordan uncomfortable, and he knew it affected the way he interacted with her. The danger, however, was that she held information to herself so that she could be the one to tell him.

Oh well, it appeared she was with them again and he'd handle it better this time. He'd be more careful how he spoke to her, keep in mind she could be easily offended, make sure she felt included. He didn't need this. He needed to be able to concentrate on his poor dead victim not mollycoddling adults who should know better. He could, of course, say he didn't want her on his team. If he did, he would probably never find a civilian assistant willing to help him again. His paperwork would be delayed, his internet searches would somehow be lost or forgotten, endless disruptions. No, Beverly was here again. So be it. He took a breath, walked to the whiteboard which naturally became the default place from which to address the room, like a teacher. She was gazing at him, a small smile on her face and when he glanced towards her, she blushed. *Great.*

"Okay. The images are disturbing, but we keep them on the board. It'll remind us just what we're working for. I'm going to the post-mortem examination later but what we think at the moment is that this is an elderly woman, white, a suspicious death obviously. That's it right now for facts, that's about all of it. As you can see someone has tried to burn her body. There are a couple of reasons they might do that. To send a message, a warning. But we see it more often with gangs, and with a woman her age – well, we have to keep an open mind, but it doesn't feel right. As far as it goes, we are not aware of any other incidents of this nature recently in this area, but someone needs to get into the HOLMES system and look for reports of burned bodies. Terry, could you do that as a matter of priority while we are out this morning? The other reason is pretty obvious, and probably more likely. To cover up what has been done to the poor woman and obliterate evidence. We'll have to wait for Dr Grant to tell us just how successful that has been. I want you to bear this in mind while you're knocking at doors and reviewing responses. Beverly, could you make sure all the reports are collated as soon as they come in. I remember you were really good at that?" He was doing it already, wasn't he? Treating her differently. She nodded at him and beamed at the others around the room. Terry was doing the eyebrow thing.

"Why are you so convinced it's an elderly victim, boss? I heard she was pretty much unrecognisable." This from the rain-soaked constable he'd spoken to earlier, in the dark.

"Well, Constable Howarth, I don't know if you had a look?"

There was just a short shake of the head in response.

"Understandable," Jordan acknowledged. "As you can see from the images, we only have the lower body to go on from at the scene, the top was too badly damaged for much examination out there. I'm thinking they are an older woman's shoes. Clunky and fastened with Velcro, plain, really a bit ugly. Not what you expect a younger person to wear. Also, there is what's left of the clothes. The skirt just says elderly to me and the tights. I know they are grubby and ruined but you can see they have been a tan colour. Not that I'm an expert but again they say mature female. The ankles are thickened, which is something age can do. Then there is the ring on the wedding finger." He pointed to a close-up of the piece of jewellery. "It looks worn, the top is flattened as though it has rubbed against another ring for many years. Possibly an engagement ring. All this is hardly more than supposition at this point, but we'll know more by this afternoon. I am pretty convinced, though, at this time. Right, that's all I've got for now. Organise yourselves with desks, those who'll need them. The computers are all up and running and the internet connections have been tested while you were all snoring in your beds. The rest of you, get out there and find me some witnesses. Ros, you're with me. I'll meet you outside as soon as you're ready. We'll take my car."

They knew it would be unpleasant and Rosalind Searle, who hadn't seen the body yet, gave a quiet gasp when the bag was unzipped, and the corpse exposed. "God, that's nasty isn't it?" she muttered. "I'm glad they've got a viewing room here. Do you think it smells – you know – cooked?"

Jordan didn't answer, he didn't want to go there.

The burning to the upper body was very extensive but what was left was treated with the respect Phil Grant always showed to her '*patients*'. Her voice was calm and quiet as she recorded her findings. The little gold ring clattered slightly as it was placed in a plastic bowl.

* * *

"So." Phil Grant had changed her clothes and brought a cup of coffee with her to the office. "You watched, I suppose?"

Jordan nodded.

"You were right in your assumptions. She's an older lady. I'd say well into her sixties, possibly even older. I'm being cautious because of the damage to the body. I've sent off blood and samples for DNA. It'll help with identification if you need it, but you know it takes a while, so I hope you find out who she is sooner than that."

"I didn't think you'd be able to get blood, with her being burned," Rosalind said.

"Oh, you'd be surprised. I was able to get urine as well. The lower part of the body wasn't too badly damaged at all. It takes a lot of heat to burn a body, and time, neither of which seem to have been available. Anyway, things I can tell you right now: She was dead before the body was burned. There was no smoke damage to the lungs or trachea and the position of the limbs are strongly suggestive of that. Thank goodness, the alternative doesn't bear thinking about. The fire didn't destroy all the body, in fact in real terms it didn't destroy all that much. There was some evidence of heart disease and she was rather overweight. You already know from the fire officer's report that an accelerant was used, so the burning was definitely deliberate. However, I imagine they knew that they were never going to be able to generate enough heat to destroy the body completely, so what was their intention? Maybe they were disturbed, maybe they were sickened by what they were doing. Fortunately for me, that's your job, Jordie."

Rosalind registered the use of Jordan's nickname, glanced at him and back at the medical examiner. She shrugged off any idea they might be more than friends. It was well known the boss was happily married and besotted with his little son.

Jordan nodded. "Well, at least we can rule out suicide – self-immolation. Any idea about cause of death then, if it wasn't the fire?"

"I need to consult an expert. I know someone at the University. I couldn't find any evidence of wounds from a sharp object and again, you'd be surprised just how obvious they can be, even in a burn victim. There's no suggestion of shooting. Poisoning, well – we'll have to wait for the toxicology reports. However, the hyoid bone was fractured."

"Strangulation then?" Jordan said.

"The burning complicates things. Bones fracture in the heat, so just to be sure it's pre-mortem other than just a result of the burning I'm going to confer. Mind, I'll be very surprised if I'm wrong. I'm taking the head and neck to a colleague this afternoon and I'll let you know as soon as possible what he thinks. I'm sorry, Jordan, Ros, this is going to be a hard one to pin down. You've got your work cut out."

"Well, I reckon the first thing is to identify her, so we'll concentrate most of our effort on that for the time being. Thanks, Phil, I'll wait for your call when you've spoken to your bone expert."

"Oh yes, just before you go," Dr Grant called after them. "We do have partial dentures, damaged of course but they may be of some help."

"Brilliant, can you send pictures?"

"They're on the way, and I'll ask the lab to let you have casts as soon as somebody has a chance to make them. Shame it's not more usual to have them marked here in the UK, in some other countries the answer would be right there. Ah well."

They headed back to the car. It was turning into a clear bright day after the damp start. The leaves on the few trees around the car park were new and bright, birds were noisy and excited by the sunshine. The contrast between inside and outside was stark. Jordan called home and had a quick word with his wife before she left for work and listened while Harry babbled at the phone. Sometimes this job tore at your soul. His extended family assumed he was hard, that the work didn't bother him, but they had no idea. Only Penny knew. Well, Penny and Nana Gloria.

Chapter 7

'Molly, Molly. Really, stop crying. You're upsetting the baby." Gary sat on the settee jiggling little Jakey on his lap.

Molly rocked back and forth, back and forth. The tissue clutched in her hand was shredded, leaving tiny pieces on her dark trousers. They hadn't slept, she looked haggard and ill. There were dark rings under her eyes, like bruises against the pallor of her skin. She had sat in the lounge all night hugging Mam's blanket around her. Gary had stayed up with her as long as he could and then gone to lie on the bed in the spare bedroom. After a couple of hours, he'd given up, clattered back down the stairs and spent the rest of the night with his sister, hunched in front of the electric fire, listening to the clock ticking, and the sound of cars passing in the road outside.

Jakey woke early and she brought him down and fed him. He picked up on the mood and became fractious and difficult. Gary didn't know why people still had kids. They were always demanding, always a pain just when you had to think about other things. Molly could have got rid of this one. His dad was long gone, and she said she never wanted to be with him long term anyway. She wouldn't even tell them for sure who it was. So, why lumber yourself with a kid? She was too young. She was lovely, had always been slender and slight, fit-looking. Now she was beginning to get her figure back, but he thought she'd lost something of her beauty, her carefree spirit. He looked at Jacob, all red-faced and snotty. If it wasn't for the desperation in his sister's eyes, he'd just go home. His flat was quiet – he'd be able to think.

"Why aren't you doing anything? God, Gary, it's Mam. She dead, Mam's dead and burned up on the field and you won't do anything." As she spoke the hysteria grew and the baby joined in the howling. There was a thud on the wall, the old woman next door making her thoughts felt about the cacophony.

"We don't know, Molly. Nobody knows."

"I do, I do – I know. It's Mam. A blue skirt with little flowers on, that's what Davo said. Black shoes, he said. Oh it's Mam, I know it is."

Gary wanted to reassure her, he wanted to tell her that they had to wait and see. He couldn't do it. Although he was trying to keep control, to be the strong one, he was sick inside. He was almost certain she was right. He knew the clothes. Mam only wore a few different outfits, a black skirt and jacket for church, a pair of trousers for when it was really cold and she had to go up the hospital, and her blue skirt with rosebuds all over it. The rest of the time she wore her dressing gown or some nasty tracksuit bottoms with sloppy tops. She didn't go out in them, they were scruffy and poor-looking. They'd talked about it, him and Molly, he'd told her all about the stylish woman she had been when they were little. She'd always been well turned out, quite glamourous really. His sister didn't remember her like that. Mary had already been into her forties when the surprise of a baby had shocked them all. His dad had been coy about what that meant but thrilled. Having a child to look after had kept Mary young for a while, mixing with the other mothers at the school had been good for her. But once Dada died the years of worry and the loss of the strong right arm had turned her, seemingly overnight, into the dowdy woman she had become. Ill health and boredom had finished the job. Making her old before her time. Her children had grown up and didn't need her anymore. She put on weight and stopped caring about her appearance. She'd lost interest in a lot of stuff. She still enjoyed the grandkids and the odd Sunday lunch at the pub. But really, she just sat in her chair, watched the programmes on the television and let them all go on with their lives around her. Lately the only trips had been to the hospital or the blood clinic. It was pretty miserable, but she told them she was fine. She played with little Jakey and still enjoyed her dinner and a few drinks on the occasional nights when they'd all come round.

Thinking about her, about the family, was a step too far and Gary let the sadness and the fear overwhelm him. He lowered his head and snuggled it into the baby's shoulder. He was warm and smelled the way only babies could, an odd mixture of milk and powder and something sour. He didn't cry, not like Molly, still roaring beside him, but he let the emotion have its way just for a minute or two.

He straightened, lifted his head and turned to place the baby on his sister's lap. "Take your baby, Molly. I'm going to ring our Eddie."

At the mention of their older brother Molly stopped crying. She gulped back sobs and reached out for her son. "Eddie?"

"Aye. I have to tell him."

"So, you do think it's her, don't you?"

"I think it might well be. We don't know for sure but I'm sorry, Molls. Yeah, that's why I won't do anything, do you see? No point until we know for sure. I need to phone Eddie. Then I suppose we should call Sandra, just to sort of prepare her."

"How will we find out? Davo said she was burned up. The woman in the field, burned up so you couldn't tell who it was. So, how will we find out?" Molly wound the disintegrating tissue round and round in her hands, dabbing at her eyes and nose with the tiny piece of soggy paper. She juggled Jakey up and down on her lap and he settled now, sucking his thumb, and gazing up at his mother.

"I don't know. I don't think we should do anything. Not until I've talked to Eddie. He'll know what we should do. He might know somebody who can help us. He'll have contacts."

"Can't we just ring the bizzies? Ring the station or Crimestoppers or something – can't we do something? I need to know, Gary. I need to know for sure."

He was shaking his head before she finished speaking. "No, we can't. Best to wait and see what Eddie says. It might not be her." Gary didn't believe it and knew Molly didn't either, but he felt it was his job now to calm her down, to take control. At least until his big brother told them what they should do.

"I'll put the kettle on, Molls, then I'll ring Eddie." He left her sobbing quietly as she rocked the baby who was drifting off to sleep now his mother had him. He walked through to the back kitchen and filled the kettle. As he turned, he saw Mam's pinnie on the back of the chair. He picked it up and held it to his face. It smelled of bacon fat and there was the hint of cigarette smoke. She wasn't supposed to smoke but they all knew she did. It hit him like a knife to the belly. His Mam was gone.

Chapter 8

"Did you talk to him, did you reach Eddie?"

Molly had put Jakey in his play pen where he lay on the floor chewing at a soft toy. She stood in the kitchen doorway watching Gary brewing tea and cutting bread for toast. She wouldn't be able to eat anything, but it was giving her brother a job.

"I left a message. It went straight to voice mail. I just asked him to ring back – soon as. No point trying to explain. I'll call Sandra. I've been trying to pluck up the courage, to be honest. She'll fall apart. She'll want to come."

"Course she will. I'll go and make the bed in the back room. Tell her not to bring the kids though, eh. Brian'll have to step up and look after them. We can't do with kids around just now. Gary?"

"Yeah."

"I was looking out of the window while I was putting Jakey down. The police are up the street. They're knocking on the doors. All the doors. They're going to come here, won't be long. What are we going to do? Can we ask them if they know who it is? Who they've found? What are we going to tell them – about Mam?"

"Okay. Look, let me do it. When they come. I'll do it."

"Won't they want to speak to us both, you know, everyone in the house?"

"They might. I can tell them you're in bed. Why don't you go up and get into your nightie?"

"No. I'm not doing that. I have to be here. I want to talk to them." She started to cry again.

"Oh, hell. Okay, but look, be careful. Don't say too much."

They waited, standing in the kitchen, sipping at the tea neither of them wanted. The toast sat cooling and unnoticed in the toaster. They heard the quiet rattle of the gate, the knock on the door. Gary put down his mug and walked along the hallway. He made a point of looking closely at the warrant card as soon as he opened the door. "What do you want?"

"We're investigating a serious incident in the neighbourhood. I just have a few questions, sir. Is that alright?"

"I don't know anything. I don't live here." As he spoke, Gary realised he'd made the wrong start. "Not all the time, anyway. My sister lives here, with her baby. I'm visiting." He needed to stop. His nerves were making him gabble. He'd just told Molly to be careful and here he was, his bloody mouth running away with him. He dug his nails into the palms of his hands, sniffed and moved half a step backwards into the hallway and reached out to push the door closed. He didn't think for a moment that he would get away with it, but it was worth trying.

"Right. So, how long have you been here, visiting?" The bobby was ticking off questions on a piece of paper. If he just answered what he was asked it could be okay.

"Just this morning. Just a quick call. I'm about to go."

"Could I speak to your sister?"

"Well, she's still in bed."

The policeman glanced at his watch. "Nearly ten o'clock. Bit late, is she okay?"

"None of your bloody business, but yes, she's okay. She's tired, got a baby and he's teething."

"Does she live here on her own with the baby?"

"Yes."

"No partner then?"

"Yeah, and that's some more 'none of your business'. Look, we've been nowhere and seen nothing, so if that's everything."

You had to give it to Molly, she had perfect timing. She chose just that moment, just as he was closing the door in the rozzer's face to appear in the hallway. The policeman didn't actually put his foot in the door, but he moved inwards so it couldn't be closed without hitting him. He leaned forwards around where Gary stood to speak again.

"Could I have a word, love? Just a quick couple of questions, then I'll leave you to go back to bed."

Molly glanced at the clock on the wall, back at the two men who were watching her. Gary gave one short shake of his head, and pursed his lips.

"Okay. What do you want?"

The policeman went through the start of his spiel again. Gary had no idea how much his sister had heard. This could all go very wrong, right here, right at the start and who knew where it would lead. The tea soured in his stomach and he had to swallow back the bile.

"I haven't seen anything. I haven't been anywhere. The baby's not well." She was doing okay. Gary held his tongue.

"Didn't I see you up at the spare ground later on last evening. You with a baby in a push chair?"

"No. I've not been out."

"You live here on your own?"

"I said," Gary interrupted.

"That your coat is it?" The policeman pointed to the hat stand, Mam's raincoat, obviously far too big for the young woman.

"No." Molly tossed her head slightly as she answered, lifted her chin. "It's my mam's."

Oh shit.

"So, could I have a word with her?" He was scribbling now on the sheet of paper.

"No. You can't – she's dead."

Gary couldn't breathe, his throat had dried. *Shit, Molly, what are you doing?*

"I'm sorry for your loss."

When did people start saying that? It sounded so fake, so false, like an American TV programme? Gary opened his mouth to tell the copper to bugger off, it might not work but he had to do something.

"Not long ago. That's why I can't move her things. It's too soon." Molly began to cry. It was obviously easy for her. She let go all the tension of the last few hours in the loud sobbing, the flood of tears. The young bobby looked away and coughed, embarrassed and awkward.

"Okay. Look, if you think of anything you've seen lately, anything odd – cars loitering, anyone hanging about – can you just let us know? I'll leave this with you, the number is on the top." He thrust the A4 sheet into Gary's hands and turned to stride back down the short path.

"Shit, Molly, I thought you'd dropped us in it there, but you were brilliant." Gary pulled her into his arms and hugged her, let her cry, the tears soaking his hoody.

Chapter 9

Jordan drove back to the scene, but the crime scene manager was adamant he couldn't enter the field. "I don't want anybody else tramping around. Sorry, Jordan, I know this is frustrating, but you have to let me finish. This sort of locus is always problematic. Give me a nice domestic setting every time."

"I know, Doug, and I understand but I'm kicking my heels a bit. We don't know who she is yet, we don't know where she's from – nothing."

"I really don't think you'll get anything much from here. The grass isn't even scorched. You'll have my report as soon as possible, but I can say pretty conclusively she was killed and burnt somewhere else and then just dumped in this place, poor old biddy. Whoever did it must have had something to carry the body, a tarp maybe, a blanket, a piece of wood. There are marks near the gate that could have been caused by something being dragged. We haven't found anything yet to tell us what it was, I'm afraid. We've looked for footprints, but the place is used by teenagers for" – he shrugged – "teenage stuff. It's a favourite with dog walkers and even people on off-road bikes. You can see there's fly-tipping and all of those bags will have to be searched. As I say, this sort of scene is difficult. Have you found nothing on CCTV?"

"There're no cameras here. There were when the site was active, but the builders took those away. So, for us at the moment, she turned up out of nowhere. We could have film of her being transported from pretty much anywhere in the country and we wouldn't know. I can't have people just viewing videos with no clear idea of what they're looking for, it's not a good use of manpower. I'm hoping the house-to-house will turn up something – a strange van or a car parked up or whatever – but, well, you know the problems with that. Nobody ever sees anything. There has to be a reason for her being left here, surely. It's not handy for the motorway, nothing like that. Someone had to come here pretty deliberately, so why? How has it been here for rubberneckers?"

"Oh, just as you'd imagine. Kids with cameras, a few bored old boys. Nobody who made my hackles tingle. To be honest, there's not much for anyone to see, just the team walking about picking up fag ends and litter. One of those shrines has been set up by the gate."

"Yeah, I saw it. Flowers, candles, a couple of soft toys. Weird when nobody knows who she was."

"The local paper was round earlier taking pictures."

"Right. I'll give them a call, ask for copies. It's surprising sometimes what you pick up in the background."

"Frankly, interest is already waning. There not enough going on to entertain the masses," Doug Crawley said.

"I'll leave you to get on with it. I'll be available if anything crops up. I'll have a word with the lads by the entrance, see if they've noticed anyone hanging around," Jordan said.

It was getting late and he might as well go home. He could do his book and review the little information they had. After that he could have a beer, play with Harry for a while, give him his bath. Phil Grant rang as he was driving back to Crosby with confirmation that the cause of death had been strangulation. "You should have the casts and images of the dentures by now, Jordan. I hope it'll be of help. They were sent over about an hour ago."

He called Terry Denn. "You've got the dental stuff from the mortuary?"

"Yeah. They're sitting grinning at me right now."

"Okay, so contact all the local dentists as soon as possible. With a bit of luck, we'll catch them before they finish for the weekend. If there's nothing from this area, we'll have to go national."

"Already on it, boss."

"Good man."

He headed for home. Tomorrow would be better. It had to be. He was getting nowhere fast.

* * *

The incident room was still dark when Jordan arrived next morning. He fired up the coffee machine and was hit by a craving for a bacon sandwich. He shouldn't, and it made a mockery of the healthy muesli and fruit he'd shared at home with Penny, but it wouldn't be ignored. Just once, it wouldn't matter, surely. He ran his hand round the waistband of his trousers. His dad had died while he was still at school and although he remembered him, it was in short snatches. Christmas Day sitting with the other men, laughing and having a few drinks, or at a wedding, singing in the church. He had a lovely rich singing voice. There had been so many weddings back then. The family had never gone away on holiday, it was too expensive for all of them, but his dad hadn't stayed round the house much when he wasn't working at the market. Jordan didn't know where he'd gone except some of it was the dog racing, some of it was the bookies. The gambling hadn't been a big problem, but it kept him away from the family.

What he did remember, though, was his dad's belly, carried before him, straining at his belt, and popping open shirt buttons. It was the belly fat that had killed him. A massive heart attack, out of the blue. One day he was there, the next gone and his devastated mother berating herself for the diet she had fed them. The pastries, the curries, dumplings and Jamaican patties. Stuff to remind him of home and the sunshine. It was all delicious but after his father died there were more vegetables, more salads, lots of fish and much more thought about health. She made them go outside, play football, and she went to aerobics herself. It had done the trick and they were all fitter. The time she and her eldest son spent together in the kitchen had strengthened the bond between them. But they had still lost the head of the household. It was an irreplaceable loss and he didn't want to inflict that on his little family. Still, today he wanted the bacon. He'd have salad for lunch – or skip it altogether. The smell of breakfast as he approached the canteen had him salivating and the treat lifted his spirits. He'd take it back to the office. If he worked while he ate, he might not feel so guilty.

"Morning, sir." The voice came from behind him in the queue.

"Constable Howarth. Do you live here?" Jordan grinned.

"Shift change. I'm on days for a bit now. Sir, can I just ask – I wouldn't mind doing a bit extra, helping with your murder? If you could swing it. I've applied for detective training. It's what I really want, and I've done three years in uniform. I could do some time voluntarily if necessary. I'd just appreciate the experience, working with you, sir."

"Let me speak to the DCI, I think we should be able to arrange something. It's good you're keen."

"What did you think about the girl?"

"Sorry?"

"The one I mentioned in my doorstep enquiry report. She's been on my mind a bit. There was something off there. She was lying about not being at the scene. I mentioned her at the time. She was the one crying and carrying on."

"Sorry, I don't know which girl you're referring to."

"Oh, right. I gave the report to your civilian clerk. Ms Powell, is it? I asked her to make sure you were aware."

"When was this?"

"Yesterday about lunch time. Just before I went off duty."

"Right. Well, look, leave it with me and if I need to get back to you, I will."

In the incident room things were much livelier. Jordan logged on to his computer, searched the reports. There were none of the house-to-house enquiries transcribed.

"Bev. Have you got the doorstep reports for me?"

"I'm collating them now, sir. Shouldn't be long."

"Was there one from Constable Howarth, one he thought should be highlighted?"

"Oh yes. I had a look. I didn't think it was urgent, I've put it with the 'could be interesting' pile, the yellow folder. I'll fish it out for you now if you like or just send it to your machine in a while."

There was Terry doing the eyebrow thing again.

"Soon as you can, yeah." He was going to have to have a word.

Chapter 10

Gary McCardle had stayed with his sister. She'd prepared the room for their other sibling, but Sandra couldn't make it until the following morning.

Molly wasn't fit to be left alone. She still kept bursting into tears out of the blue. She had spent much of the evening sitting in her mother's chair with the cushion clutched in her arms. It smelled of Mary, and Gary wasn't sure whether she was finding it a comfort or a torment. He was out of his depth with it all and wanted it to stop. He was convinced by now that the body on the field had been their mother. After all, if not, where was the old woman? He needed to speak to Eddie yet every time he tried, the call went straight through to voice mail. He was becoming more and more desperate. He needed his older brother to tell him what to do. He needed him to come. Eddie had always taken charge even when they were kids. Of course, it would take a while for him to arrange it. The season was just starting in Spain and his bar would be getting going now. He'd need time to organise things and book flights – all of that and yet he hadn't even been able to reach him.

He tried the landline for the bar. The phone was answered by one of the waiters Gary remembered from when they'd visited.

"Oh, hello, Mister Gary. Are you coming again soon?"

"No, I don't think so, Cesar. I need to speak to our Eddie, though."

"He is not here. He has not been here maybe six days."

"Well, where has he gone?"

"We don't know. He has gone and we are just waiting. It's all fine, really. We are doing good trade, and everything is organised."

"Listen, Cesar. If you hear from him, you ask him to call me, yeah? It's urgent."

"Okay. Maybe we see you soon?"

"Yeah. Maybe."

There was nothing more he could do now but wait.

When there was a knock on the door mid-morning, they assumed it was their sister Sandra, and Molly ran down the hall with the baby in her arms. Jordan and Terry Denn held up their warrant cards, introduced themselves.

"I wonder if we can have a word?" Jordan said.

"Gary. The police." She half turned to call back into the house.

"It's alright, love." Terry held out a calming hand. "We just need a quick chat. It's about that poor woman up on the spare ground. You'll know about her, yeah? Maybe we could come inside?"

The skinny figure of Gary McCardle appeared in the gloom at the end of the hallway. He pushed a hand through his dark hair, flicking it away from his forehead. "What do you want?"

"Is this your husband?"

"No, it's my brother, but what's that to do with you? I've already told the other bloke, the one who came before. I don't know anything."

Jordan nodded his head. "Yes, Constable Howarth said he'd spoken to you. Thing is Mrs…"

"Miss. McCardle – I'm Molly."

"Okay." Jordan smiled at her and reached out to touch the baby on the hand. The little boy grabbed at his finger and giggled as Jordan wagged it back and forth. "Hello, what's your name?"

"He's Jakey. Jacob. You were saying?" She twisted sideways, effectively cutting off the contact between her son and Jordan.

Jordan winked at the little boy and then pulled his hand away.

"Our colleague was a bit concerned about some of the answers you gave him. We just wanted to clarify things. If that's okay."

By the time he had finished speaking Gary McCardle had moved nearer the door. He pushed Molly behind him, just a step but the message was clear. He was taking charge.

"Okay, I want you to leave now. We've already answered your questions and we've nothing further to say. It's time for Jakey to have a nap so we'll just get on." He began to push the door closed.

Terry stepped closer. "I think you might be best off talking to us now, mate. We're investigating a serious crime here and you don't want to be seen as uncooperative, now, do you?"

Before he had the chance to respond, Molly interrupted them. Her eyes filled with tears. She was hugging the baby tightly to her, ignoring his squirming. "Who is it? Do you know who it is? The woman." Now she lost the remains of the slight hold on her nerves and began to cry in earnest.

Jordan bent down so he could look into her face. "Why not just let us in, love, and have a chat?"

"No." Gary pushed her further into the hall and then stood four square in the doorway. "That's it now, she's easily upset, and you need to stop it. Go on, bugger off, just leave us alone."

They had no choice but to leave. As Jordan and Terry stepped away from the slam of the door they could hear the baby's distressed crying and raised voices from inside the little house.

"Okay, that was odd," Terry said.

"Yeah. I think Howarth was right. We need to get a warrant, have a look around that house. See if we need to have either of them in to have a more official chat. At the least they are behaving obstructively. I'll have a word with DCI Cross."

Chapter 11

Sandra arrived shortly after Jordan and Terry had left. There were tears and hugs and questions and, looming over it all, there was fear. Molly went through it all again, rehashing the facts, looking for reasons and torturing herself with regret. Blaming herself for not caring enough, telling herself and the others she was a selfish cow and winding herself up into hysteria.

Sandra pulled her younger sister into a hug. Spoiled and pampered because she was the youngest by far, they had all treated her as if she were fragile. It had started with Dada who idolized his little girl and the whole '*we have to look after Molly*' thing had rubbed off on the rest of the family.

"Hush, shush. It'll be okay," she said.

"No, it won't. She's dead and it's my fault because I didn't bother to look for her."

"You couldn't have done. You didn't have any idea. You didn't know there was a problem. Stop being silly. We just need to decide what to do for the best now. First of all, we need to be sure, don't we? Has she been worried the last few days? Was she upset about anything?"

Sandra moved them both across the room towards the settee. Molly was a wreck. Her soft trousers were stained around the hem where they dragged on the floor. Her top was smeared with baby puke and there was the faint smell of sweat when she moved. How quickly she had fallen apart. How were they going to manage her now?

But she wouldn't let it go. Over and over again she told them what had happened, what she had done and what she now thought that she should have done. She insisted it was all her fault and that she could never forgive herself.

Sandra tried to wrap her arms around her sister, but Molly shrugged her off to bend forward and rock back and forth and give in, yet again, to the noisy sobbing. Gary grimaced and shrugged.

"I can't do anything with her, she's been like this the whole time. Listen, Molls. We don't know for certain the body in the field was Mam. I mean you've jumped to conclusions, haven't you?"

"A blue skirt, Davo said, with flowers on." Molly sniffed and wiped at her face with the back of her hand.

"Yeah, and Mam isn't the only woman to have a skirt like that. Shit, she got it from the supermarket, there must be dozens of them, hundreds probably. Listen, have you even looked in her cupboard to see if it's gone?"

Molly stopped crying. She glanced back and forth between her brother and sister and then, before either of them could move, she had run from the room and they heard her pounding up the stairs.

"It's Mam, Sand. I know it is. It's got to be," Gary muttered.

"But why, why after all this time?"

"I don't know. That's why I've been trying to talk to Eddie. He's vanished though."

"Right."

The sound of Molly charging back down the stairs brought them both to their feet. "It's not there. It's not. I told you. It's Mam and you won't listen to me and you won't do anything." She turned away to grab the blue blanket from the end of the banister rail. "I'm going out. I'm taking Jakey for a walk."

"No, come on. You're not in any fit state." Sandra tried to grab her sister's arm.

"I'm going. I can't sit here and just wait and do nothing. I can't."

"Let me come with you," Sandra said.

"No. I want to be on my own." She tucked the blanket around the sleeping baby and then bounced the pram down the step.

They watched her go.

"Gary, maybe we should go to the police and tell them that we know whose body it is. Leave it to them to deal with it."

"No. If we do that, if we go anywhere near the rozzers, we'll all end up like Mam. You know we can't. We'll wait until Eddie gets in touch. He'll know what we should do."

Chapter 12

Jordan wasn't looking forward to his meeting with Richard Cross. He needed to have a look around the McCardles' house. But persuading the DCI that a search warrant was justified was going to be an uphill struggle. All he had was a woman who hadn't yet been reported missing, an emotional young mother, and a body still in the process of being identified. Apart from that, it was little more than a suspicion Molly and her brother were hiding something. Even if he did manage to persuade him, he knew from bitter experience the sloping shoulders of Cross would ensure Jordan would be the one in the mire if it all came to nothing. However, he had no choice. They had to keep pecking away at the edges of this thing until it all broke open and made some sense. Without knowing for certain who the victim was, finding reasons for what had happened was impossible. Without reasons, finding the bad guys just wasn't happening. They drove in silence back to the station.

* * *

They trudged into the incident room and were met with an atmosphere of tense excitement.

"What's happened?" Jordan asked.

"I was just about to ring you, boss." Rosalind Searle strode across the room waving a sheet of paper in front of her. "We reckon we have an ID. Dentist in Kirkby. He's matched the dentures with a patient of his. Mrs Mary McCardle."

"Boom," said Terry. "I bet the address is where we've just been."

"It is," said Jordan holding out the report. "I guess Constable Howarth can give himself a pat on the back. Shame we didn't have this earlier." Beverly didn't react, so maybe the comment was lost on her. "We need to go back. Now, I reckon. I'll ring the DCI on our way. Once we give the McCardles the news, they'll likely be more amenable. Sorry, Terry, but I think it's best if you stay here. You come with me, DC Searle. There's a young woman there who seems a bit fragile. We'll arrange a family liaison officer as well. Terry, get onto that, would you? Let's just get this done. This is great stuff, well done, people." He directed his words at the room in general.

"There is one thing, boss. It's odd," Rosalind said.

"Yes?"

"There is a comment in the report by Howarth. The young woman, Molly, told him her mother was dead. But according to records, this woman is mother of Edward, Sandra, Gary and Molly. She's a widow but not reported dead. Well, she wasn't until just now. She's also the owner of the house."

"Okay. That is strange. Look, we've got a step forward, a puzzling step but we'll go and have a word. I still wonder why they didn't report her missing. Perhaps they thought they knew where she was – whatever, let's get on with it."

Rosalind Searle was rushing to keep up as Jordan stormed down the corridor. She'd taken just a few seconds to grab her jacket and bag but by that time he was already out of the door and on his way, his long legs carrying him further and further out of earshot. He glanced back and appeared to suddenly see the problem. He stopped and waited for her to catch up with him. He tried hard to keep the grin from his face, but she saw and smiled in return.

"Thanks. My dad always said I was munchkin-sized. He told me it was cute, but I promise you it does have drawbacks. I only just made it into the job. Isn't it odd to say your mother's dead when she isn't?"

"Yeah. Unless, of course, Molly knew she was."

"Yes. That's it, isn't it? Horrible to think of but that's it."

"There was something off about the young woman. She was very emotional. But she has a baby and I know from my own experience that hormones can play havoc with your nerves."

"It was enough to alert you though, wasn't it?"

Jordan nodded.

"How old is your little one? A boy isn't it?"

"Yes. Harry. He's coming up to eighteen months now and things are great. But it was tough at the beginning, so we have to bear her situation in mind and be gentle. The brother is pretty antsy though. He could be difficult."

* * *

Sandra answered their ring at the door. "Did you forget your key? Oh – sorry, I thought it was my sister. We don't want anything, thanks." She began to step back inside but paused as they held up their warrant cards.

"I thought you were selling something. Sorry."

"It's okay, Miss...?" Rosalind said.

"McCardle. Just call me Sandra. What can I do for you?"

"Could we come in, do you think? We'd like a word. Do you live here?"

"No, I'm just visiting. It's my mother's house."

"Right, well. We need to speak to you and your brothers and sister."

"Molly's not here. She's taken the baby out for a walk." Sandra stepped forward to glance up and down the road. "No, can't see her. Sorry, come on in. Gary's here anyway."

In the lounge, Gary sat in front of the electric fire staring at the rug. The room felt overwarm and stuffy. It was furnished with a grey three-piece suite and a coffee table, which was littered with baby paraphernalia. There was a row of small porcelain cats in a line on the windowsill, a couple of vases of silk flowers; a bit dusty. It was dull and uninspiring – very ordinary.

As Jordan and Rosalind Searle entered the room, Gary groaned and shook his head. "Oh, bloody Norah. Not you again. What the hell do you want now?" He stood. Sandra had paused in the doorway.

"Please, Mr McCardle, Sandra, won't you sit down?" Rosalind waved a hand towards the empty settee.

"No, just tell us what you want and then go away." Gary had taken a couple of steps towards the door attempting to herd everyone from the room.

"We have some upsetting news for you. I'm sorry, I really think it would be better if you sat down," Rosalind said.

Although Gary stayed where he was, his sister pushed past him and lowered herself slowly onto the sagging cushion of the nearest chair.

"We believe the body found locally was Mary McCardle. She has been identified by her dental records. This is the address we have for her. Is that correct?" Jordan said.

They had expected tears, perhaps shouting. Sometimes people reacted violently to the worst of all news. There was a short silence and then Sandra spoke, quietly. "He's sure, is he, the dentist? I mean Mary didn't have many teeth. So how would he know?"

"According to the report, Mrs McCardle had three teeth on the bottom and five on the top and the denture we have fits that perfectly. Luckily for us your mother's dentist is one of the few who marks the dentures he provides. Not all of them do but it helps if the person has to go into care, or into hospital. However, I'm afraid it means there is no doubt they are Mary's."

Sandra pulled a handkerchief from her pocket and dabbed at her eyes. Gary had still not spoken. Jordan and Rosalind waited but there was no reaction from either of them apart from a quiet sniff from Sandra. Jordan glanced at his detective constable, she shrugged back at him.

"You didn't report her missing. Were you not concerned about her?"

"We didn't think she was missing," Gary said, his voice dull and flat.

"The body was found late in the evening on Thursday. That's two days ago. A woman's body was found nearby yet you weren't alarmed or concerned that your mum wasn't home. So, where did you believe she'd gone?"

"We don't live here. Molly's the only one who lives here – with her."

"Mr McCardle, why did your sister tell one of our officers your mother was dead?" Jordan leaned forward on his seat, staring directly at the younger man.

There was another short silence. Sandra watched her brother.

"I know what Molly said to the copper who came to the door. You have to understand. Molly is having a hard time right now and she was a bit panicked by everything that was going on. She was a bit hysterical," Gary said.

"But why would she say that?" Jordan said. "And, if your mum was missing from here, why did you not consider reporting it?"

"I've told you we didn't think of her as missing. Well, that was why Molly was feeling guilty," Gary snarled. "Molly and Mam had been arguing. Molly was being a bitch. Mam had stormed out and that's all there is to it. Look, you need to leave us alone. We need to get our heads round this."

"Where is Molly now?" Rosalind asked.

"Out for a walk." Gary rubbed a hand over his face.

"I'm sorry, Mr McCardle, I'm going to have to ask you to come down to the station and give a statement. We need to clear this up. You have a brother. Eddie? We will need to speak to him as well," Jordan said.

"Good luck with that. He lives in Spain. He's got a bar over there. Been there for years. We went over there once to see it. So soz. Anyway, there's nothing to clear up. My sister's away with the fairies at the moment. Post-natal whatchamacallit. She said something daft. Look, just leave us alone. We have to think about all of this in peace."

"I'm sorry, I can't do that, and we need to bring in a team to have a look at this house. Sandra, is there anywhere you can go and stay while we do our job. You said you don't live here, could you go to your own home? I'll need Molly to come down and speak to us as well. Do you know where she is right now?"

"No, she just went for a walk. I don't know. But what about the baby?"

"We'll arrange for someone to look after him, if necessary," Jordan said.

"Oh no you bloody won't. We're not having him with the social services. I'll take him. He can come back with me. You're not taking him anywhere. This is all wrong, I don't know why you need to go carting poor Molly off anyway." Sandra stood and walked to the window. She pulled aside the net curtains to look outside.

"Well, if you would just give us her number and we'll give her mobile a call."

Jordan dialled and there was quiet while he waited. He shook his head. "It's engaged. Is there anywhere she likes to go particularly?"

"No, she just goes out, round the streets."

"Okay, we'll try and get a few people looking for her."

"Am I under arrest? Do I need a lawyer?" Gary's face was pale. For the first time the bravado wavered, and he gulped.

"No, just come in and let's get this sorted out," Jordan answered.

"Can I see her? Can I see Mam? It still might not be her," Sandra asked.

"I don't think it would be a good idea really. The body was badly damaged. I don't think you'd want to see her like that. And please, just take my word for it. It's your mother."

The last statement proved too much and at last there was a reaction. Sandra flopped into the chair and began to sob.

"Detective Constable Searle will stay with you for now, Ms McCardle. We might well have some questions for you later, but for now why don't you just pack a few things for the baby and wait for your sister to come back?"

Rosalind followed Jordan into the hallway. "I reckon Viv Bailey and her team will be here pretty quickly. In the meantime, don't let Ms McCardle into the mother's room. Help her to pack the baby's things but that's all, okay?"

"Boss. This is weird, isn't it? I mean, I don't have much experience, but this feels weird."

"Yep. It's very bloody weird."

Chapter 13

Molly bent forward over the handle of her pram. She tucked the blanket closer around the baby. The tears that had been washing down her cheeks dripped from her chin and landed on Jakey's hand and she rubbed them gently away. He was a bit cold and she was shivering now in her short jacket and jeggings despite the weak sun dipping down behind the houses.

It was time to turn around and go back. She didn't want to. The thought of the long evening in the house with Sandra and Gary was horrible. They would sit in silence staring at the walls, not doing anything, not really talking. Mam was dead and they'd done nothing. She didn't understand what was going on and, as always, there was the feeling that her brother and sister knew so much more. It had always been like this. She was the youngest by a good few years and throughout her childhood she had known she was excluded from something. All she had were vague hints and half-truths from as far back as she could remember. Conversations that ceased when she entered a room; comments, and remarks she didn't understand but that caused Mam's forehead to crease with worry and Dada's temper to be more frayed, more explosive than usual.

It had always been there, the promise of a threat, the idea they were somehow all living in dread of a reckoning. Whenever she tried to find out more, she was put off with platitudes. She wasn't to worry, they said, it was just life. Life was difficult and she should just be glad they were dealing with it. Then when Dada died, the sense of foreboding had lessened. Mam, Gary, and Sandra relaxed as if a great weight had been lifted. Eddie had gone. Years before, he had appeared one morning at the bottom of the stairs with his bags and told them he was going away. It had been ages until they heard from him again. Years of Mam standing by the window with the net curtains pulled aside, watching, just waiting for her first born to come home.

Then they received tickets in the post for all of them, tickets to Spain. It was a budget airline out of John Lennon Airport, but it didn't matter, they were going abroad. When they got there, he had rented them a villa and they stayed for five days in the sunshine with her big brother. It was the very end of the season, but they still spent their days lazing by the pool or strolling round the old town. In the evening there was eating and drinking at his bar. At Eddie's bar. Mam had cried because Dada had never seen it, but it had been the best time of Molly's life.

Where was she? Where was Mam? Lying somewhere on her own in a hospital basement or a mortuary. Would she be in one of those horrible metal drawers they showed on the TV? Would she have a label on her toe? Molly couldn't bear it. This couldn't go on. She was going back to the house and it was time for them to tell her just what they knew, what they feared. It was time for them to explain why, when this terrible thing had happened, they weren't screaming from the rooftops, demanding action from the police. Why they weren't doing something.

Her phone rang. She didn't bother to read the screen. She couldn't see through the mist of tears anyway. "What?" It would be their Gary.

It wasn't.

"Molly. It's me."

"Eddie. Is that you, Eddie?"

"Yeah. Are you okay, Molls?"

"No, no I'm not. Eddie, something awful has happened. It's horrible. You have to come back. Our Gary has been trying to phone you."

"I know. I know. Listen to me, Molls. Listen."

"I'm listening. But really, you have to come back. It's Mam. Oh, Eddie, she's dead."

"I know. I know, love."

"You know? How can you know? We haven't been able to tell you?"

"Never mind that for now. Just listen. Where are you right this minute?"

"I'm out with Jakey. I had to get out of the house. I had to get some air."

"Right. Okay, good. Now then, you need to keep going. Don't go back to the house. Just go away now. Do you understand me?"

"No. What are you talking about? I can't go away. Listen to me. Mam was killed and she was on the field and Gary wouldn't let us tell the police. I don't know what's happening and I can't go away, don't be so daft."

"Yes, you can. You must. Look, take the baby and just leave. Go somewhere and stay in a hotel or something. Don't let anybody know. Turn your phone off as well."

"Don't be stupid, I can't. I've got the baby. I'm out in the street. Tell you what, maybe I could come to you; to Spain."

"Molly. I've put some money in the bank for you. You've got your purse, haven't you? You've got your bag?"

"Yes, course I have but, Eddie, I don't understand."

"I know. I know, love, but just do what I tell you. Don't go back to the house. Go as far as you can. Maybe Scotland, the Isle of Man, something like that. I have to hang up now."

"What about Gary, and Sandra? They're at the house."

"I know. Don't worry about them. Just you go away, you and the baby. I'm switching off now. Do as I tell you. Turn your phone back on at ten o'clock and let me know where you are. Tomorrow, buy a cheap phone. There's enough in your account, the one where I sent your birthday money. Buy a cheap pay-as-you-go and use that to call me."

He was gone. Her brother was gone. The street was empty, and she was scared and alone. Molly looked around her. What the hell was she supposed to do now?

Chapter 14

Jordan didn't take Gary McCardle into an interview room. The man was already wound up. He picked at the skin of his fingers and chewed the inside of his cheek. Sitting in the low chair, he bounced his knee up and down and shifted edgily on the thin upholstered cushion. Jordan wanted answers, not a solicitor advising 'no comment' as the reaction to everything. Apart from that, this bloke had just been told his mother was dead. Jordan couldn't begin to imagine how it must feel. So, although there was definitely something odd going on, for the moment at least he was in the more comfortable 'lounge'. Terry Denn sat beside him, slouched on another low chair, his legs stretched out in front of him, casual, relaxed.

There were precautions they did have to take.

"Do you mind if I record our talk? If you prefer, I could have someone in to make notes," Jordan asked.

"Do I need a solicitor? Am I under arrest?"

"No, as I told you back at your house, we just want to clear up a couple of things which have us puzzled. I'm sure you're just as keen as we are to find out who did this terrible thing and why." Jordan paused.

"Well, it wasn't me. If that's what you're thinking. I know that's what you do. You assume it's family. I've seen it over and over on the TV, in films. Anything so you can to tick the boxes and clock up a result. Like I said, it wasn't me."

Jordan ignored the outburst. "I still don't understand why you didn't report your mother missing."

"I told you already, we didn't think she was missing. Our Molly thought she was with me and I didn't know she wasn't at home."

"Okay. I understand that, but when you realised you were both wrong and then the body was found at the building site you didn't come forward."

"No – well, we didn't ever think it could be Mam. Why would we think that? That would be horrible."

"One of my colleagues reported seeing your sister very distressed at the crime scene and then later she told him your mother was dead. Now, you can understand how that looks odd to us."

"I've already said. Molly is upset right now, she's on pills from the doctor. The baby is getting on top of her and I suppose he was winding Mam up as well. It's not easy. Have you got any kids?"

"I do and I know it can be very difficult, but nevertheless this all seems strange."

Gary shrugged. "Can't help you, mate. I need to go now anyway. I need to get back to the house. Have you heard if Molly has turned up yet?"

Jordan glanced at Terry who shook his head. "Still looking for her, boss. It's getting late. Have you no idea where she might be, Gary?"

"No. I reckon I should get out there and look for her. I'm off."

They could have asked him to stay, they could have asked him to make a formal statement. They could possibly have gone further and interviewed him under caution, but it didn't feel right. Not yet. Once they started down that route they were committed and they needed more, much more to try and convince the CPS that Gary McCardle had anything to do with the death of his mother.

"I'll arrange for a car to take you home," Jordan said.

"No thanks. The neighbours would love that. No, I'll get a taxi."

"Mr McCardle, keep us informed about where you are until we have a chance to find out what's happened."

Gary didn't answer, he lifted his jacket from the back of the chair and stomped from the room leaving the door to swing closed behind him.

"What are your thoughts, boss?" Terry asked.

"Honestly?" Jordan shook his head "I haven't got a clue. There's something off but I can't see what it is. One thing, though. We need to find Molly and I think we need to hurry up. She could be a danger to herself, or she could be in danger. From whom or what I can't even imagine but I'm going to see if we can mobilise more troops."

Chapter 15

Molly turned towards home. Maybe Eddie was there, he hadn't said where he was. He'd just told her not to go back. Well, that couldn't happen. He had no idea. She had the baby with her. You can't just up and disappear with a baby.

It was almost dark now and it was chilly.

He'd sounded scared. He'd asked her where she was. Oh, wait. If he had to ask, then he couldn't be at the house. He said there was money in her account. How had he done that? He was clever. He was probably the cleverest of them all, even though Sandra thought she was the cat's pyjamas with her qualification in bookkeeping or whatever it was. Hadn't got her very far, though, had it? Okay, a house in The Wirral and a car of her own. But she worked all the hours god sent for Brian and his heating business and he still hadn't married her. But their Eddie – he lived in Spain, in the sunshine. He had a flat in a compound, with a pool and a gardener. He was the most successful. Mam had been so proud of him. He sent her money, regular.

So, if he told her not to go home, maybe she shouldn't. These things that were happening. This horrible thing that had happened with Mam. The police, Gary a nervous wreck and all he could think was he had to talk to Eddie. So, maybe she should do as she was told. She turned the corner. She'd go up to Picton Road. There'd be a shop there and she could get some stuff. She had the changing bag, always there hanging from the handle of the pram. There'd be nappies in it and a change of clothes for Jakey. She was still breastfeeding him so that wasn't a problem. She needed another bottle of water for herself. She could do with something to eat as well. As she walked it began to dawn on her that she was doing as she had been told. As usual. As she always had.

She wasn't going back to the house.

But where the hell was she going?

The bus arrived as she drew level at the stop, and she took it as a sign. It was the seventy-nine into the city. She'd go there. There would be shops open still and she could get something to eat. Maybe she could stay somewhere there in Liverpool. That didn't feel right though. The only hotels she could think of were big ones, expensive ones. She didn't know how to behave in those places and she felt scruffy and grubby. She needed somewhere small like they had at seaside places. Okay. So, she'd go to Lime Street. From there she could get a train to Blackpool or Southport. She'd been to Southport a lot when she was a bit younger. They'd loved it for the clubs and the funfair – that was until she'd fallen pregnant. That'd put a stop to all the fun. Anyway, there were sure to be little places there, bed and breakfast, guest houses. She could just walk into those places and ask if they had rooms. She'd get the first train that came in, either Blackpool or Southport.

Jakey started fussing on the bus and she had no choice but to feed him. He was overdue, poor little bugger. An old woman glared at her and tutted, but Molly just stared her down. She turned her shoulder in a bit and pulled her skimpy jacket over her, but it was all she could do. The woman got up and turned to her. "Disgusting. When I had mine, we stayed at home, we didn't go showing our tits to all and sundry. You've no shame. Poor little lamb, what is he going to grow up like?"

Molly was determined not to show she was upset so she dipped her head and watched Jakey whose eyes were closing with the movement of the bus lulling him to sleep.

"Leave her alone, yeah. She's got to feed her baby. If you don't like it, don't look you old cow. Mind your own business." This from a young woman sitting a few seats away.

"Oh yes, you'd think. Where you come from, they walk round all day naked."

"What, Kirkby? They bloody don't." With that the black woman burst into loud laughter and a couple of the other passengers grinned at her.

The old woman knew she was beaten and with a final glare she thumped down the bus.

"You alright, love?" the woman asked Molly.

"Yes, thanks. I can't help it. He's hungry. I didn't mean to be out this long."

"Hey, don't worry about it. She was a cranky old biddy. He's lovely anyway. What's his name?"

"Jacob. Thanks."

"Oh, go on – I didn't do nothing."

Molly was glad to see the other woman reach over and press the button to tell the driver to stop. She was going to cry if she carried on being nice to her. She wanted a good cry. She wanted to be at home, in her room with Jakey in his cot, and she wanted to lie down and cry it all out.

Chapter 16

"This girl, what's her name?" DCI Richard Cross made a perfunctory rustle of the papers in front of him.

"Molly McCardle, sir," Jordan told him.

"Right, McCardle. She's not missing. She's a grown woman and she's gone off in a bad mood. There's no justification at all to start some sort of hunt for her."

"But, sir, I really do believe there is a risk to her wellbeing."

"No. You're overreacting, Detective Inspector. She'll come back when she's got over her strop. If we started some sort of furore every time a woman got herself in a bit of a tizzy we'd never do anything else. No. No justification at all for an alert."

"I'm sorry, sir, and with respect, I disagree. Her mother has been murdered and she is fragile and vulnerable."

"No. High maintenance, that's what they are nowadays. We didn't have all this when my wife had our children. We just got on with it. No. If she hasn't turned up after twenty-four hours you can come back and see me but in the meantime my decision is made."

There was no more he could do, and Jordan left the office without another word. The corridor outside was empty and he allowed himself a single expletive as soon as he was out of earshot of the secretary who was packing up to leave.

Terry and Rosalind were still in the incident room.

"Okay, no luck with getting some help looking for Molly. I'm going to go over there and see if I can't help to find her. It's up to you whether you want to come as well. It won't be overtime. It's been decided to wait before we do anything official. Have you tried her phone again, Terry?"

"I did and it's going straight to voice mail. I reckon she's turned it off."

Jordan knew they could pick up on the hidden message about his run-in with the DCI and he wasn't surprised when both detective constables followed him out to the car park. "We'll start at the building site. She might have been drawn back there."

She wasn't there. A quick word with the constable kicking his heels at the entrance to the site confirmed she hadn't been seen.

"Any idea how long we're going to have to keep covering this site, sir?" the constable asked Jordan.

"Shouldn't be much longer. Once we're sure the whole scene has been searched that'll be it, I guess. It's up to the crime scene manager. Are people still bringing flowers and candles?"

"No, not really. A few people stop on the way past, take a picture or read the little cards but there's not much interest anymore. It's all starting to look a bit tatty to be honest. That's the problem with these 'cellotaphs' as they call 'em. But in the end, somebody has it all to clear away. We'll have to move it soon, I reckon. Only one today. Someone left that." The constable pointed to a bunch of long-stemmed roses.

Jordan crouched down to read the card that had been tied to the flower stems. He drew out his phone and took a picture.

"Did you not see who left it?"

"No, it was early, before I came on."

"Okay, thanks. Make sure when it is cleared away that they keep the little cards and notes. Just until we make sure there's nothing there that might help us. Anyway, tonight, keep your eye out for this young woman, would you, and if she does come here, ask her to call her brother or me as soon as. Take my card so you can give her my number. Don't upset her."

As they moved away, he showed the image on his phone screen to the others. It was a small cream card with a picture of a crucifix and a rose in the corner. There was just one word – '*sorry*' with a letter X below it.

"What do you reckon?" Rosalind said.

"Could just be someone who doesn't want to be too obvious, I suppose. Someone who doesn't actually know the family but wanted to pay their respects. It's an expensive bunch of flowers though. Not like the ones from the local garage, you know what I mean?"

Jordan slipped the phone into his pocket. "Okay, we'll split up, I'm going to just walk up and down the streets, have a look down the back alleys. It's more casual than I would have hoped but she's on foot so she can't have gone far. Her brother might be still out here searching as well. Let me know if you see him."

"What about the buses though?" Rosalind Searle said. "There are a couple of stops round here. Can we request footage of the on-board CCTV?"

Jordan was torn. It made sense to him and yet it would involve staff to view the video and the request would need to be made officially. If DCI Cross became aware, then Jordan would be on the carpet and the insubordination would be undeniable. His gut reaction was pretty much *sod Cross* but it could backfire hugely and see him suspended.

"It's a good idea, Ros. I'll take it to DCI Cross first thing in the morning if we still haven't found her. For now, let's just hope she's still around here. Tell you what, though, if you see any houses with private security cameras it wouldn't hurt to ask for a look. Mind, I don't imagine there'll be many. It's not really Kensington and Chelsea round here, is it?"

"Wouldn't know, boss. Never been there." This from Terry who was grinning at the other two. "We're not all from that London."

Jordan quirked an eyebrow at the teasing. "Okay, keep in touch, we'll give it an hour or two and then we'll go to that pub we passed, and I'll buy you both a curry."

"Make mine fish and chips and you're on," Ros said.

Chapter 17

Gary had walked the streets for more than two hours. Surely, Molly couldn't still be out pushing her pram along the pavement. He had asked Sandra to let him know immediately if she came home but there had been nothing.

He was becoming really scared now. All these years they had spent shielding her, hiding stuff from her that Dada had said was too hard for her to deal with. 'I want just one of my kids to grow up without the fear,' he had said. Gary remembered as if was yesterday. The tear that had trickled down his cheek and the way Mam had put her arm around his shoulders.

Perhaps it had all been a mistake. Perhaps Molly, like the rest of them, should have known about the hidden horror. Okay, it was probably why Eddie had left, they knew it had shortened Dada's life and there was no doubt in his mind it was the reason for what had happened to Mam. But Molly, she had no clue. Had that put her in danger? Okay, she was street-smart the way they all were. They all knew better than to have their phones on show and wear jewellery too ostentatiously – it was all just part of living in a city. But did she listen for the footsteps on a dark street the way he did? Did she check up and down the back jigger before she put the bins out and lift the net curtains to peer outside several times a day, just in case?

No.

He felt the fear run up and down his spine. If something had happened to Molly, to Molly and little Jakey, how would they ever live with themselves?

Perhaps Sandra was right, and it was time to tell the police. After all these years they could bring everything out in the open. Maybe that would make it go away. Now Dada and Mam were both gone, perhaps the rest of them could enjoy some sort of peace.

But first he had to find Molly. Nothing could happen until he had his sister and his nephew home. So, he trudged on, around and around the warren of streets with his collar pulled up against the chill and his hands thrust deep in his pockets.

A group of lads gathered in the doorway of the Wellie pub in Picton Road called out to him. "Hey, Gazza, ya'alright, la?"

"Hiya, Stano. Hey you haven't seen our Molls, have you?"

"Yeah. About an hour ago. She was up near the tattoo place. She's got her figure back, hasn't she? Looking lush. Had the sprog with her, but she didn't let on."

"Thanks. See ya." He trudged on. Where the hell had she gone and why had she turned her phone off? He was scared and shocked and felt panic building. He hated this. He hated everything about his life and now Mam had gone he was calling it a day. He was going to do what their Eddie had done and bugger off. Go somewhere he could sit in the sun and drink till the early hours and not have to look behind him in the dark.

He speed-dialled Eddie. He was the oldest. It was his job to sort this. They all had to get together and decide what to do, but Eddie had to come over and be a part of it. He couldn't swerve his responsibilities anymore.

The phone went straight to voice mail. Gary cursed, loudly, and he kicked out at an empty drink can lying on the pavement. It flew across the road and hit the rear window of a passing car.

"Sorry! Sorry, mate," he yelled.

But the car pulled in at the kerb the front doors sprang open and two blokes shot out. They were big and burly and there were two of them. Gary was small and wiry and tired, he knew he'd be no match for them in a fist fight, and he'd just kicked a can at their car. Every bloody thing that could go wrong was going wrong and he was sick of the lot of it.

He turned and shot down a side street, over a brick wall into a small back yard. He vaulted over the next wall using a plastic bin as a launch pad and over the next. There was a narrow alley between the houses, he sprinted along it, splashing gritty water up his jeans and into his trainers. He skidded into their own road and glanced back, there was no-one around. He dragged out his key and let himself in through the front door. There was no pram. No short jacket hanging on the newel post. No sign of his sister and now he couldn't go back out there until he'd given the car driver time to give up and drive away. He lowered himself to the bottom steps, hid his head in his hands and tried to block it all out. He hated his life, and he hated Dada.

Chapter 18

Jordan stood at the bar ordering drinks, a pint of lager for Terry, red wine for Ros and a Talisker for himself. He wouldn't normally have drunk spirits so early in the evening, but he was cold after the trail around the darkening streets and he was frustrated and worried about Molly McCardle. He was convinced they should have patrols out looking for the young woman. They should have put an appeal out on the evening news asking her to get in touch and there should be someone at the house supporting the family and on hand in case she came home.

Gary and Sandra had refused to have a family liaison officer staying with them and they couldn't be forced. They had promised to call him if Molly came back but he wasn't convinced they would stick to their word. There was the baby as well. It was cold now and there was rain in the air, a young baby shouldn't be out in just a little buggy. Although there was definitely something off about the whole set-up, Molly had seemed to be a caring and loving mother. What would persuade her to have Jakey out in the cold streets now. Nothing good, it couldn't be.

Jordan turned and looked across to the table in the corner where Gary and Ros were reading the menu. They were subdued and he had the feeling they were only there because it had been the agreement earlier. They were as puzzled and worried as he was.

He took the drinks back to the table. "Listen, I am going to get on to the bus companies, start the ball rolling with a request for the CCTV on the buses from Picton Road."

"What about DCI Cross?" Terry asked.

"I'll have to go and talk to him in the morning. In the meantime, when we've had something to eat, I'm going back to the shops. Some of them will have security cameras. They might have picked her up walking past. You guys can get off home if you like. It's been a long day and there'll be another one tomorrow. We still have the murder to deal with and this missing woman is a sidebar."

"I'm free tonight," Ros said. "I can do some if you like. We need to find her. I guess she might have had some sort of breakdown or whatever. She's not safe to be out on her own, I don't reckon."

"Count me in," Terry said.

Jordan just nodded at them. "Thanks, guys. Now what are we eating?"

"I'll tell you what, boss. I think I'd rather get on with things. I'm happy to get back out there." Rosalind took a big gulp of the wine and pushed the glass away from her.

Terry glanced at her and finished three quarters of his pint in two massive gulps. "Come on, let's get on with it. Sooner we start, sooner we finish, as my old granny used to say."

"Cool. I owe you one," Jordan said.

"Did she really say that?" Ros was sliding her arms into her jacket and turned to look at Terry.

"What?"

"That. What you just said about starting and finishing. Only it doesn't really make much sense. No offence to your granny, like."

"No, I don't think so. Didn't know her much anyway."

"Oh, okay. Bit of an odd thing to say if you ask me." And with a grin she turned away and made for the door.

The two men watched her go for a moment and Terry shrugged and followed. Jordan reached and picked up his glass, gulped down the last of the whisky and followed the two detective constables. They had gelled really quickly, and he had the warm feeling they were a team. When he went back in the morning and spoke to the DCI, he would be grateful to feel he had their backing. Cross was wrong. Jordan didn't know why so many of his requests were refused but it seemed to be developing into a routine. He pushed away the thought niggling at the back of his mind. Racism was a huge deal in the force and not something he could even suggest unless he had much more proof than just not getting his own way – even when he was so obviously right.

He shrugged into his coat and went back into the night.

Chapter 19

Molly was at home in the city centre. It had been her stomping ground for as long as she could remember. They used to come as a family, shopping and riding on the ferry across the water to New Brighton. Like going on holiday really. Then, when she was older, with her mates lying about their age to get drinks in the pubs, giggling in the pictures and sitting for hours in the cafes eating chips and flirting with lads.

It had changed a lot over the years, the famous old Infirmary used to stand in a warren of terraced houses. She barely remembered it. But Mam had worked there and they were always made to notice it. There was a new hospital now and the old place was some sort of private organisation. The shops changed all the time and Mam had been upset about the loss of the old names. They didn't mean much to Molly, there were still the cheap fashion shops and the ones selling earrings and bags. Mam said the quality had gone but they'd laughed at her a bit. That was in the days when she cared about how she looked and spent money on good clothes.

The thought of Mam brought a lump to her throat, but she swallowed hard. She had to get away. Their Eddie had said so and he'd sounded so scary. She looked at the baby fast asleep in his pram. The main thing was to keep Jakey safe. She didn't understand what was going on but for now she'd just do as she was told and wait for Eddie to call.

Outside Lime Street there were a couple of girls wrapped in grubby quilts; one of them was pregnant. They looked at her with dead eyes and though they didn't speak, one of them held out a hand. She fished in her purse and brought out a couple of pound coins. She was scared and cold now but at least she knew she had a home to go to. Didn't she?

Eddie had said don't go back but he didn't mean not ever. He couldn't have done. She thought of her room with the cot in the corner. The warm living room and the kitchen where there was always something to eat in the fridge, and beer, and wine. She knew she was lucky. They'd always done okay. She had a job for a while, just a shop assistant in the local chemist but he'd suggested she do some more study, told her about jobs in pharmacies and she'd been interested. She could go and work in a hospital, he'd told her. Then she'd fallen pregnant and it wasn't going to happen. She'd had high blood pressure and they'd made her give up working. Then she'd had trouble coping when Jakey arrived and Mam had told her not to worry about it. There was Jobseeker's Allowance and other benefits, but Mam had seen her right. She just gave her money when she needed it and Molly had never really thought about where it came from. It was there and she took it.

Looking at the scruffy women sitting on the pavement outside the station she thanked her lucky stars. But it made her wonder. They weren't rich. Dada hadn't been a doctor or a teacher or anything. He'd worked at the container base in Bootle when she was small and then he'd stopped and she wasn't sure what he did really afterwards. There'd always been plenty of money, though, she had never questioned it. Not until now when she was questioning everything.

She went to the hole in the wall in the station. She put her card in the machine and was shocked when she asked for her balance. Eddie had said he'd put some money in there but there was over five thousand pounds. She'd had a couple of hundred already, but this made her stomach flip. Where had he got that sort of money and how come he could afford to just give it to her? Maybe he didn't expect her to have it all. Maybe he just wanted her to look after it for him until he got to Liverpool. She glanced at her watch. It was just after eight and he said she had to ring him at ten. She'd find out then just what he wanted her to do with all this money.

In the meantime, she'd find somewhere to stay. Just for tonight and then she was going home tomorrow. The homeless girls had frightened her, not because they'd been threatening but because they'd been so lifeless, no spark to them, just dull acceptance. She needed to go home. She needed her family.

The train to Southport was already at the platform and it was warm inside. She was glad of the sit-down. Even though he was still asleep, she lifted little Jakey out of the buggy and hugged him to her with the soft blue blanket tucked around him. The flickery movement of his chest as he breathed and the warm baby smell of him was a comfort. She put her head back on the seat and closed her eyes and when the train left with a little jerk, she let the hum of the motor and the low murmur of the other passengers lull her into a daydream. It would all be okay.

It had to be.

Chapter 20

"So." DCI Richard Cross leaned back in his chair. A huge mug of tea steamed on the blotter. Next to it a greasy bag gave off the smell of sausages and tomato sauce. Jordan had been in the office since five thirty and still had not had breakfast. His stomach growled. He coughed to cover the sound.

"This is not what I wanted to be doing this morning, DI Carr," Cross said. He leaned forward and pulled the bacon roll from the bag.

Jordan waited, watching him chew and wash down the sandwich with a swallow of tea and then wipe red sauce from his lips with a tiny paper napkin.

"No, I was planning on a morning in the garden. A round of golf later, and then a couple of drinks with friends. Am I there, enjoying my Sunday?" He waited, Jordan wasn't sure whether or not he was expected to respond. He decided silence was the best reaction but gave a small nod to show he was listening.

"No, I'm not. I'm here waiting for you to come up with some sort of progress report with this murder. I don't appreciate having to come in at the weekend. I had years of weekends and nights. I did my time. I don't appreciate a call on a Saturday afternoon from the Assistant Chief Constable wanting to know what I have to tell him and having to admit there has been no real action. Am I making myself clear, DI Carr?"

Now Jordan nodded more vigorously. "We are working on it, sir. The team are all in and going through reports."

"Reports of what?"

"Well. We have been viewing images taken at the site. The local paper were there and we've been reviewing those pictures. We've been to see the family of the deceased. Actually, sir, that's been the main thrust of our efforts."

"How so?" Cross had finished his bacon roll and now screwed the debris together and dropped it into the waste bin. He loosened the button on his jacket and swivelled in the desk chair to peer out of the window.

Jordan carried on despite the pantomime. "We've been trying to find the girl. We picked her up on CCTV boarding a bus to the city centre yesterday evening. I would like to requisition the footage from the bus company and have a look at the town centre cameras. I've had the younger son in for an informal interview. We've had SOCO go through the house. They've found nothing of any help, but they have taken away Molly's computer. I would like to requisition Gary's as well but it's not in the house, it's at his flat so we would need a warrant."

DCI Cross heaved a sigh as he turned back to look at Jordan. "Carr, stop arsing about, your first priority is to find me a murderer, do whatever you have to, but don't lose track of the main issue here. I have been given a preview of the lead in the *Echo* tomorrow – we do not come out of it well, DI Carr. 'Local police baffled. No justice for Mary.' Oh yes and one local blog has started talking about 'witch burning'. We need something before all the loonies come out of the woodwork. It's not good enough. Get this sorted, man. Oh, and don't even think about putting in overtime for your lot for last night. You can go."

* * *

Terry and Ros took one look at Jordan's face when he stomped back into the incident room and threw himself into his chair and both found things to do that entailed keeping their heads down and their eyes on their screens.

He gave himself time to calm down. Okay, the meeting had been a horrible experience. But much as it pained him to admit it, the DCI did have a point. They had got practically nowhere with the murder and they had now lost Molly.

"I'm going back to talk to Gary McCardle. Terry, you're with me. The family home first and then his flat if he's not there. In the meantime, Ros, go through the cards from the flowers that were left at the site. Look at the one from the bunch of posh roses and see if you can find out who bought it. The address of the flower shop might well be on there. If they paid with a bank card, we need a name and address."

"What about Molly, sir?" Rosalind Searle asked.

"Get on to central, ask to view footage of the bus terminal and let's see if we can find out where she went. Ros…"

"Sir?"

"I'm sorry to put this on you, but can you do that on the QT?"

"No probs, boss."

Chapter 21

Terry rang the doorbell and he and Jordan stepped back to peer at the windows of the McCardles' house. The net curtains in the living room were lifted and Gary glared out at them.

When he eventually opened the door, he didn't speak but neither did he move aside to let them in.

"Mr McCardle," Jordan said, "have you heard from your sister?"

"No." Although the answer was short and belligerent, there was a flicker of worry in his eyes. "What did you want now? You people have torn the place apart, gone through all my mother's belongings and taken away Molly's computer. You've no respect. We're in mourning here."

"I am sorry about that. But I want to find out who killed your mother. I want to help to find your sister and this is the only way we can do it. If you know anything, anything at all that might help, please just tell us. Help us to sort this out, Gary." As he spoke Jordan stepped forward and, with a sigh, Gary McCardle allowed him into the narrow hallway.

"I've nothing to tell you."

"Have you tried ringing your sister again?"

"Of course, I have. I've been up all night trying to contact her. Nothing."

"Could she be with Jakey's dad?"

Gary paused for a minute, glanced out into the street and then closed the door. "I don't think so."

"Have you spoken to him?" Jordan asked.

"No. Look, we don't know who he is. She never told us, refused to even tell Mam. She said he was unimportant, and he wasn't on the scene anymore. In the end, Mam said we had to let it go. She said it was her choice. So, no I haven't bloody spoken to him. I want you to go now. I want you to get your nose out of our business. Just go."

Though he knew they really should leave, Jordan spoke again his voice low and calm. "Mr McCardle, who is there who would want to hurt your family? Can you not think of anything to help us here? Has there been trouble with neighbours, anything in the past with your extended family?"

"What? Are you asking me if some cousin over in Ireland came and killed Mam over a broken jug years ago? Is that the best you can do?"

"Of course not. But anything you can tell us, even if it seems unimportant to you, might just give us what we need to move this along."

"Well, the answer is still no."

"And your brother Eddie. Where is he now?"

"I've told you. He lives in Spain."

"But is he not coming over to support you?" Terry asked.

"I haven't had a chance to speak to him yet."

"Is that unusual?" Jordan had flipped open his notebook. "We've got a mobile number for him, is there a landline?"

"I've tried his home, and his bar. He's not there just now. He's probably gone on holiday. He does that sometimes. It's about to move into his busy season so maybe he's taking a break first. He doesn't get much chance once it's summer. Anyway, I've sent him texts and I've messaged him. He'll be in touch when he can."

"Mr McCardle, two members of your family missing, your mother dead. Don't you think it's time to try and help us find out what's going on?"

"I've told you. I don't know anything."

"Okay. Has your sister gone home? Sandra, isn't it?"

"Yes, she's got kids to look after, they have a business to run. We're in touch."

"Okay. We'll leave you to it. Are you going back to your own flat?"

"No. I'm staying here until our Molly and Jakey come back. I don't want her walking into an empty house."

Jordan and Terry headed for the building site. The little display of flowers and cards was sad and grubby-looking after the overnight rain and a woman with a toddler was removing some of the dead blooms and pushing them into a black plastic bag.

Jordan introduced himself and flashed his warrant card. "That's a messy job for you. It's kind of you."

"Well, I liked Mary. She was always nice to me. I went to school with their Eddie and we were close for a while. It's terrible what happened."

"Do you mind telling us your name?" Jordan asked.

"Laura, Laura Clark and this is Jennifer." She smiled at the little girl.

"Did you know Molly?"

"Yeah. Not so much because she's quite a bit younger but she was always around, in the house and so on. Spoiled brat she was, to be honest. Her daddy's favourite. I couldn't understand it. Their Sandra was cleverer and prettier I thought, but there we are. He was so grumpy most of the time – the old man. Very strict. Between you and me, he wasn't beyond giving them a walloping now and then. Still, mustn't speak ill of the dead and he doted on his little girl."

"Are you still in touch with Eddie?"

The woman straightened and gathered her things together, hoisting the child onto her hip. "No. Not anymore. He's not the same and anyway he lives away, doesn't he? Nice to see him back though, for his Mam."

"How do you mean?" Terry asked.

"Well, him being back to help the family. I suppose there's a lot to arrange. All hands on deck, times like this, isn't it?"

"When did you see him?"

"Day before yesterday. Only from a distance, like. I didn't let on. As I say, we're ancient history and I wouldn't have anything to say to him. I hope you find out who did this to Mary. She didn't deserve it. Poor old biddy. After all she put up with through the years."

Chapter 22

It had been a long night. Molly barely had a chance to lie on the double bed. Now, she sat propped against the pillow sipping at a cup of instant coffee as she watched the light grow in the gaps around the flowered curtains. Jakey was beside her, chewing his fist and drooling. She slid from the bed to go and open the drapes. It was cloudy but at least there was no rain.

This was a nice room, clean, warm, and pretty, and the man who had checked her into the small hotel had been kind. He made sure she had everything she needed for the baby. He made her a sandwich even though the kitchen had been closed for over an hour and then offered her a T-shirt to sleep in. "They're just advertising things we had made a while ago for our dining room staff to wear. This one is new, still in the bag," he said.

Molly accepted it gratefully. She could tell by his face he didn't believe her story about losing her luggage on the train. He probably thought she was a battered wife, running away, or just a woman leaving for any of the dozens of reasons women left home. He didn't pry, he was just kind.

Jakey had cried and cried. He was obviously picking up on her mood and even though he was still only tiny, she believed he knew he wasn't in his own cot. She didn't have the little blue teddy that always lay alongside him. Mam had said he was too young to appreciate the cuddly toy but maybe Mam was wrong. She had rocked him, fed him, and walked the floor with him. All the time she had worried someone would complain about the noise.

At ten o'clock she had called Eddie, but he hadn't reassured her. He had barely spoken but simply taken the address of the hotel in one of the side streets in Southport and then told her, again, to get a new phone the next day and send him a message so he'd have her number.

"Don't worry. Try and enjoy yourself. You always liked Southport; God knows why but have a break, pretend it's a holiday. I really wanted you to go further away but it might be okay."

He had no idea. No idea what it was like to be stuck in a strange room on your own with a fractious baby and nobody to help.

"What do you want me to do with that money, Ed? I don't know what to do with all that much."

"I don't want you to do anything with it. Just use it, that's all. Don't go short of anything, Molly, not for you or the baby."

She washed her hands and face. She'd washed her knickers and dried them on the radiator. They were still a bit damp, but it wouldn't have to matter. She dressed, put Jakey into his buggy, and jiggled it back and forth until he dozed. Once he was asleep, she pushed him into the clanky old lift and went down to the dining room.

She was only halfway through the bacon, eggs, beans and toast and gulping down a second cup of coffee when he woke and started to grizzle. She hoisted him onto her knee and tried to lean around to continue eating.

"Here, let me take him for you." There was a tall, dark-haired man standing beside her. He smiled and held out his arms.

"No, it's fine. I'm fine, thanks though."

The bloke leaned closer. "Honestly, it's okay. I know babies. I have three nephews. Here. Let me have him. My name is Patrick. It's nice to meet you. He'll be good with me."

He took hold of Jakey and swung him up out of Molly's hold. She didn't want him to take her son but there were other people in the dining room. She didn't want to cause a fuss. There was an older couple at a table in the window who had shaken their heads and tutted as she had wheeled the pram into the room. Their disapproval made her want to sink into the ground. She dredged up a smile. "Oh well, okay. But please, sit here with him."

"Of course." He hooked a foot around the leg of one of the other chairs and pulled it away from the table. As he sat, he rocked Jakey and the baby had quieted. Maybe her mood was affecting him more than she realised or perhaps he was simply intrigued by this new presence.

Molly finished her breakfast. She was on edge and uncomfortable with her child in this strange man's arms and in just a few minutes she pushed the plate away and stood from the table. She held out her arms. "Thanks. That was kind of you. I'll take him now."

The man stood and bent towards the buggy. "I'll just put him in here. Why don't you go and get your coat and we'll take him out for a little walk? It's not too cold and the fresh air will be good for him."

"No, I have to go. I need to pack. I'm leaving today."

With one hand on the handle of the pram and the other stuffed into the pocket of his jeans, the stranger shook his head. "No, I don't think you are, Molly. Tell you what. I'll meet you outside." He snatched up the brown leather jacket that had hung on the back of the chair at the adjacent table. He draped it over the hood of the buggy and then swung the thing around in the narrow space. He grasped Molly by the arm and propelled her from the dining room. "Off you go now. Just get your coat and meet me outside. I expect you have a bag with the baby's things in. Best bring it, and your handbag. Oh yes and before you go, just give me your phone."

"No. I'm not. How do you know who I am? Who are you?" Molly was afraid, she looked desperately back and forth, searching for some help. There was no-one near enough and she really didn't want to cause a fuss. "Give me my baby back."

"Outside. Quick." With the final command the pram was pushed down the hallway and out into the small porch.

Molly followed reaching forward, trying to catch hold of the buggy handle but unable to squeeze through the narrow space between the man and the wall. "Give him back."

"Molly, go and get your things. I am waiting here."

She stood for a moment in terrified indecision. She could fight for possession of the child and the pram or she could run upstairs and fetch her things. She could stand in the porch and scream for help – but she didn't.

She couldn't leave Jakey, couldn't turn her back on him.

A woman crossed the parking space towards them, she smiled at the baby. Molly was about to call out, to beg for help but before she had a chance, Patrick handed over the pram to the new stranger. He turned and took hold of Molly by the wrist.

"Come, don't make a scene. Let's go to your room. We will bring your things. No need to be upset."

He pushed her back into the hallway and then up the narrow stairs to her room.

Chapter 23

Penny didn't interfere with Jordan's work – ever. She listened when he wanted to talk and rejoiced with him when he had a success but that was all. But on Sunday night she had taken his tablet computer away from him.

"Leave it, love," she said. "Sitting here going over and over it isn't going to help. You're exhausted. Come on up to bed. Get some sleep. Nothing is going to happen tonight and even if it does, they know how to contact you."

She was right. He knew it and he followed her up to the bedroom where she helped him to strip off his clothes and then, while she checked on Harry, he had a shower and slid under the covers. It was warm and comfortable and once Penny was beside him, he was able to switch off for a short while and let the worry go. He pulled her close and breathed in the clean, fresh perfumed scent of her and as he held her the tension and worry drained away and he drifted into the darkness.

He had just over an hour's sleep before his mobile chimed and he grabbed it quickly before it woke his family.

"Boss, it's Ros. Really sorry to disturb you but I've found Molly McCardle. Well, I've seen her anyway."

"Brilliant. What have you got? Hey, hang on, are you still in work?"

"Well, yes. I didn't want to give up on this and I had to do it on my own, so it took a while. I had to flannel a bit with the bus company, but I reckon if we get her home safely it won't matter. Am I right?"

Jordan reassured her and hoped they were right.

"Anyway, it was worth it I reckon. To be honest, from what I've seen this might be able to wait until you come in. She was on her own. She didn't look disturbed or frightened from her body language. She had the baby with her, of course. I picked her up on the bus from Picton Road. She went all the way into the city. She caught a train at Central and travelled to Southport. I was able to follow her leaving the station. She walked along Lord Street, went into the supermarket and came out with a couple of bags. Then she turned down Hill Street and I lost her. Really, boss, I don't think there is anything much we can do right now. Maybe she just needed to get away, you know, have some *me time*."

"Go home, Ros. You've done brilliant work, thank you. At least we know she's okay. But now you go home, get some kip. I'll get in touch with Terry and we'll take over. We still need to find her and find out just what has been going on. I reckon we could request information about her bank card use, and whatnot. Going walkabout after what has happened to her mother makes her a person of interest. I'll have a word with DCI Cross in a while, we need to put out an appeal – ask her to contact us. We also need to have the Southport bods involved."

"I'll go home, get a shower and a quick nap then I'll be back in later. Call me if you need me," Rosalind said.

"I will. Thanks again."

Jordan left a note for his wife, grabbed an energy bar from the tin in the kitchen and rang Terry on the handsfree as he drove through the quiet Crosby streets and out to Wavertree.

* * *

By the time Jordan arrived at the station, Terry was already there, scanning the report and footage.

"Can't get onto the bank yet, boss. We need to contact the brother and find out which one she uses."

"Call him now."

"It's a bit early."

"It's his sister. If he's asleep, I'd be surprised. If it was my sister, I'd be walking the streets and I'd do anything, anything at all to find her. Sitting in the house waiting for her to come back isn't good enough. Get on to him. Find out if they have any relatives in Southport, which bank she uses, which cards she has. Oh, do you know what, bugger it – let's go and talk to him ourselves. I want to put out an appeal. Let's ask if he wants to be a part of it. They have more impact with a concerned relative on screen. I know that's a bit cynical but it's also fact. Come on."

Terry gulped back the remains of his cup of coffee, pulled on his jacket and they stomped off down the corridor. The station was still night-time quiet, a couple of drunks were lolling in the reception area on the plastic chairs and the desk sergeant appeared to be playing some sort of game on his phone. However, Terry and Jordan were firing on all cylinders as they swept past and headed for the car park.

Chapter 24

Gary McCardle was red-eyed and dishevelled. The curtains were still drawn across the windows and as he dragged open the front door, the stink of cigarette smoke swept past in a cloud.

"Christ, not you again? Leave us alone, can't you? It's seven in the morning there must be some sort of law about this. It's harassment."

"Mr McCardle, we did offer to assign a family liaison officer – that would have avoided some of the visits, but you declined." As he spoke, Jordan pushed forward and for once Gary didn't bother to try and stop him entering. They walked down the hallway and into the kitchen. After just a few days, the place had deteriorated into a shambles. There were dirty mugs and plates on all the surfaces. A loaf lay beside the toaster with the wrapping screwed closed and a jar of peanut butter was left lidless on the table with the knife abandoned alongside. There were crunchy yellow stains across the tablecloth.

"We have some better news for you, Gary. But first of all, I need to ask if your brother Eddie is here."

"No, I've told you. I haven't seen him in a couple of years. I don't know where he is."

"It's just that we met Laura Clark up by the memorial for your mum and she told us she thought she'd seen Eddie."

"Aye well, she's talking through her arse, isn't she? How could she see him when he's not here? Do you really think I wouldn't know? Anyway, what's this better news you've got? I could do with some."

"We've seen CCTV of Molly."

"Where! Is she alright?"

"We think she's okay. We tracked her on CCTV to Southport."

"Southport? What the hell is she doing in Southport?"

"We were hoping you might be able to tell us," Terry said.

McCardle shook his head, his lips pursed. He reached for a pack of cigarettes which were lying on the table. Jordan was about to ask him not to smoke while they were there, to point out they had that right. But he looked at the dark rings under Gary's eyes, the fingernails bitten to the quick and kept his thoughts to himself.

"She likes Southport. Always did," Gary said. "When she was younger. She was a bit wild, they used to blag their way into the clubs there, her and her mates, like. She loved the funfair as well. I bet she hasn't been since she had the kid though."

"You've no relatives there?"

"No, bloody hell, no. A bit too rich for us. Well, it used to be anyway. All those big houses, the posh shops."

"We need to find her. We could look at her bank accounts and see if she's used her card, that might give us an idea what she's up to at least. She must have stayed somewhere last night. She could have spent the time in the open, at the railway station or even in the bus shelters, something like that. But we haven't seen her on any of the cameras. My instinct is she had somewhere to go. She would need to with the baby, after all."

"I'll go. I'll go and look for her. I don't want your lot tracking her or whatever. Just leave me, let me get myself together and I'll head off."

Jordan shook his head. "That's not the best idea, Gary. Really, leave this to us. We'll be quicker and more efficient. We have access to technology that'll help. We won't frighten her. I promise you. Look, we could have her located and back home with you while you're still trying to find a parking place in Southport."

The tongue-in-cheek comment diffused some of the tension. Gary raised his head and stared at Jordan for a minute. "You promise, you won't scare her? You're not going to arrest her or something?"

"No, of course not. We would like to talk to her, obviously. But the main thing right now is to make sure your sister and the baby are safe. I know you understand that."

"Okay, what do you need."

"Bank details, card numbers if you have them. Then we can get on with tracking any spending. Any idea at all that you think might help. I need to get back to the station and put things in motion. But you can call my mobile any time and if you can't get through, try Terry here or our colleague DC Searle. I'll give you her number. There is just one other thing. If we don't manage to track her down quickly, I would like to arrange an appeal for help. You know the sort of thing I mean. Just a short section on the news asking her to get in touch or anyone who might have seen her to let us know. Would you be willing to take part in it? I'm sure you've seen them yourself?"

"No, bloody hell no. Don't do that. Whatever you do, don't do that. Please. You have to promise me you won't." As he cried out, Gary McCardle sprang from the table and grabbed hold of Jordan's arm. "Don't do that."

Chapter 25

"Gary was panicked. What was that about? I thought we were getting through to him." Terry Denn was driving them back to the station while Jordan messaged the team with information about Molly's bank cards.

"It did seem like an overreaction, I have to say. I'm not reading too much into it right now. He's an odd character anyway and he's under a lot of stress. I still want to go ahead with an appeal if we can't trace her today. If he doesn't want to take part, then there's nothing we can do. I suppose we could approach Sandra."

"Yeah, that's a good thought. Maybe it's not going to be a problem though. If we trace her through her plastic – job done."

"We have to be careful here, Terry. We are focused on finding Molly, and I think that's right. She's still alive and she may be in danger. At the very least her behaviour is odd. But we still have a murder to solve. We can't let the original investigation get away from us. I've asked Beverly to look into the background of the family. Anything she can find could be a help in tracing just why that poor old woman was killed. Up to now we haven't found anything.

The SOCO team have drawn a blank at the crime scene. Except of course to say it's not actually the original crime scene but simply the place where she was left. Vivienne Bailey has sent a report in. They believe the flames…" Jordan compressed his lips. "Sorry, I can't think of another way to say it. Anyway, they were extinguished with water. Not potable but something more likely from a lake or a pond, that sort of thing. They will try and find out just where, but that means taking samples from all the water sources in the area. But it means they never really intended to let the body be totally consumed. This leads us back to it being some sort of message, but we don't know who for or why. She also highlighted the presence of residue on the shoes. Apparently, there is something in the tread on the sole. A bit of a puzzle, she said. She's still working on it."

* * *

The incident room was quiet, everyone was focussed on their screens, either scanning CCTV of Southport and looking for live images of Molly and her son, or reviewing the film of her the night before. Jordan had asked them to go over it to see if they could pick up anything suspicious around the young woman. "Just ask them to look for people who are on all the images, who took the same bus, the same train and then turned up in Southport," he told Rosalind Searle when he spoke to her on the way back from the McCardles'.

"Anything?" he asked the room at large as they arrived. There was a chorus of negative responses. "Okay, well, carry on. If anything shows up from her bank card it'll help to tighten the search. But this is all good stuff."

"Can I have a word, sir?" Beverly Powell had come up behind him and spoke quietly into his ear.

"Have you found something?" he asked. "If you have it's probably best to share it with everyone. The more information we all have the better."

"Erm. No. I just need a word in private."

Terry stood by the table making himself coffee, he was doing the silly wiggling thing with his eyebrows again. Jordan glared at him.

"Okay, Bev. What is it?"

"Can we step into the corridor, sir?"

"Is it really necessary?"

"I'd prefer it."

He had no choice but to follow her out into the space outside the incident room. She turned and closed the door behind them.

"If this is a personnel matter, you really should speak to HR, Bev," Jordan said.

"No. No, of course it's not, sir. I have no problems. It's great to be working with you again. No, it's just something odd about the family – the McCardles."

"Okay."

"Well, you know you asked me to have a look at their background?"

Jordan nodded.

"I can't."

"Oh. I'm surprised. I would have thought that sort of thing was right up your street. You're good with records and what have you."

"Yes, well, thank you, sir. It's not that I'm not able to do it, although it sort of is. It's just – well, there's nothing there. I've found records of the murdered woman owning the house. That was quite easy from the Land Registry. It has been in her name for a long time. Since the seventies. There was no record of a mortgage on it which I found surprising but anyway you would expect her to own it outright now, given her age. I found a record of her working as an auxiliary nurse at the Royal Infirmary. I think they call them something different now – health care assistants, I believe. There was some employment information about her husband at the docks and at the container base in Bootle. I can't find any record of her at any other hospital though. The kids have got school records and health service cards and all of the usual documentation but none of it goes back to the beginning. It seems very odd."

"What do you mean *the beginning*?"

"I can't find an address for her before the current one and actually no marriage certificate. The father's name on the birth certificates is McCardle and it says they are from Liverpool. I don't want to let you down, boss. I just wonder how much time you want me to spend on it. I could look for all the certificates and even census records, it is very time consuming."

"Well, maybe it's not so odd. It could be she never married. Maybe unusual in someone her age with so many children but not impossible. I'll see if I can get more information from Gary McCardle, he must know where she came from and her maiden name. He did mention a cousin in Ireland so perhaps that's it. Maybe her records are all there and he didn't specify whether it was North or South and to be honest I didn't think to ask. It didn't seem very important at the time. As you say, it's going to be a challenge. Leave it for now but let me see what you've got, and we'll decide whether or not it's going to be something we need to follow up."

"Okay, sir. I'm sorry, I feel as though I've failed."

"No, not at all, let me know how you get on."

Chapter 26

Rosalind Searle strode over to the whiteboard where Jordan was reviewing the latest notes. "Sir, I reckon we've found her." She held out her tablet so he could see the screen. "She's paid with her card at an hotel in Southport. Queens Road. She used it in the supermarket as well."

"Excellent." Jordan grinned at her and made to hand the computer back.

"There is something else. If you look at the credits on her account." She pointed at the screen.

"Blimey. Where did that come from? Five thousand all in one lump. I don't think it's her Jobseeker's Allowance, is it?"

"No, I reckon not. We are on to the bank. Bev is chasing them to find out where it came from. They are being a bit cagey at the moment. But we'll keep working on it."

"Great stuff. Come with me, will you? She may be upset when we turn up and it'll be less frightening if she sees a woman."

"Right, boss."

"I'll meet you in the car park. In the meantime, ask Terry to call ahead and let the hotel know we're coming."

"Do you want to send a local bobby round to keep an eye on her till we get there?"

"No. I don't think so. We don't have any proof she's done anything after all." He turned to the room. "Okay guys, we need to monitor the live feed cameras in Southport, particularly around Queen Street. We are heading out there now but if you do see our woman out and about you need to let us know, soon as. Yeah."

* * *

The sat nav offered two routes with only minutes difference in the timings. "I reckon going via Formby will be easier, boss. The A565, less wiggly. Take the M62 down past Prescot and Knowsley."

"Fair enough." Jordan judged it enough of an emergency to use the integral blue lights and the outside lane of the motorway for the first part of the drive. But he stayed within the speed limits. It wasn't a chase, and he had no backup. "Let's hope Molly likes a lie-in and a leisurely breakfast," he said.

"What, with a little baby? Any sleep at all is probably a bonus," Ros said.

"What the hell is she doing in Southport? Is she meeting someone? What is all the money about? This is all looking a bit dodgy for her, but I just can't imagine how. I can't believe she had anything to do with her mum's murder. She was gutted. She's barely more than a kid. Still…"

He didn't need to say more. They both knew that age and gender was no barrier to violent crime. He didn't believe it though, surely not that small fragile young mother. He hoped not. The job knocked a lot of the sentimentality out of you very quickly, but he would be sad if they were to find Molly McCardle was a murderer.

* * *

"That's it there." Rosalind pointed to small hotel standing in a tarmacked car park. The walls were rendered and painted white. There were heavy-looking drapes at the windows and hanging baskets of pansies outside the porch. It had been a grand house in the past and now it was just one of hundreds of similar small hotels in every seaside resort in the UK. Jordan liked the look of it and could see why it had appealed to Molly, not as daunting as one of the big chain places. More homely, friendly.

There was a young girl behind the reception desk wearing a black skirt and white blouse. "Good morning, do you have a reservation?" As she spoke, she turned her computer monitor so she could read the screen and she jabbed at the keyboard.

When she looked up from the desk, Jordan and Rosalind had their warrant cards held in front of them. "I'm DI Jordan Carr and this is my colleague, DC Searle. We need to have a word with the manager."

The girl stared at them, her eyes popping, and then without a word, she jumped from her stool, held up a finger in a *hang on* gesture, and shot through the door behind her. They heard her screeching in the room behind the reception. "Mr Bromley, the police. It's the police. Out in reception."

Jordan looked down at Ros and gave her a grin. "Not often we get that sort of reaction these days, eh?"

She laughed.

* * *

"Ah yes, I was expecting you. What can I do for you, officers?" Roger Bromley wasn't as fazed as his young employee had been. He smiled at them as he lifted the heavy wooden flap which allowed him access from the reception desk and out into the hallway.

"We won't keep you long, sir," Jordan said. "We believe you have a young woman staying with you. She has a baby with her. She checked in last night. Molly McCardle. We just need to have a word with her."

"Oh right, yes. Nice young thing. Arrived quite late, hungry. I made her something to eat. Didn't have any luggage – so I assumed, well, I thought perhaps..." He shrugged. "I hope she's not in any trouble." He waited, obviously hoping for information, a bit of gossip. When none was forthcoming, he went back behind his counter and moved the mouse to wake the computer. "Yes, here we are. I put her in room twenty-four. First floor, easier for her with the pram. Though we do have a lift."

"We really do need to speak to her, sir. As soon as possible," Rosalind said.

"Ah, well. I'm afraid you missed her. She went off just after breakfast. In a bit of a rush, to be honest. I was surprised. She handed her key in at reception and left without so much as goodbye. I did wonder if everything was okay. There was a man with her, according to Karen, and she said she seemed a little... flustered. Yes, that was the word she used. Flustered. I wondered if it was the husband. I hope she's okay."

"What time did she leave, do you know?" Jordan asked.

"Well, as I say, just after breakfast – before nine anyway."

"We need a word with Karen." Jordan glanced at DC Searle. She nodded. "Okay. My colleague here will have a word with your receptionist. See if she can help us with a description. Do you have CCTV?"

Bromley blushed and shook his head. "There's a camera, out in the car park. To be honest, it hasn't worked for a couple of months. We need a new one, I want to upgrade the system. I'm hoping for a good summer season to pay for it. We leave the other one there because it makes the guests feel more secure but..." He shrugged his shoulders.

"Great." Jordan turned away and went back out to the car, leaving Rosalind Searle to begin to interview the girl.

He called Terry Denn. "Too late, Terry. She's gone off with someone. Could be Eddie, I suppose. Can we try and get an image of him from Gary McCardle? Failing that, see if we can get a copy of his passport photograph. I'm going back in to speak to the girl here and then we'll go straight to the McCardle house. I'm hoping it is Eddie and she's gone home with him. I'm really hoping that."

"Do you want me to ask Gary if she's there?"

"I don't think so. If she is, we'll find out soon enough and if she isn't, it's only going to cause him more stress. It can wait until we have more information."

Chapter 27

Karen, the hotel receptionist, looked like a startled hare. She had pulled the sleeves of her blouse down over her hands and twisted and pulled at them, popping a button in the process.

"There's nothing to be alarmed about, honestly," Rosalind Searle told her. "All we want to know is what happened when Miss McCardle left this morning. Did she say anything? Did she tell you where she was going, for example? How did she seem? Happy, upset, worried?"

"Like I told Mr Bromley, she seemed just a bit flustered."

"Can you explain what you mean?"

"Well, she looked as if she'd had to go in a rush. She had her baby bag with her and her jacket and handbag but that was all. No suitcase. But, I don't know what she brought originally, I wasn't here when she checked in yesterday. She just put the key on the counter and said, thank you, and that was it. Then she went out. The man followed her. He didn't speak at all. Well, it was alright because I knew we had her card details and she'd paid the deposit and she hadn't been here long enough to have anything from the bar or the restaurant. So, she just went. Normally people say whether they've had a nice time. They say they'll come back again – or something. Friendly, you know. But she didn't. I wondered where the baby was. I looked out of the door, but they got into a car, so I assumed it was there. I know you shouldn't do that, leave them in cars, babies. So, I just thought that was why she was a bit panicky. Seems odd because she could have kept him with her, couldn't she?"

"Okay. So, this man who was with her," Jordan said. "What can you tell us about him?"

"He was quite tall, about the same as you, about the same age as well. Dark hair, slim erm…"

"Yes, you're doing very well, Karen. You are being really helpful. Anything else? What about his clothes?"

"Oh right. He had jeans on and a grey top, a sweatshirt. And that's about it really. No coat or anything. I had seen him earlier in the dining room and he had a brown jacket with him then. I didn't realise at the time he wasn't a guest, not until Mr Bromley said. He was sitting with her, holding the little baby. I thought they must be together. Were they not?"

"To be honest, we don't really know at the moment, but you have been a huge help. Thank you so much."

Jordan's phone chimed. There was a text message from Terry Denn.

Sorry Boss. Gary M refused to provide a picture of his brother. Working on a passport photograph or social media. Nothing yet.

Jordan went back to the girl. "Now, this car they left in. What can you tell us about that?"

"Not much. Sorry. I don't know about cars."

"Okay, don't worry. What colour was it? Do you know?"

"I think it was dark. I only saw the back of it. Dark blue perhaps, yes it was dark blue."

"But you don't know what sort it was? If we show you some pictures, do you think it will help?"

"No, I only got a quick look. I just saw she got in the back and they put the pram in behind the seat. She had the baby on her knee, that's not right, is it? But that was all I saw, then it went. Anyway, the phone was ringing, and I had to dash back inside. I'm sorry."

"You didn't see the licence number?" Rosalind Searle wasn't hopeful, but the question had to be asked.

Karen shook her head. Tears welled in her eyes and she scrabbled in the pocket of her skirt for a tissue.

Jordan leaned towards her. "Please don't be upset. You've done nothing wrong at all. Look, we're going now and I'm sure when we find Molly, she'll be fine. If you do think of anything else, just give us a ring. I'll leave my card with Mr Bromley. Perhaps you should just have a cup of tea." He glanced at the hotel owner who nodded at him.

"Anything else we can do for you – just let us know," Bromley said.

"Thanks, we will. It's alright, honestly, Karen. Look, we don't know there's a problem yet. We just want to talk to Miss McCardle and make sure she's alright. She's had a couple of problems lately and we are a bit worried for her," Jordan said.

"It was just the way he pushed her that upset me." Karen sniffed and wiped at her eyes.

"Sorry, what did you say?" Ros asked.

"The tall bloke. When they got to the car. She stopped and looked in, I thought she was checking on the baby, but he just opened the door and sort of pushed her. Not hard, not so she'd fall over but just by her arm, you know."

"I thought she had a problem. Right from the start. She just seemed… tense… you know." This from Bromley.

"Aw poor thing." With these words Karen dissolved into a full-on crying session and Jordan tipped his head towards the door. Rosalind Searle followed him out into the car park.

"Well, that was interesting. I don't know how much of it was just looking for things to up the ante on the part of the receptionist. She seemed to be a bit of a drama queen, don't you think?" Ros said.

"I'm glad you said that and not me."

"Well, I know. But it was all a bit intense. I wonder if he really did push her, or maybe just helped her in."

Jordan pointed at the defunct camera on top of its useless pole. "I wish there was some sort of regulation about those things. If you're going to have them, they should bloody work. I don't suppose there are any traffic cameras down here, it's a bit off the main drag. A dark-coloured car, maybe blue, isn't much help." He unlocked the car and slid into the driving seat. "Right, let's get back to Wavertree and find out why Gary McCardle is so hesitant to supply a picture of his brother."

Chapter 28

"So, you haven't found her?" Gary McCardle was shouting. He had flung open the door when Jordan and Ros arrived but then had leaned out into the street, looking back and forth. "Where's Molly?" he'd asked.

"We don't know. We know where she was overnight, and we have spoken to people who were with her this morning. Right at this minute, all we know is that she was well, and the baby was okay."

"You're bloody useless, aren't you? Dada was right. You have to look after yourself. You can't rely on other people and especially not the police."

"I'm sorry, Mr McCardle, Gary – I know you're upset but why don't you just sit down for a minute and we'll talk about this." Jordan tried to usher the younger man into the living room. He refused to move out of the hallway, and they stood in a line squashed into the small space.

"There's nothing to talk about. I wanted to find her myself right from the start, but you put me off. Leaving me here just waiting. I thought you had all sorts of technology. That's what you said. Well, fat lot of good it's done us."

"We found her, Gary. But by the time we got there, to the hotel, she'd gone."

"So, use your bloody technology and find her again."

"Gary," Rosalind spoke quietly. "She went off with someone. Now, the best thing you can do is help us to find out who it was. We wondered if it could be your brother."

"I told you he's not here."

"Well, you don't know where he is, so perhaps it was him. Do you really not have a picture of him? What about the holiday you all had? You must have taken some snaps then. Happy memories and all that. Maybe your mum had some here. Where did she keep those sorts of things?"

"She didn't. We don't do much of that."

"Really? These days everyone takes pictures all the time. With their phones and then put them on the internet and so on."

"Well, I don't." He sighed. "Okay, I do have a couple of pictures but I'm not happy about giving them to you. Not without talking to our Eddie. That's not right. I don't know what you'll do with them. How do I know they won't end up in some database?"

"What about his bar in Spain, doesn't he have a website?"

"Yeah, he does."

"Let's have a look at that then. Maybe he's on there."

"No, he's not. It's just pictures of the inside and the view. Some of the parties they organised."

"What are you not telling us, Gary? There's obviously something here you're not talking about. We need to know. If you want us to find out who killed your mum and maybe even where Molly is then we need to know about your family," Jordan said.

"No. I know what you're doing here. You're trying to turn this around. Trying to make out I wouldn't help you. You're just covering your arses. I'm not daft. I'm not giving you pictures of my brother."

"Okay, I can't force you. The girl at the hotel said the man who Molly left with was tall, dark-haired, about my age."

"Well, in that case it wasn't our Eddie."

"How can you be sure?"

"He's a ginger and before you say anything, he wouldn't have dyed it. Anyway, I wouldn't call him tall, he's about the same height as me."

"Okay – not your brother. But does it sound like anyone you might know?"

"Nope. It's time for you to leave. I'm going to Southport to find my sister."

"Really, Gary, I have to advise against it. You don't know where to start and we don't know what's going on. If she is at risk, you could make things worse for her. Anyway, you could put yourself in harm's way. I wish you'd be honest with us. I know you're not being and unless you trust us then you're tying our hands."

"Trust you? Ha! Yes, that'd work, wouldn't it? I did trust you, and see where it's got us. Look, I just want you to go. I've had enough of you."

"There is something else we need to ask you, Gary, and then we'll go. We've been looking into your mum's background. It's routine – we are looking for anything that might help us trace someone who possibly had a grudge against her. That sort of thing."

"I've already told you, there's nobody."

"Well, that might be true, but have you got copies of your parents' birth certificates? We're having trouble obtaining copies. It would help if we could confirm dates and locations."

"No. I haven't. A load of stuff was lost. Something about a box that got tossed by mistake once when they were having a clear-out. They didn't bother to replace them. Mam said she didn't need bits of paper to tell her how old she was."

"What about when she went abroad? Only she would have needed a passport for going to Europe."

"Yes, she had one when we went to Spain. We had to get them, but she already had one. I don't know why. Didn't think about it at the time. I suppose she'd used it once and then just kept it up to date in the hope."

"In the hope?"

"Yes, that she'd have the chance to go and see Eddie. Well, in the end she did. Too late for Dada but we all went over. Eddie booked a place for us to stay. It was lovely and just what Mam needed at the time. Molly was quite young, still at school."

"Okay. So, what do you know about your past? Were they born in Liverpool, your parents? Didn't you say you had a cousin in Ireland?" Jordan asked.

"A cousin, no I don't think so."

"Yes, you did," Jordan insisted.

"Well, I was upset, who knows what I said. It was Liverpool, yeah. As far as I know. We didn't talk about it much. They had no relatives. Mam was an orphan brought up by her auntie who died when Mam was a teenager, and Dada's parents were killed in the war and he stayed with some people at a farm somewhere. Well, that's what the story was anyway. But we were never bothered. They didn't make a fuss about it and that stuff – it's irrelevant, isn't it?"

"Well, it's one way of looking at it. I like to know about my family, though. About where I came from," Jordan said.

"Aye well, maybe it's more interesting. You coming from…" There was a short pause. "Well, from Africa or wherever."

"Jamaica. My family, originally," Jordan said.

"Well, that's more interesting than bloody Wavertree, isn't it? Like I say – there's no papers, no pictures. It all got tossed and nobody was bothered. We had each other and it was enough for us. Haven't a clue whether she still had the passport. She wasn't a big one for keeping stuff like that and she hasn't been well enough to travel far for a while now. It would have been out of date by now anyway. Look, Mam's dead. It stinks, and of course I want you to find out who did it, but you have to find Molly and Jakey. You just have to, at least try and do that."

"If you hear from her, let me know." It was all Jordan could say and they had no choice but to leave and head back to the station with their tails well and truly between their legs.

"We're not going to get anywhere until he starts to tell us the truth. I know he's hiding something. It's an odd set-up all round."

"We should have a look at Molly's Facebook account. She must have one, surely – or one of the other platforms. I'll get on to the forensic data laboratory. They might not have got around to looking at her machine yet. They're always pretty backed up, but they can give us her social media information so we can have a look for ourselves."

"Yes, get onto that will you, Ros. Push them if you can."

"I'll send Bev a message, ask her to get some of the civilians started with it as well. Just online searching. Not very efficient but we might be lucky."

"When you've done that, contact the office and get me an appointment with DCI Cross. He's got to agree to a national appeal now."

Chapter 29

Beverly Powell was waiting for them. "I've got everyone started with the trawl through Molly McCardle's social media usage. I don't know if we'll be able to cover even half of it without knowing what sort of things she was interested in."

"What about the parenting sites? Probably one of the most important things that's happened to her was having the baby," Rosalind said.

"Oh yes, good thinking. I'll pass it on to the team. The brother was no help then?" Beverly asked.

Jordan shook his head and rubbed a hand over his face. He looked around the room, everyone was working away but it seemed it was getting them nowhere. They needed a breakthrough, fast. He had an hour before his meeting with DCI Cross, just time to go through his reports. And, as if he'd wished it upon himself, the first one was from the Detective Chief Inspector.

> *Report on my desk by noon today. Preferably with some progress.'*

He groaned aloud. Uttered an expletive. He'd walked into that. There could be no excuse not to attend now – he had initiated a meeting. Cross would be expecting an update and he had virtually nothing to tell him except they had missed catching up with Molly McCardle. Well, that would go down like a lead balloon, especially as he wasn't even supposed to be looking for her. He hated being on the back foot with the DCI but he was going to have to do some grovelling this time.

Vivienne Bailey stood before the whiteboard and she turned when she heard the swearing. "Oh dear. Somebody's not happy." She walked over to Jordan's desk. "Any chance of a cup of coffee? I smell real coffee. Get me a decent drink and I'll try and cheer you up a bit."

"I'll do it," Terry said.

"Oh God. Well, I hope it's better than your usual."

"Yeah, well, this isn't instant. This is good stuff. Black, no sugar, right?"

"Oh. You remembered. How sweet."

"Now then." She turned back to Jordan. "The dead woman's shoes. They had thick soles, you probably noticed. Old lady shoes. Non-slip. A gift to us as it happens. As I mentioned in my report – I assume you bothered to read it?" She tilted the chair onto the two back legs and swung her feet round on to the corner of Jordan's desk. Rocking back and forth.

He lifted the sheets of paper and wagged them at her. "I was just going to. I've been out," he said.

Terry joined them. Vivienne sipped at the coffee and lifted her eyebrows in surprise. "Hey, Denn, this coffee's not bad. You been taking lessons?"

She didn't wait for a response. "Where was I? Oh yes, shoe soles. There was residue in there; turned out to be grain."

"Grain?"

"Yeah, you know, the stuff your bread gets made from."

"Flour then?" Jordan said.

"Not exactly."

"Could it be from her kitchen?"

"No. God, will you just let me finish? This is imported stuff. I've had a colleague look at it. He reckons it's from the EU. We import quite a lot of grain into Britain, and Liverpool has a long history of the trade. Have you ever seen the Corn Exchange? It's a lovely old building. Course they're effing it up now by converting it into a sodding Aparthotel or something. Anyway. We need to go to where they store this stuff. The place to start will be the container base and bulk storage ports. They have all manner of things there and my opinion is that your lady could have been there before she died," Vivienne said.

"Bulk storage?"

"Yeah. Big ones are down in Seaforth – nice and handy for the docks and then for the Ship Canal and up into Manchester. That isn't very far from where your old lady lived, is it? Pretty straightforward route, quick twenty minutes in a car. Of course, there are plenty of other options, flour mills for example. But we have to start somewhere, so where it comes into the country makes sense to me, and especially as that's close to the deceased's home."

"So where does this grain come from?"

"Germany, France – a lot from France until we screw it all up leaving the European Union. We export it as well, once we've faffed about with it a bit, to Ireland, that'd be Eire."

"How come you know all this?" Terry asked.

"Ha! Because, my little coffee-making friend, I listen. As I said, I consulted a colleague and he's very knowledgeable," Vivienne replied. "Verging on boring, truth be told, but there we are. Each to his own. Anyway, I need to go down there, and I expect you'll want me to keep you informed."

"When do you think you'll be going?" Jordan asked.

"This affie. Mind you, it's probably not going to be a quick job. I reckon I'm on to something but don't expect news in the next few hours. To be honest, our best bet is spotting something interesting on their CCTV. Place is bristling with cameras, obviously. Then if we're very lucky, we might have a clue where to start searching. Right, that's it. I'm off. Stay safe. Be good. We still haven't had that drink, Jordan. I don't think you want to go out with me."

"I do, it's not that at all. Of course, I want to have a drink with you."

"Well, okay. But I'm beginning to wonder. I think you're scared of being seen with us '*ladies*'."

Jordan looked up at Vivienne, her eyes twinkling, a smile twitching her lips. He nodded and grinned back. "Yeah. Soon as this is all squared away, for sure," he said.

She gave a quick wave and swept from the room with Terry gazing after her. "I still can't believe she's not straight, boss. I'd be in there, no danger."

"Stop kidding yourself, DC Denn, she's way out of your league even if she didn't have a very lovely partner." Jordan turned to look at the door, stood quickly and strode across the room. "Vivienne."

The SOCO sergeant turned. "Missing me already?" She laughed.

"Always. Looking at the CCTV, just keep in mind a dark-coloured car, possibly blue, would you?"

"Oh, yeah right, because they're so rare, aren't they?"

"I know but– well..."

"Make, model, plate number?"

"Sorry." Jordan shook his head.

"Bloody Norah, don't hold your breath." She raised a hand in acknowledgement as she swung back and continued her march down the corridor.

Chapter 30

"So, not to put too fine a point on it, DI Carr, you have made no progress with the murder investigation and I think it's mainly because you've been chasing after this other bloody woman. I distinctly remember telling you to concentrate on Mrs McCardle. She may be dead, DI Carr, but she is deserving of our full attention. Already the local papers are giving us a barracking. There have been comments on Radio Merseyside and I don't appreciate having awkward conversations with the chief constable." Richard Cross was standing in front of the window. He had his back to Jordan, his hands clasped behind him.

"I wouldn't say we haven't made any progress, sir. Sergeant Bailey is following up a very promising lead which may well tell us where Mrs McCardle was killed. I still feel, sir, that the disappearance of Molly McCardle is closely linked to her mother's murder. It has to be. It doesn't make any sense otherwise."

The DCI turned and slid into the swivel chair behind his desk. He opened a jar of humbugs and stuffed two into his mouth, rattling the boiled sweets between his teeth. He sucked noisily. "Do you think this girl killed her mother?"

"No, sir, I don't."

"So, why are you chasing her all over Merseyside?"

"I wouldn't say that exactly, sir."

"Well, I bloody would. Let it go, Carr, let her go. Forget about appeals. Unless you have some strong evidence she is actually involved, forget about her. Do I make myself clear? You did well on the last murder, you are now hanging onto the residue of that success but let me explain something." He paused and crunched at the humbugs. "Unless we start to see some genuine progress, things might very well change. I don't want to have to bring in someone else, but it's not beyond the bounds of possibility. Now, go and do the work you are paid for. Missing persons have the details of this Molly woman, leave them to do what they do – unless, of course, you would be happier moving from major crime into that department. You can go."

"Thank you, sir." Jordan walked along the corridor, back straight, chin up. Inside, he was seething. As he made his way back to the incident room with the thoughts swirling in his mind, he knew, no matter what DCI Cross said, no matter how much he railed and threatened, no matter how much he was putting his job on the line, he was going to continue to look for Molly McCardle. He truly did not believe she had killed her mother but that was only a part of this thing and he wanted her and her baby home safe. Yes, the missing persons department were aware of her, but she wasn't underage, she wasn't ancient and suffering from dementia, she wasn't any sort of a priority for them and, more than likely, her name was on a list in a database and that was as far as it went.

He threw himself into his chair, closed his eyes and breathed slowly and deeply, attempting to slow his pounding heartbeat.

"Rough was it, boss?" Terry was beside the desk holding out a cup of coffee.

"It wasn't fun, Terry. I get where he's coming from, I really do. But in here," – he tapped at his forehead – "and in here," – he patted his chest – "I just know the two things are tied together. I understand she could just have run off because she's upset and grief-stricken, but it just doesn't gel. She's a bit sheltered, mollycoddled – excuse the pun – and spoiled. However, her place of safety is that house and when you're upset that's where you go. I'm right, aren't I?" As he asked the question, he wished he could swallow it back immediately. Not only was he putting the DC in a difficult position but showing weakness in command was the worst thing he could do. "Of course, I am," he said.

"Of course you are, boss." Terry winked at him.

"Right answer."

He was rescued by the phone ringing. "Sergeant Bailey, give me some good news."

"Okay."

Jordan put the phone on speaker with the volume reduced. Terry leaned in closely.

"You know your blue car?" Bailey said. "The one you didn't know the make, model or plate number of?"

"Yes." Jordan frowned up at Terry.

"Well… I found it for you."

"Bloody hell, do you really think so? How on earth could you do that?"

"Okay, don't blow a fuse. Too much excitement is bad for a bloke your age. Let's just say there is a dark blue car on the CCTV here, it's left-hand drive, but seeing as you gave me so little to go on I don't know if that's important or not. Lovely Barry, the Port of Liverpool officer who is sitting here beside me, doesn't recognise it even though it must have had a gate pass to get in. It entered the port late on Wednesday night. Barry wasn't on duty then, but I imagine it will be interesting to find out just who was – sorry, Barry." There was quiet muttering. "My friend Barry says you'd better make sure you've got your ducks in a row before you start throwing around any sorts of insinuations. I said I'd pass on the message. For his part, I want it noted he's been really helpful and, bright spark that he is, remembered this one because it was the time that puzzled him. Late for anyone attending a meeting. All the offices would be closed. Not shift change time, just a bit random, etcetera. We followed it around the site on the footage, and I reckon now is the time when I tell you to get your arse down here and come and see what we've found. Bring a hat – it's draughty by the river."

"What have you found?"

"Oh, no. I want to see your pretty face when I show you. Come on, DI Carr, I'm waiting for you."

Chapter 31

Sergeant Bailey was indeed waiting for them at the gatehouse. She had a mug in her hand. Steam curled upwards as she sipped at the hot drink. She slid the window aside. "Alright, Jordan. Won't be a minute." She gulped back what was left of her tea and with a touch on his arm, and a smile at Barry, she stepped out of the little shelter. "Follow the road down there and park next to my lot's van. You will need to suit up, but I promise it'll be worth it. I'll walk down and join you."

The evening was drawing in and the port began to take on a surreal atmosphere. Ships lining the docks swung at their moorings, reflected lights danced on the waves. Floodlights were activated and shadows around the cranes and containers changed the place into something almost otherworldly. Jordan stood for a while watching the play of lights on the river and the scud of clouds across the sky, underlit by the glow from the city.

He turned back to the job at hand and pulled on the shoe covers, gloves and the mask they had been given. Bailey led them down a gap between massive warehouses and under suspended walkways. It was a strange and alien world. The drizzle that had begun earlier glittered silver as it fell past the floodlights. From nowhere came the thought that little Harry would be entranced at this 'fairyland'. The thought of his son brought into Jordan's mind the missing Molly McCardle and her baby. He hoped whatever it was that Vivienne Bailey had to show him wouldn't be to do with the young woman. He shook the thoughts aside as they entered the building and he focused on his surroundings.

There were piles and piles of stuffed sacks lying on wooden pallets. Though attempts had been made to keep the floors clean, he noted the pale grit in corners and around the edges of the stacks. It began to make sense now. There was a prefabricated office in one corner of the warehouse, and it was crowded with white-suited SOC officers. There was the flash of a camera as pictures were recorded. Pushed up against one wall there was a small desk and chair. A metal filing cabinet stood alongside. Evidence tents had been placed on the plastic floor tiles and a safe route created with metal stepping plates.

"Come on then, Carr, have a look at this. I'm moving it as soon as you've seen it, but I thought it would be useful for you to get the whole picture. Don't say I never think about you." Sergeant Bailey was pointing at a small white object lying on the ground. It was a handkerchief, white cotton with a lace edge. In one corner was a tiny, embroidered shape. Sergeant Bailey picked it up with tweezers. Before she slid it into the plastic evidence envelope, she held it closer so Jordan and Terry could see the thing more clearly.

"It's a leaf or a flower," Terry said.

"Actually, it's a shamrock." Bailey stuffed it into the bag, labelled it and handed it to one of the technicians to stow safely away in the crate. "So, I'm thinking older lady – most people use tissues these days. Okay, now come with me." She took them outside to a narrow car park at the edge of the dock. "According to the log Barry showed me, the security lights in this area were faulty on Wednesday and the maintenance crew reported broken bulbs. The last recorded image of the vehicle was just over there." She pointed towards a larger parking area around the corner of the building. "The problem with the lights is not unknown apparently. This is a very heavy work area, big equipment moving about and accidents happen. But this was noted as unusual with all of them being out at one time and there was mention of possible vandalism. The camera was also out of service for a while and they found a broken cable." She flicked air quotes around the word 'broken'.

A scene tent had been erected and the generator hummed noisily in the background, the echo rattling off the corrugated steel sides of the warehouse. They could only just hear the gentle ripple and gurgle of the water sliding past.

On the ground inside the protective cover, Vivienne Baily pointed to a darkened patch of tarmac. "I reckon if we'd found this a couple of days ago there would have been more debris. In my opinion, something has been burned here, there is evidence of the surface beginning to melt and then reset."

"A picture is beginning to form, isn't it?" Jordan said.

"I rather think so. I wonder if the intention was to dump the body over the side or, was it just a safe place to do the evil deed? One thing's for sure. When we find that car, the boot is going to be a cornucopia of evidence. I'll send you a full report as soon as we've finished processing the scene, but it will take a day or two at least. There's a lot of stuff to move inside. But, Jordan, I truly believe we have found your crime scene. I'll come clean and admit it was actually an informed lucky guess on my part. My uncle used to work on the docks and my aunty was always complaining about the muck on his shoes. There were so many other options for the origins of the residue, but it just rang a little bell in the back of my mind."

"Well, thank goodness for your uncle, and your aunty and, for that matter, the little bell in the back of your mind. Thanks so much, Viv. At least now I've got something to report. I'll have a word with Barry before I go. We need to start some investigation into how they got in and I'm afraid that's not going to make us very popular with the port police."

"No, but a bent copper is a bent copper, Jordan, and I don't have any sympathy. Oh yes, in case you were going to ask. The cameras do have ANPR but guess what – the number was obscured."

"Well, that's hardly a surprise, is it. Still, thanks again for this. It's another step in the right direction."

Chapter 32

Gary McCardle was no longer antagonistic when Jordan and Terry knocked on the door. He stood aside silently to allow them entrance and then turned and slogged his way into the kitchen. His hair was greasy, there were stains on his sweatshirt and the distinct smell of body odour trailed him. He had been difficult with them up to now, but Jordan was moved by the state of him.

"Is there anything we can do for you, Gary? Do you want us to contact anyone? You don't have to stay here if you would rather be at home. As long as you keep us up to date with where you are. You might be more comfortable in your own place."

"Thanks. I can't go home. Not until our Molly's back. You haven't found her, have you?"

"Not yet. I'm sorry," Jordan told him. "I have something I want you to have a look at, Gary. It might be upsetting."

"Ha, nothing new there then."

"No. Sorry. Do you recognise this?" Jordan held out his phone with the image of the handkerchief. He scrolled to a close-up of the embroidery.

Gary didn't say anything. He left the kitchen and they heard him run up the stairs and then the creak of floorboards as he walked about in the bedrooms. When he joined them again, he was holding a small white handkerchief in his hand and he simply placed it on the table in among the dirty plates and jam jars. They didn't need to pick it up to confirm that it was a partner to the one from the warehouse.

"Bought them for her for Christmas. She hated paper hankies."

Jordan nodded and pushed the phone into his pocket. "We are getting a clear idea now about what happened to your mother."

"Where did you find it?" Gary pointed vaguely towards Jordan. They knew what he meant.

"I don't want to get into that with you right now, Gary, and to be honest it's opened up more questions. I promise you, later on you'll know all about it. Just one thing though, and it may seem odd. Your dad used to work at the docks, didn't he?"

Gary didn't answer. He stared at them for a minute and then, with a huge sigh, he lowered his head into his hands. "Yes. He did." They could barely hear him.

"Are you in contact with anyone from back then? I know it's quite a while ago now but, sometimes, family friends keep in touch, don't they?"

"Ha. Family friends. No, we are not in touch with anyone from back then."

"You still haven't heard from Eddie?" Terry asked.

"Nope."

"He hasn't been in touch with Sandra?"

"Nope."

"Okay. Well, that's about it for now. Keep us informed if you hear anything. Look after yourself, Gary." Jordan was tempted to reach out to the hunched shoulders with a reassuring pat but physical contact was a minefield and so they turned away and left him sitting in the mess at the kitchen table running the tiny handkerchief back and forth between his fingers. As they passed the living room, Jordan glanced in to see a little row of soft toys lined up as if they were sitting on the sofa.

"Poor bloke's losing it," Terry said as they clambered back into the car.

"Yeah. We're letting him down. Shit." As he uttered the expletive Jordan thumped at the steering wheel. "Where the hell is she? Where's Molly and the baby?"

Terry didn't speak. There was nothing to say after all and that was the problem.

* * *

They had been back in the incident room just moments when Jordan's phone chimed with a message from Vivienne Bailey.

> *Can open – worms everywhere. Better get your butt back down here smartish. Things just got complicated.*

Chapter 33

It was fully dark now and the rain was heavier. The officer on the gate had been briefed and didn't hold Jordan up any longer than it took to examine his warrant card. "Sergeant Bailey wants you to park where you were this afternoon, sir. She'll meet you there."

There was more activity than there had been earlier, more vehicles, and more people. As they stepped away from the car a figure approached from the doorway of the warehouse, hand raised in front of him. Jordan and Terry took out their ID and were surprised at the close scrutiny it received.

"Sergeant Bailey will meet you. Just hang on by the door for a minute, sir."

"Armed!?" Terry hissed as they splashed through the puddles towards the warehouse. "What's that all about?"

"Dunno. But I reckon we're about to find out."

They didn't have to wait long.

"What's going on, Viv?" Jordan shook his head, flicking aside the raindrops from his hair, and swiped a hand over his face. The rain was heavy now and he wished he had brought his overcoat.

Vivienne Bailey took pity on them. "Come on and sit in the van. I can't let you in there without you suiting up." She jerked her head backwards in the direction of the storage facility. "You can go in later if you really want, but it's a bit busy right now."

The back of the SOC van was warm – the engine running to stave off the chill. Vivienne Bailey perched on the top of one of the boxes. "Sit down. They're tough, these crates, you'll be okay. Right – now then. Your case is about to become much more complicated, mate. So be warned."

"Okay," Jordan said.

"You noticed the pallets when you were here earlier?"

"Yes, of course."

"Well, as you already know, they're grain sacks. We found evidence of bodily fluids on and around them, in the aisles. She was carried through here when she was dead, or maybe dragged. But look at this." She opened an image on her phone and pointed to a shot of one of the pallets and the plastic wrap which had been sliced open. "This wrapping is the way that they are transported to keep the stack safe when it's moved. They are only part way through their journey here, so why would you split that, making it unsafe? It's wrong and we had to look into it. Well, that's when things became really interesting. Look." She held out her phone.

"Oh, bloody hell."

Jordan handed the phone to Terry Denn who let out a low whistle. "That explains the visitors," he said, jerking his thumb backwards towards the guard at the warehouse door.

"Yes. We're waiting for officers from Serious and Organised and I have a feeling Anti-Terrorism may come in on this as well. Better make sure all your I's are dotted and T's crossed, Jordie. You are about to come under some scrutiny."

"The stuff in that sack, though, the packing?" Jordan pointed at the screen image. "That's not grain."

"Ha, well spotted, Dr Watson. No, it's sawdust."

"So, where do we go from here?" Jordan muttered.

"It's turning into a foul night. There doesn't seem much point in you hanging around here for the moment. My advice would be to go back to your place. Get Denn to make you some of his coffee." She grinned at Terry. "Then go through your reports and wait for the call. Sorry, Jordan, this has just become very much bigger than your little dead lady."

Chapter 34

Back at the police station the civilians had left for the day, but Rosalind Searle stood in front of the whiteboard reviewing the notes and now and again adding something.

"So, what's the news?" she asked, turning as she heard the door.

"Ha. You're never going to believe this." Terry hung his damp jacket across the back of a chair and walked over to the whiteboard. He picked up the marker. ARMS CACHE IN THE WAREHOUSE. He underlined it and stepped back and then turned and looked across to where Rosalind was staring open-mouthed.

"For real – what? Where?"

"Guns in the sacks. Hidden in the grain. They had unwrapped the one we saw but there are others still all bundled up. Well, not really in grain, which is interesting," Jordan said. "They don't know how many yet, but it sort of doesn't matter, one is too many and they haven't really begun to search. It's a massive job."

"So, what does this mean for us?" Rosalind wanted to know.

"Right now, we haven't a clue. They were expecting the heavy mob down at the warehouse. The Serious and Organised Crime squad were on the way. Vivienne Bailey was waiting for them. We came away. There'll be dogs and goodness knows what else and actually nothing for us to do. It was good of Viv to give us the heads-up so quickly. It means we have the opportunity to go through what we have and make sure it's ready to hand over."

"Hand over?" Searle said.

"Yes. I don't see any way we'll be investigating this. Sergeant Bailey reckons there may well be anti-terrorism involved. No, this is more than likely no longer our case and I won't pretend otherwise. It pisses me off. But we have to be realistic here. God only knows what connection a little old lady from Wavertree could have to arms smuggling, but I guess there's something."

"Warning," Terry Denn said.

"Sorry?" Jordan said.

"Back at the start, you said one reason they could have burned the body and left it on the field was as a warning."

"Yes. But are we saying here the McCardles are mixed up in international arms smuggling? It's a bit of a stretch." Rosalind was shaking her head.

"Is it? Why do we think that? Because they're not rolling in money? Because they aren't walking around like Bond villains? You just can't tell these days," Jordan said.

"But guns, boss?" Rosalind said. "The old woman and Molly?"

"That's a point," Terry said, "what happens now about Molly?"

Jordan flopped into one of the chairs. "Molly, sod it." He blew out a long breath. "I'll be honest, I don't know. Right now, I have no idea how this is going to be handled. I'll bet we'll be sidelined. I suppose we have to accept it no matter how much it hurts. There are things here needing skills and knowledge we just don't have. I expect there'll be a meeting with the DCI. We'll know more afterwards."

"But, Molly," Terry said again. "She's still out there. This is going to cause all sorts of delays and complications and in the meantime – she's still out there."

"Is it possible," said Jordan, "we might have been misguided about her? We've assumed she's in danger and being kept away from home against her will, but does this mean we've been wrong all along?"

"Right now, we're thinking, and I reckon it's understandable, we're all thinking Mary McCardle and Molly are somehow mixed up in this new thing, this guns thing. What if they're not?" Rosalind said.

"Oh, come on, Ros. What? You reckon there just happened to be guns in the same place Mrs McCardle was probably killed and there's no connection. Get real," Terry snapped.

"Yeah, I suppose you're right. It's just that I can't see it. I mean, why?"

"Well," Jordan said. "Until we're told otherwise, I'm going to carry on looking for Molly and Jakey. I'm not turning my back on her and letting her become a footnote to some sort of huge international investigation. She's still out there somewhere. We can't do anything about Mary McCardle, it's already too late for her. But Molly – I'm going to keep looking. If she's a crim then so be it. I'll have egg on my face. But we need to know. You guys can call it a day if you like but I'm staying for a bit. I'm going through some of the CCTV from Southport. That bloody car didn't just disappear. We need to find it and see where it went after the hotel. If we're wrong about Molly, it'll get us some brownie points with the heavy mob and that'll please DCI Cross. What's to lose?"

He knew they'd stay.

Chapter 35

After a couple more hours of peering at CCTV footage with no result and then checking all their paperwork was in order, they called it a day. "Anyone fancy a quick one? We've got time to get in before last orders at the Durning," Terry said.

Jordan glanced at the wall clock. Penny would be in bed. Since she had started back at work, the whole working mother thing was wearing her out. He hated to see her so tired, but she insisted she was fine and she'd soon get used to it.

He pushed thoughts of the baby away. The pub was a typical local boozer. It would be noisy and busy. It would be a distraction.

"Why not? Are you up for it, Ros?"

"Yeah. I'm still trying to get my head round all this, to be honest, and I don't think I could sleep if I went home now."

It was good in the end. There was karaoke and though they didn't actually join in, the laughter and jeering applause took them out of themselves. They were glad there wasn't any need to struggle to make conversation that didn't involve guns and missing or murdered women. As they were leaving Terry pulled out his phone to call for an Uber. "I'm going to meet a few mates, in town. I don't suppose you want to come?"

Jordan shook his head. But Rosalind glanced at her watch and nodded. "Go on then, just for an hour. I'm still wound-up. It's time I met some of your mates anyway, Terry. I'll just send my mum a quick text to let her know I'll be late. She worries otherwise."

* * *

Jordan called at the McCardle house the next morning. Gary was sullen and unresponsive. It occurred to Jordan after a few minutes of stilted and difficult conversation that he shouldn't have come. It wasn't going to help, and he was too aware of hiding an awful truth. He gave up. "I just wanted to touch base with you. Just to reassure you that no matter what, I'm still looking for your sister and the little one."

"How do you mean, no matter what? There's nothing bloody happening as far as I can see. You'd be better off doing your job than coming round here at the crack of sparrow fart bothering me. When can we have Mam's body anyway? We need to organise things and we need to start to find a way out of this mess."

"I don't know, Gary. I'm sorry."

"Well, I can't understand why they still need to keep her. What the hell good can come of it? Poor bloody woman. That's something you could be doing instead of trying to ease your conscience visiting me."

"I'll find out what I can. If there's anything I'll let you know."

Jordan left feeling depressed and sad.

Although he'd been expecting it, the message on his phone to report to the DCI's office felt like the final straw. This had all become so complicated and Richard Cross wasn't to be relied on to help to sort it out.

Rosalind was already at her desk. She looked a bit bleary-eyed and there was a bottle of water and a mug of coffee close to hand. But she looked up and smiled when he came in.

"Good night?" Jordan asked.

"Well, I'll say one thing for Terry and his mates, they can put the booze away. Jesus, I left them to it after a couple of hours. I can't wait to see what sort of state he's in when he arrives. What do you reckon will be the next thing here, boss?"

"I've got an appointment with the DCI. Until then your guess is as good as mine. Is there anything from Sergeant Bailey?"

"No, not as far as I've seen."

The door opened and they both turned expecting to see a worse for wear Terry Denn. It wasn't him at all.

"Can I help you?" Jordan asked.

"Looking for DI Carr? Would that be you?"

"Yes. And…"

"DCI Griffiths, David. Serious and Organised Crime." As the newcomer walked further into the room, he held out a hand, shaking first Jordan's and then Ros's.

"I've not got long, have to get down to the port pretty sharpish. But I thought it could be useful to have a chat as soon as. You can bring me up to date with things from your end. If you have time now. Then we can work out how we're going to play this. I expect you'll want to stay involved. It was your dead lady that led to this after all?"

Jordan didn't look at Searle, but he imagined she was grinning widely.

"Excellent. Can I offer you coffee?"

Chapter 36

Terry arrived as they were giving David Griffiths a rundown of the case.

"So, this Eddie, the older brother," Griffiths said, "how much do you know about him?"

"Not very much," Jordan said. "He has a bar in Spain. It's one of the big holiday destinations. Seems to have done okay but there's been nothing from him at all since the discovery of the mother's body. We have tried to contact him via mobile phone, and we did speak to someone at the bar. He left there a couple of weeks ago and they haven't heard from him since. They're beginning to be a bit concerned as it's moving into their busy period and nobody else does the ordering etc."

"Hmm. I reckon we'll get someone to go and have a look at his bar in person. Do you have his Spanish address? And a recent picture?"

"Address is in the file, no picture. There was a possible sighting of him by a neighbour up near where the body was found. But Gary was insistent it must have been a mistake. To be honest, we haven't spent a lot of time on him and Gary was antsy when we asked for photographs.

Of course, that was before yesterday, and he didn't seem very important. Did we slip up there?" Jordan asked.

"Don't beat yourself up about it. This is a developing situation, it's no good looking at what-ifs. I fully get your thinking. Anyway, leave him with me, yeah. I may be able to help you out with some of this," said David Griffiths.

"Okay. In the meantime, I'm intending to carry on with our search for Molly. That won't step on anybody's toes, will it?" Jordan said.

"No, seems like a plan, actually. Keep me updated with any developments. What have you got going? Have you put an appeal out?"

"I have discussed it with my boss and we agreed to hang fire on it for a while but I'll run it all by him again, I don't see a need to wait now." He was aware that Terry was looking at him with his eyebrows raised but the young DC would learn that there were times to speak out and times when it was best to keep things to yourself. "I'll get on to it this morning. I suppose it's too late to use Gary now. He was against it anyway."

"Yes, I'd prefer to have him to ourselves," Griffiths said. He glanced at his watch. "In fact, I've already sent a couple of my mob round there. They'll be with him right now. We may well need to commandeer one of your interview rooms. I assume I can rely on your help with him if necessary, Jordan? He's familiar with you."

"Of course. Anything."

DCI Cross arrived just as Griffiths turned to leave. Jordan made the introductions. It was obvious he'd come down because someone had alerted him to the presence of the visitor. It became clear he knew at least some of what was going on, but he was surprisingly tight-lipped.

When Griffiths left, DCI Cross spent a couple of minutes reviewing the whiteboard. By now the whole team were in and there was a background hum of excitement as word of the discovery spread.

"Well, you'd better pull your finger out, Carr. Find that girl you've been rattling on about. I need a word." The DCI jerked his head in the direction of the corridor.

"I've decided I'm handing over as Gold on this one. A DCI from Serious and Organised is going to be in overall control. I've already got more on my plate than is reasonable."

Jordan didn't respond, apart from a brief nod. They both knew this had been a foregone conclusion once the second team was brought in and possibly why he had been unusually quiet while Griffiths was still there.

"I still need to be kept informed, mind you. You are still my officer. I don't want you thinking you can by-pass me and take all this to your new friends in St Anne Street. I still have an important role to play here. No need to make a fuss about this either. The rest of the team will become distracted and confused. They'll have no need to interact with DCI Morton who has taken over. We've already had a conversation and he was happy to assume overall control."

"Sir." There was nothing else Jordan could say. They both knew how much it must have smarted to have this case whipped out from under him, and even though Cross could tell himself it was pressure of work, lack of experience in the particular discipline, it wasn't going to be his name on the reports or, down the line, him standing outside the court giving the *team effort* statement to the press.

Once Cross left, Jordan contacted the press office regarding the appeal for information about Molly. "I'd like the whole nine yards with this. Notice boards around the area where she was last seen out and about: Lord Street, Southport and in Picton Road. More of them should be placed in the city around Central Station and the bus stop. I'd like something on the television and of course the social media platforms."

Once that was under way, he found a quiet corner in the corridor outside and rang Vivienne Bailey on her mobile phone. "Just wondering what's going on down there, Viv?"

"I've not been here long. I had to get some beauty zeds. I was here until the early hours. Anyway, at the moment the place is like a fairground. We have a fleet of vans and trucks to take stuff away. We have a whole bloody squadron of technicians to check and move the sacks and of course that includes forklift trucks, and all the rest of it. I can't get into the little office to do much about your dead woman. It's a pantomime and no mistake. They've found more guns. They've already started an investigation into the port police so as you can imagine we're about as welcome as a ham sandwich at a synagogue. Sorry, Jordie, not much help to you at the moment. On the upside, I reckon it's got to all be connected so maybe the Serious and Organised section will solve your murder for you and all you'll have to do is stand there and look pretty on the television reports."

"Thanks, Viv. Anything startling, give us a bell, yeah?"

"Of course."

Terry appeared in the doorway of the incident room. "Boss, they need you in the interview suite. They've got Gary McCardle in there and he's refusing to speak to anyone but you. A bit worked-up apparently."

"Right. I'm on the way."

David Griffiths met Jordan outside the interview room. "He's very agitated. We have told him it's to do with the investigation into his mother's death. Which it is at this point. So, he started ranting about you being the one in charge of that. He's right as far as it goes so, I reckoned it was best if you have a chat and I just sit in."

"Fair enough. Have you found anything to suggest he knew about what was at the warehouse? Up until yesterday we didn't know where Mary McCardle was killed."

"We need to talk. There's some stuff here that you don't know. Is there somewhere quiet where we can get a cup of coffee?"

Chapter 37

The canteen was busy, and Griffiths insisted they needed somewhere they wouldn't be interrupted or overheard. In the end, they bought a couple of cups of coffee and a bacon sandwich each, left the station and went to sit in Griffiths's Range Rover.

For a few minutes, there was just the distant swish of tyres on the main road at the front of the building and a few sparrows arguing in the shrubs.

"It's a health hazard, this job," Griffiths muttered through a mouthful of bacon and bread. "I try to stay in shape and then times like this it's all takeaway pizzas, fish and chips and these bloody things. I just can't resist them. Anyway, moving on. Gary McCardle – well, the McCardle family really. I know you tried to trace their background. That was in the report you let me have."

"Yes, we did but we came up against a bit of a brick wall, to be honest. The records were incomplete and when we asked Gary it was hopeless. He waffled and blustered."

David Griffiths pulled a file from the backpack he had stuffed into the footwell. "Have a look at this."

Jordan wiped his fingers on the skimpy napkin and flipped the folder open. He read through it in silence.

"Bloody hell. No wonder we couldn't get very far."

"Yeah, well, you weren't supposed to. It goes without saying that this is on a need-to-know basis. The family had been safe for a long time. Once they were relocated from Eire and settled and the cases were over" – he shrugged – "they were pretty much left to themselves to make the best of it. They were doing okay, weren't they? The older children would probably remember some of their previous life, but the parents seem to have done a pretty good job at keeping them quiet. Molly, well, she was tiny. She wouldn't remember anything about it. There's a couple of pictures in there but nothing very current."

"So, what did he actually do? I mean, I see from this that he was in the protection programme but was he just a grass or actively involved with the terrorists."

"Yes, he was in on a lot of stuff that would have seen him locked up for a long time. There was blood on his hands and no mistake. But he got himself a deal and the people he pointed the finger at were more valuable than he was. Okay, they are old now, some of them were old even when he betrayed them. But they were still connected, and their memories are long and their punishment harsh and merciless."

"Gary will remember his early life in Ireland, but does he know just why they moved and what his father was?"

"Well, I guess there's only one way to find out."

"Yeah, but hang on. The old man has been dead for a while so, what does him being involved with the Irish terrorists have to do with what's happening now?"

"Intriguing, isn't it? As I say, memories are long. If it had just been the killing of Mary McCardle, you would probably never have known about this. That's the whole point of witness protection after all. So, the discovery in the warehouse has done you a favour. It's saved you from having an unsolved murder on your ticket. On the other hand, it's complicated things and, I'm afraid, pretty much taken the case out of your hands to a large extent. I have to say, though, I'm impressed by the way you've handled this. I'll do everything I can to keep you involved and we'll start with now. I'll give you a couple of pointers about what we need from Gary from our side. You'll just have to wing the rest of it and get whatever you can to help you with the search for Molly. We have no reason to hold him as yet, so I'd prefer to keep this as 'friendly' as possible. He's probably been waiting long enough now. Shall we get back and have a word?"

Chapter 38

Gary McCardle was chewing at his fingernails. A plastic cup in front of him was half full of coffee, scum forming on the top. Jordan dismissed the uniformed officer who had been by the door of the little room and he and David Griffiths took their seats at the other side of the Formica-topped table.

"Are you okay, Gary? Have you got everything you need? Can we get you some water?" Jordan said.

"What the hell is going on? Who is this bloke and why am I here?"

"There's been a bit of a development, Gary. Things have become complicated and DCI Griffiths is from another section who have had to be involved. We want to clear things up as quickly as possible so if you just answer a couple of questions now and I'll be honest, there'll be more later. But we'll get you home again as soon as we can. I need to record our talk, okay?"

"Am I under arrest? Because if I am, they didn't do it properly. They didn't read me my rights, didn't tell me what I'm supposed to have done. Which is nothing, by the way. I'm a victim here. I'm a grieving bloody relative. They just asked me to come in, made it clear I didn't have a choice and stuck me in a bloody car. The neighbours'll be loving that. This is police brutality."

Jordan held up a hand, the palm towards Gary, who was shifting and shuffling on the chair. "No, you're not under arrest. You can leave at any time."

"Right, well, I'm off then. I'm going to the papers about this."

"Oh no, I don't think so. I don't think you'll be making any waves, Gary. You don't do that, do you? You were raised to keep your head down, weren't you? To keep your mouth shut and be unnoticed. It must have been tough. Having to watch what you said all the time, having to be alert and aware. Not a good way for young lads to live. It must have been a struggle for you and your Eddie. I bet you cursed your old man at times, didn't you? Forcing you into that sort of life."

"Don't. Don't go bad-mouthing the old man. He did his best. He got us out. He found a better way for us." Gary stopped speaking. He closed his eyes and hid his face behind his hands.

"It's okay," Jordan told him. "I know about it all, you can talk about it in here."

Gary raised his head. "Nothing to talk about. You've obviously been told where I'm from and why I'm here, in Liverpool, so there's nothing else to say."

"I don't think I could have done it, not when I was a little kid. You were very young. How did they manage to make you understand, your mum and dad?"

"They made it plain what was at stake. We weren't daft. They drummed it into us, and they showed us pictures. Pictures of what could happen if we opened our mouths, if we blabbed about the past. You see pictures like those, you don't forget – not even when you're a little kid. I remember our Sandra couldn't eat for days after."

"Is that why you didn't report your mother missing, Gary?"

McCardle sighed. His shoulders slumped as the last of the bravado leaked away. He nodded. "It was like a nightmare coming true when I heard what they'd found, up on the building site. It was as if we'd been waiting for it all along. As if it had just been a matter of time. Did she know? Mam, did she know what was happening?"

Jordan glanced at David Griffiths who gave a small nod. "Your mother was strangled, Gary. She was dead before the fire."

"Thank God. It's been torment. I kept thinking about her, about her being afraid."

"Well, I'm sorry but she was probably afraid, there's no getting around it but we are sure she was dead before the fire. Gary, there are still so many unanswered questions around what happened to your mum. Now you're able to talk about it, would you work with us and try to explain some of it? Your dad found the strength to do the right thing in the end, this is your chance."

"No, we're not doing that. We're not going to lie about it. Dada did what he did because he was scared. He was scared for himself but mostly for us. It was nothing to do with 'the right thing'. He believed in the cause and never really changed his views. He just got us out of it because he didn't want us all to end up dead. It was a big sacrifice for him. He felt like a traitor."

Jordan was aware of David Griffiths tensing beside him. "And you? Do you believe in the cause?"

"I didn't grow up there."

It was a strange non-committal answer. Jordan left it.

"Okay. From what we know there was no sign of a struggle at your house. You told us Molly didn't even raise the alarm with you when she found your mum gone. Have you any idea why that might be? I mean, she was an old lady we know, but after a life of being careful would she just go off on her own without telling anyone?"

"She had a letter, in her bag."

"You didn't tell us she had a letter," Jordan said.

Gary simply shrugged his shoulders. "As you say, after a lifetime of being careful, well you don't blab about stuff."

"But you knew she'd been murdered. Surely you wanted to help us. We went through her things, there's no mention of a letter."

"I threw it away. I didn't know what else to do. I tore it up. I didn't want Molls to see it. I was scared shitless, if you must know. I was sure we were next."

"Can you remember what the message said."

"Of course I bloody can."

They waited.

"There was a picture of Molls and Jakey, just in the street. Outside the house. It said: 'Here's a fine Irish lassie. Shame if anything were to happen to them. Wait for the knock.' So, I guess she did, and they came, and they took her."

Chapter 39

They had to take a break. The declaration about his mother was too much for Gary McCardle. He tried for a while to fight off the tears but in the end the whole thing got the better of him. He sniffed and wiped at his face with the tissue Jordan handed over, but he couldn't form a coherent sentence. They brought him tea and left him to himself for a while, giving him room to get himself together.

"How are you feeling now, Gary?" Jordan and David Griffiths had waited for ten minutes in the corridor, but they were impatient to extract what information they could.

"How the hell do you think I feel? I'm bloody shattered."

Jordan was strangely pleased to see the spark of rebellion back. They had no reason to think the lad had done anything wrong and he and his siblings had been robbed of so much already. Jordan pitied him.

"Okay. But listen, we need to find Molly. We are regarding it as one of the main things. We need to talk about Eddie, but DCI Griffiths is probably the one you should do it with when he's ready. I just want to find your sister and bring her home. Okay?"

Gary nodded. "Listen, I honestly don't know where she is. If I did, I'd tell you. Now this is all in the open. I reckon we'll have to go away, won't we?" He glanced at Griffiths.

"It's something we'll have to talk about, yes. But there's a lot to sort out first, I reckon."

"Well, whatever. If I knew where Molls and Jakey were, I'd tell you. All I know is she was niggled with us. She went out for a walk and she never bloody came back. If those bastards have hurt her, after Mam gave herself up like that. I'll slaughter every last one of them." He stopped. He knew it was a hopeless claim and he knew the two men sitting opposite to him were well aware of that.

"There's nowhere she would go? She didn't have any friends she might stay with?" Jordan asked.

"You still don't understand, do you? Our life hasn't been like other people's. Mam and Dada wanted us at home where they could keep an eye on us. Dada might have saved us all, he might have found a better way, but it wasn't good, it wasn't ordinary. All my life, for as long as I can remember, I've been looking over my shoulder and wondering if somebody trying to make friends with me was genuine or not."

"Okay. So, you can't think of who it could have been she went off with from the hotel?"

"No. It wasn't Eddie, and it wasn't Sandy's partner. He's a fat bloke, that's the first thing anyone would say about him. What are you doing to try and find her? Seems to me you're just sitting on your arse asking bloody stupid questions."

"We're looking at CCTV. We're going to put an appeal out on the television. We've got notice boards up in Liverpool and Southport and we're putting it on social media. We are doing everything we can. If the people who have her are the people who took your mother, then they already know all there is to know. We're not putting her in more danger. You do see that, don't you?"

"I guess."

"Okay, I'll organise a car to get you home. Stay in touch and I promise as soon as we know anything, I'll let you know. Do you want us to contact your older sister?"

"No, I'll do it. Before I go, though. You haven't told me what this other stuff is – why this bloke" – he pointed at Griffiths – "is involved now."

"No, we can't discuss any of that with you right now."

"It's always the same, isn't it? You want me to tell you everything but when it's the other way round there's nothing you can say. Don't bother with a car. I'll walk. I want some fresh air. Some that doesn't smell of pork." He stood, grabbed the jacket from the back of his chair and stormed from the room leaving the door to slam back against the wall.

"Nice to have him on our side," Griffiths said with a grin. "Okay, I'm off down to the port. Do you fancy a drink later?"

"Yes, why not. I'll bring Terry and Ros along. If you see Vivienne Bailey in your travels, I owe her a drink as well, maybe you could ask her."

Chapter 40

It had been so long since the landline in his mother's house had rung that at first Gary didn't recognise the noise. He had forgotten where the thing was kept. Eventually he found it on the shelf behind the television. He wasn't going to answer it. It could only be a sales call anyway. But the house was empty, the night was lonely, and it might be one of his mother's friends who hadn't yet heard about her death. They would be shocked and sympathetic and say kind things. He lifted the receiver.

At first there was nothing, a bit of white noise, some crackles. He was about to hang up when he heard the noise of a motor, the swish of tyres on the road. There was the mutter of passing voices, a distant burst of laughter.

"Hello, who is this? Stop arsing about."

"Gaz. It's me."

"Eddie?"

"Yeah. Listen, are you on your own?"

"I am. Eddie, where have you been? Really shit stuff has been happening. Eddie, Mam's dead."

"I know. I know all of it. Look, I haven't got much time. Is the back gate unlocked?"

"I don't know – probably not. You know Dada screwed it closed years ago. Back when he went through that really paranoid phase. When those blokes were thrown in jail in Dublin."

"I need you to get it open. Now. I need to come to the house. I'll have to come the back way and I'll need to be nippy. Can you do it? Do it now."

"I suppose so."

"Go on, la. I'll be there soon."

"Eddie, what's going on?"

"Open the gate. We can talk after."

"Okay. I'll sort it. I'll see you in a bit, yeah."

"Don't answer the door, Gaz."

"What do you mean, Eddie, why not answer the door? What's going on?"

He was gone. Gary stared at the plastic handset for a minute and then clicked the off button and laid it on the coffee table.

Dada had plenty of tools, he kept them in the cupboard under the stairs in tool kits and cardboard boxes and old shopping bags. He needed the biggest screwdriver to take the fixings out of the brackets they had used. Three of them and the screws were rusted. By the time he'd finished, he was sweating, and his hands were aching and bruised. But the three lumps of metal clattered to the paving stones. He heaved on the handle and it came off in his fingers and he realised the wood had rotted and all that had been necessary would have been a good kick and the whole thing would have collapsed. He'd need to get it fixed. Or maybe not, maybe it was time to call it a day with this place. Leave it and go somewhere with no memories and no reminders. Not yet, though. Not until Molly was back.

He heard the scrape of shoe soles in the alley. He turned the big torch in his hand, hefting it by the long handle. He pulled the rickety gate closed by what was left of the metal fixings and waited.

Chapter 41

The queue of trucks outside the port was astounding. David Griffiths had mentioned it in the pub the night before. The talk had been mostly about the case and nobody had been surprised, or inclined to try and change the subject. After the introductions, the ordering and the food arriving, Molly and Mary had become the main topic of conversation. Of course, the rest of it, weapons and smuggling, had figured large but the start of it all had taken centre stage. However, the murder of Mary McCardle had been sidelined by the disappearance of her daughter and grandson. It wasn't that they didn't care, but Molly was still alive. At least that's what they were all banking on. But the talk was overlaid with the unspoken knowledge that the longer she was missing with no word from her then the more chance there was of an end for the young woman and her baby none of the people around the table wanted to think about. But they did, and they examined all the possibilities and, though it was good to get together, the night was tainted with the spectre of the missing girl.

Arriving at the port, Jordan wasn't prepared for the scale of the problem. He had driven to Seaforth straight from home. Griffiths had suggested it at the pub. "Come and have a look, we are almost at the winding down stage, I reckon. Viv is hoping to finish processing the little office space, I think." Sergeant Bailey had nodded and muttered her agreement through a mouthful of chicken korma.

"We should have moved all the pallets by the day after tomorrow and we need to give the place back to the port authorities as soon as we can. Any hold-up costs them a fortune and the truck drivers are livid. Understandable, really, because they are on such tight schedules, and I don't think their bosses are very interested in reasons when the deliveries are late. Trouble is, if the tachograph says it's time to stop, they have to stop, and if they haven't made their delivery it's a major problem for them."

There were huge articulated lorries backed up along the dual carriageway and traffic officers were fighting to keep one lane free and ensure a flow for the other cars and vans. Jordan drove past and pulled onto the wrong side of the road to access the port. DCI Griffiths was waiting for him in the gatehouse.

"You can leave your car here. It's a bit congested further in."

"It's mayhem out there. How are you managing it?" Jordan asked.

"Well, we can't let them in if they are going anywhere near your warehouse. We're trying to arrange parking but there's going to be plenty of complaints. Costing people a fortune, this business. I expect there will be compensation claims flying around. Think yourself lucky it's not coming out of your budget. We had to draft in some more help, or we'd have been here for weeks. We've made an impression now, though."

"How much did you find?"

"Up to now, it seems as though the pallets down in the corner by the office were the only problem ones. They weren't grain sacks, though they looked like them at first glance. They were stuffed with sawdust and hidden in the middle of the stacks. Then of course, they were wrapped with plastic. If Viv Bailey's team hadn't been so thorough, we could well have missed them. Of course, that was the whole idea. It's good some people still do their jobs properly. Anyway, the sacks nearer to the doors had nothing unusual but unfortunately some of them still had to be opened. There's going to be losses for innocent people, I'm afraid, but it can't be helped. We've got some dogs in and that's speeding things along and cutting down on the destruction. It's someone else's job to decide whether or not they'll have to be destroyed because of the dead body in the office. I'm not worrying about things like that now."

They had reached the storage facility beside the dock. A harsh wind was blowing up the river. The water was whipped into white-capped waves and the hawsers on the ships whistled and rattled in the angry air. Jordan zipped up his jacket before he dragged on the paper scene suit and the shoe covers.

DCI Griffiths led the way to the warehouse door. "So, the thinking is now that it's been one truckload only. We have officers going through the logs and viewing CCTV and it's only a question of time before we trace the truck, which will give us the company, and that'll lead us to the driver. We'll drag him in, and we'll be able to find out where the shipment originated and who's behind it. It's pretty much just a question of going through the motions, to be honest. We've contacted our colleagues in France and alerted them to the situation. It's all happening right now, and we need to move quickly before people cover their tracks. There's still the question of the blue car and how come it was allowed in and that's grim because it's certain someone in the port police is involved. We are questioning officers and it's a bit of a bitch. We'll get to the bottom of it but it's not making us any friends round here. Anyway, Viv Bailey is back in the warehouse office with a couple of her team and I thought you might want to have another look at your own crime scene."

"I appreciate that. There has to be a connection between Mary McCardle's murder and this mess, though, doesn't there?"

"Undoubtedly. Any ideas?"

"Well, the obvious thing is that it's quite simply the same people involved in both and this was a convenient place to bring her. But why would she get herself mixed up in something like this, when you take into account the sacrifices she made to leave violence behind? I am convinced they always intended to set fire to the body. It doesn't seem to me to be the sort of thing you would do on the spur of the moment, not if you intended to dump her back in Wavertree. But we don't know yet who the warning was aimed at, if that's what it was. Gary McCardle would seem to be the obvious one. But it doesn't feel right. I mean he's a bit of a scally, but I don't see him mixed up with this sort of thing and it didn't work, did it? If it had, he'd have been long gone before we'd even identified her. He hung around, he's still hanging around, waiting for his sister."

"What about the other girl. Sandra?"

"I've had some of my people checking into her as much as we can and there's nothing. The partner is from The Wirral. Nothing in his background to be concerned about. He met her at college, and it seems they are just hard-working small business people. I've sent Rosalind Searle to have another chat with her. She's got good instincts. I don't think Molly can be there with them but it's another thing we have to confirm just to show we've covered everything."

"So…" Griffiths said.

"Yep, that leaves Eddie, doesn't it? No contact from him as far as we know." As he said the name, the light in the back of Jordan's mind flickered. "The flowers."

"Sorry?" Griffiths said.

"There was a memorial thing up at the building site. You know what I mean, flowers and candles and what have you."

"Oh yes, a cellotaph?"

"Really? You knew that's what people call them?"

"Yeah, makes sense in an odd and rather tacky way."

"I suppose. Anyway, there was a bunch of roses left there. A bit nicer than most of the filling station ones and the card just had the one word, 'sorry'. He's here, isn't he? He's here in the UK. He's been here all this time."

Chapter 42

Vivienne Bailey glanced up at the change in light from the office door. "Hello, Jordie. Don't come in if you don't have to. We're on a roll here. Got some interesting stuff for you."

"That's good to hear."

"Hair, of course, some of it almost certainly your lady. Grey, curly. But there's more. Dark, short, from over by the desk and near the door. There's some threads from fabric down here." She pointed towards the place where the handkerchief had been. I think we'll find most of it was from Mrs McCardle's clothes and there's more caught in there." She pointed to a small wooden chair. "The back is split. I think she fought. Well, of course she did. I think she fought hard, but she was sitting on there when they killed her, I reckon. I'll be writing it all out for you. Have you met the Crime Scene Manager? Dave Griffiths brought him in."

"Oh, so not Doug?"

"No, new scene, new manager from St Anne Street. Nice guy. Hey, it was good to get together last night. Doesn't get you off the hook, though, you and me have got a date at some stage. Actually, how do you feel about you and your wife coming round to ours for dinner sometime? I know you've got a sprog but you could bring him if you're into that or get a wrangler for him and come on your own. Rebecca does a mean chili."

"That'd be lovely. I know Penny would be chuffed."

"Cool. Okay. Got to go, evidence to collect."

"Cheers, Viv. No point in my hanging around, I don't reckon, but thanks for the update."

"No sign of your missing girl yet?"

Jordan shook his head. "The more we find out about all of this" – he swept an arm around – "the more worried I am about her. We'll keep looking until we find her, but I worry about what exactly we'll find, to be honest."

Vivienne Bailey didn't respond. There was no need.

Jordan left the warehouse. It was a controlled hubbub, but he could tell the initial flurry of excitement had ebbed away as the innocent sacks near the door were moved. The dogs were still snuffling around but the handlers were obviously pretty relaxed. He was on his way back to where he'd left the car when David Griffiths called him from the gatehouse.

"Hey, Jordan hang on a minute. I've got something for you." The DCI sprinted to catch up. "Okay. Let me bring you up to date. They've found the truck. It originated in Spain, drove up through France, a couple of stops on the way and then unloaded here just the day before your murder. We've actioned the international warrant to arrest the driver. Looks like I'm off to Spain. Do you want me to bring you a straw donkey back?" Griffiths slapped Jordan on the back.

"That's brilliant. So…"

"Come and look at this." He turned and strode back towards the entrance to the port. There were truckers milling around the barriers, the mood was ill-tempered and there were angry shouts as they passed. David Griffiths ignored the drivers as he ushered Jordan through the narrow doorway.

"Okay, Mick – play it again."

They huddled around the screens. "Now, this is the day the truck arrived. The CCTV has ANPR – I think you already knew that?"

Jordan nodded.

"So, here's the truck with the pallets. This numpty" – he pointed to the port police officer on the corner of the screen – "is already down in the city waiting for me to go and have a chat with him. We're unpopular with the guys here but I reckon he's going to be even more of a pariah very shortly. Stupid bugger. Anyway, that's my next action, but watch this."

The barrier was raised, and the truck rumbled on through. Then, before the red and white metal arm descended, they saw the other vehicle, the blue hatchback tailgating the lorry, sliding in close behind it without stopping. "I reckon you might well want to be in on my little chat. What do you think?"

"Brilliant. No plate number visible?"

"Nah, he's too close up behind the truck – deliberate of course."

"Okay. This is excellent."

"I still have some stuff to do here. Why don't you meet me down in town this affie?"

Chapter 43

Gary stood in his mother's kitchen, frying bacon. He had heard the shower start in the bathroom and knew Eddie would be down soon. He'd want breakfast.

He had been filthy when he'd arrived the night before, sliding in through the back gate and then insisting it be screwed closed again. He was unshaven, his clothes grubby and stinking of BO and his hair greasy and lank. "Bloody hell, Eddie. What's happened?"

"Pull the curtains on. Is the door locked?"

"Calm down. What's going on?"

"I'll explain it all in a bit. Stick the kettle on. I'm spittin' feathers. Have you got anything to eat?"

"I've got some bread – I could do you some toast."

"No, I need more than toast. Tell you what, ring for a pizza. Meat feast and some garlic bread and some fries."

"Okay, okay. But look, just take a breath – look at you, you're in a right state."

"Yeah, well. Just give me a minute. Ring for the pizza. Tell you what, run up to the offie, Gary. Grab some cans and some voddie. I need something to take the edge off. But be careful."

"How do you mean?"

"Well, you know. Make sure nobody follows you. Keep your eyes peeled – see there's nobody hanging around."

"Oh, come on, man. You sound like Dada back in the day."

"No. You need to take care. Think. Look at what happened to Mam."

"Yeah 'course but... you know, I thought once Dada had died we'd be in the clear. I really thought we were – and now this. And what about Molly? She's missing and little Jakey, I'm out of my head with worry. What's going on, Eddie? Do you know?"

"We'll talk about it all, but first you need to get me some food. Come on, I've had nothing but a couple of bags of crisps and some chocolate for days."

"But why, la? Honest to god you're not making any sense." Gary shrugged his shoulders and sighed. "Okay. Go on and get a shower, you smell really ripe. I'll order the pizza and get a bevvy in." Gary had moved forward with his arms open for a hug but Eddie backed off. "You're right, our kid, I stink."

Unbelievably then, his eyes had softened, clouded with tears. He coughed and turned away stalking from the room and moments later his feet thundered on the stairs. As the noise of the shower started, Gary made the phone call to the pizza place. He opened the front door and looked around. It was late evening by then and the street was quiet. He jogged to the off licence in the main road, his back itching and prickling, convinced he was being watched. He came out of the shop with a carrier and sprinted home. He was wound up again, just the way he'd been when he'd heard about the body on the field and had begun to believe it was his mother. He couldn't take much more of this. Molly wasn't back yet. Sandy wasn't answering his calls and the bizzies were about as much use as a chocolate teapot. He'd had enough. He was going home to his flat tomorrow. Eddie could wait for Molly. It was time he got involved in all this crap. Then when he'd grabbed his stuff, he was off. He'd go over to Germany. He had a mate over there and he could get him a job in a bar. Then after a while, when he'd got some money together, he'd go to Australia. That's where he should be. There wouldn't be any need for him to look over his shoulder in Oz. He could live normally. It's what they all should have done. Got right away from the Troubles.

They'd tied one on when he got back. When the food arrived, Eddie had fallen on it as if he hadn't eaten for days. He was calmer though, and had fished some old gear out of the wardrobe in the back room. It was funny to see him in old trakkies and a band T-shirt. But it was so good to have someone to talk to that Gary just went with the flow. They hadn't talked about Molly. Eddie asked about their mother and when the funeral would be. He was annoyed when Gary told him the police weren't releasing the remains. They couldn't do anything about it and, in the end, he had to let it go. But every time Gary brought up their sister, Eddie changed the subject. He said they'd get onto the whole thing later, they'd get a private detective if they needed to. He had money and they'd pay to find her. He said she'd always been a bit dibby, that she'd probably just run away to worry them because she was used to being the centre of attention. "She'll be with that gobshite of a boyfriend, the one who won't let on that he's Jakey's dad."

"No. I've been asking round. Nobody here has seen her."

"Whatever. We'll find her. We'll get on it tomorrow for sure, yeah. I'm tired tonight." Eddie said.

"They nearly had her," Gary said.

"How do you mean?"

"They saw her in Southport, the police. What the hell was she doing in Southport?"

"God, la, I don't know. Will you stop it with the bloody third degree."

He was vague when Gary asked him how he'd travelled, why he didn't have his posh car with him, why he was so filthy when he arrived. He skirted around the edges of why he'd sneaked in the back way, why he was so paranoid. Because that's what he was.

But he wouldn't talk about it.

He told Gary to leave it, to let him get himself together. He said he'd screwed up his travel arrangements and had to hitch and didn't want anyone seeing him arriving so scruffy and messed up. Well, it made sense, in a way. He'd always been vain and proud, but still, it didn't all hang together.

Anyway, now, this morning, Eddie was going to have to fill him in on just what had happened, and then he had to take up some of the slack. He was the oldest. It was his job to take charge. Gary cut two big doorstops of bread and poured the boiling water on a couple of tea bags in Mam's best mugs.

Chapter 44

The phone buzzed as Jordan drove back to Wavertree. "Boss, it's me," Rosalind Searle said.

"Yep, what have you got for me, Ros?"

"I've been to see Sandra McCardle. She was pretty cranky, to be honest. She said she hasn't heard from her sister and has no idea where she is. I think I believe her. She said she wanted to be told when Molly 'turned up', her words. But she says she's having nothing more to do with the family. She was quite outspoken. Had enough of the worry and the constant secrecy, she says. Doesn't intend to go back to the house in Liverpool. Isn't intending to have anything to do with their Gary anymore. She asked me to let her know when her mother's funeral will be. She's not helping with the arrangements but intends to be there on the day. I got the impression that now her parents are dead she's opting out. She said she just wants to be 'ordinary'. It was a bit sad actually. I met her bloke. Nice chap and very supportive. He knew about the family background but didn't make any comment about it except to say he reckons it's over now as far as they're concerned. They are thinking about moving away to start afresh. That's quite a big move when you have an established business but there we are."

"Okay. They hadn't heard from Eddie?"

"No, boss. I asked and they just looked blank. Insisted he was in Spain."

"I'll see you back at the station," Jordan told her. "I'm in St Anne Street this afternoon but we'll have a briefing before then."

By the time Jordan arrived at the incident room, they had hard copies of the images of the blue car, a Vauxhall. Beverly had them pinned on the notice board. "I've requested image enhancements and they reckon there's a decent chance of useable pictures of the people inside."

"That's excellent. Terry, give them a call later on this afternoon, will you. I know they're busy, but the creaking gate gets the most oil and all that."

"Creaking what?" Terry said.

"Oh, it's something Nana Gloria says. I think it's a bit made-up but it's an excuse for nagging, basically."

"Fair enough. I'll creak at them."

* * *

In the interview room in St Anne Street, the officer from the port police force was taciturn and unresponsive. It was clear he knew his career was over and there was a good chance he'd be going to jail. However, he wasn't about to give them any information about who he had allowed in illegally, whether or not he knew about the 'extra' cargo in the lorry or where the munitions were headed ultimately.

"You do know there's no way out of this for you, don't you?" David Griffiths asked him. "This is a one-way street and the best you can hope for is to claw back some jail time by helping us now."

It was a constant depressing 'no comment' response and in the end, they gave it up.

"I'll be having another go at him later," Griffiths told Jordan. "I'll keep you up to date."

"I reckon he's more scared of the people behind this than he is of us and the British justice system," Jordan said.

"Yes. He's got himself involved with some nasty people, I reckon, and even jail seems a better option than betraying them."

"Are you still intending going over to Spain?"

"Oh aye. Tomorrow all being well. We've got the address for the owners of the lorry. At the moment they're denying any knowledge of anything amiss. Could be true of course, the driver made a couple of stops in France. Anyway, he's been arrested. They are holding him under terrorism offences so he's not able to speak to anyone and he's in deep shit. Hopefully, it'll loosen his tongue. I'll keep you updated. No news about your missing girl yet?"

Jordan just sighed and shook his head. "I've got another appeal going out tonight, but she's just vanished. It's not looking good." His phone chimed. "Sorry I need to get this, and I'll get off back. Thanks for including me in."

"Wasn't much use really, I'm afraid. We should get together for a drink again soon."

"Yeah. Maybe when you get back. Bring some of that cheap brandy and come round to the house. I'll make a paella. Hopefully, we'll have something to celebrate by then."

* * *

Jordan felt the lightening of the atmosphere as he walked into his incident room. "Terry, what's happening?" he said.

"I've been down to the digital forensics department and had a word with a mate. Actually, he's related to my brother's partner. Anyway, he did us a favour when I told him about Molly McCardle and the baby, and I've now got a decent image of the passenger of the car. The driver was on the far side, so we at least know the car wasn't English, but her face isn't as clear. It's a woman though."

"Okay. Get on to immigration and send them a copy. It's a long shot but they may have caught film of them coming into the country. Tell you what, make sure and explain to them it's linked with the truck, they already have details of it. Maybe they have something from the ferry or at the tunnel. I assume if they all travelled together, the car people and the truck driver, they might well have been in a group in the port or on the train, boat – however they crossed. I know there is pretty extensive CCTV coverage of all of the customs posts and terminal buildings. I'll have Dave Griffiths send you the information he's got, just to make sure they have all they need. This is a step forward. A little one, but movement. Let's get off to Southport."

"Southport, boss?"

"Yes. I want to show the pictures to Karen at the hotel. I know she was a bit flaky but there is just the chance that she'll recognise this bloke as the one who picked up Molly. It's worth a try anyway, blue cars are not exactly rare, but you never know. If she does recognise him, we can include it in the appeal going out tonight. It'll be the quickest way to get his face out there."

Jordan took a deep breath. He felt a buzz of excitement deep in his belly. At last there was movement. After days of nothing, he really thought things were beginning to unfold. He stuck his hands in his pockets so nobody saw him cross his fingers as he walked down to the DCI's office to update Cross.

Chapter 45

By the time Eddie came downstairs Gary had his sandwich ready, his tea made, and had taken them into the living room. Mam would have had kittens if she'd seen them, greasy fingers on her chair covers and rings from the mugs spoiling her coffee table. But Mam was gone, for ever. They would have to decide at some point what would happen with the house. Gary wasn't sure whether she had a will, if she didn't then they would have to sort it out between themselves. They would need to take care of Molly and her son, but the house was worth a few bob. It would need to be discussed. He didn't see how he could bring it up now with Eddie. He should wait, shouldn't he? He should wait until after the funeral. But there was no getting away from the fact that the money would be handy. He could do with it if he was going to leave. With his share, he could go straight to Oz. Wouldn't need to go to Germany.

He looked across the room at his brother. Now he'd had a good night's sleep and a chance to clean up, he was Eddie again. Smart and neat.

"Do you want to go up?" Gary said.

"Up where?"

Gary jerked his head towards the window, vaguely in the direction of the junction outside. "Up to where they found her?"

"No."

"Oh, okay. I just thought you might want to see. There were some flowers and stuff for a while. I don't think there are many left now though."

"Leave it, yeah. Just leave it, our kid. I don't want to go up there. I don't need to."

"We could ask the police if we could go and see her."

"I thought they'd already said no."

"Well yeah, they did but that was back then. Just after it had happened."

"And why do you think it would be any different now?"

"Well, you know, they might have made her look better. She might look okay now."

"How can she look better, you divvy? She was set on fire."

"Well yes, I know but they do stuff, don't they? You know with makeup and that."

"She's not going to look better. They're not going to let us see her. You have to just accept it. We'll get her a nice coffin and a big wreath. We'll see she gets a good send-off but that's all we can do."

"How do you know? You weren't even here. You don't know."

"I know. Just believe me, they won't make her look better. Oh, don't start snivelling."

"I'm not."

"Yes, you are. Just can it, yeah? There's other stuff going on that I have to deal with."

"You don't know what it's been like. You have no idea. While you were over there drinking in the sunshine, I've had to deal with all this. With Mam and Molly, you weren't here, were you? You should have been here. You should have been doing your bit. Even bloody Sandra dropped me in it. Buggered off back to The Wirral and left me on my own. Some bloody family this has turned out to be. Dada'd be spinning in his grave."

"Aye well, it's a bit late for that, innit."

The atmosphere had become charged. Eddie picked up the plate and mug and moved towards the door.

The doorbell rang.

"Who's that?" Eddie said.

"I've no idea. It might be the bloody copper again. He's back and forward all the time."

"Shit. Don't let him in. Wait." He ran through to the kitchen and threw the breakfast dishes in the sink, grabbed the jacket he'd left on the back of a chair the night before and ran for the stairs.

"Don't let on. You hear me? Don't let on I'm here. Doesn't matter who it is. I'm not here."

"Alright, alright. Just calm down."

Eddie sprinted up the steps. Gary waited until he heard the slam from upstairs and then pulled open the front door.

The box wasn't very big, just cardboard with a fold-down top which was loosely closed. There was no-one around. Gary stepped out and scanned up and down the street but there was nothing. He pushed the carton gently with his foot, just shifting it across the flags. He bent forward and, using his fingertips, he pulled the flaps upwards. "Oh shit." For a moment he couldn't breathe. The world tilted and he had to put his hand on the wall to steady himself.

He lifted the parcel carefully and stepped inside closing the door behind him.

"Eddie, God, Eddie get down here. Oh Christ, Eddie, come down now."

Chapter 46

The weather was warm for May and Jordan followed
Queens Drive, through Bootle and past where the port
was in Seaforth. It didn't take them much longer than the
other route, but the traffic was lighter and the driving
much more pleasant. The road didn't go near enough to
see the water but the woods at Ince were coming into leaf
and there was a taste of countryside.

"I haven't been down here for years," Terry said.
"Used to come sometimes when we were kids. It's a fair
way from Kirkby on a push bike but when you're young
you don't notice it so much. We used to go to the sand
dunes now and again. Build a fire, cook some sausages,
drink cider. It's changed a bit now, all wooden walkways
and what have you, but you should take your little lad,
there's squirrels, red ones."

"Yeah, he'd like that, I bet. Maybe when he's a bit
bigger. Is this the best place for a beach then?"

"Well, the dunes are fun for kids and there's the woods.
The beach is big, flat, you can have a good game of footie
but it's not like Spain or somewhere. The sea is always
miles away, at least that's what it seems like. You can see

across to Blackpool, the tower. And if you're into that sort of thing there's the footprints. They've become a bit of a thing now."

"Footprints?"

"Yeah. I don't know all about them but apparently they're like prehistoric."

"What, you mean – fossilised?"

"No. They're in the sand. At low tide they get uncovered and then you can see where the people and the animals walked along the beach. There's a department at the university researching them. There's stuff on the web as well."

"It's fascinating. I'll have to look it up. I hadn't heard of them. Penny would be keen to see those."

"I think they have organised walks and stuff. It's not my thing, all a bit too much like school for me, but it's all on the internet."

"Cool."

They were in the town now and threading through the traffic on Lord Street, avoiding the pedestrians who'd left their caution at home while they were out enjoying the sunshine. "Okay, let's see if we can get anything useful from Karen," Jordan said.

* * *

The girl was, if anything, even more nervous than the first time they had interviewed her. Jordan tried to reassure her, but her eyes shone with nervous tears and her hands shook. "There's nothing at all to worry about, Karen. All I want you to do is look at a picture and tell me if you recognise the man."

"Who is he?" she asked.

"I don't want to say too much because I don't want to suggest anything that might confuse you. Just look at the picture and tell me if you've seen the man before."

He handed the print over and they sat in silence for what felt like an hour as she studied it.

"Well, I don't know him," she said, and Jordan felt his hopes disintegrate. But she continued, "I don't know his name or anything. But I've seen him."

"Okay. Where have you seen him?"

She glanced around the little office. "Out there, in the reception. He was with the girl you were looking for. The one who was holding the baby in the dining room."

"Are you sure?" Jordan asked.

"Oh yes. He's quite hot – oh sorry. Sorry, Mr Bromley."

"No problem, Karen. You just be sure about what you're saying," the hotelier told her.

"I am. He was the one who was with that girl and got into the car with her. I haven't seen him since, though."

Jordan handed over another picture. "Do you think this could be the car?"

"Well, I don't know. It's the same sort of colour, but I only really saw the back. Sorry, I think it could be but only because it's dark blue."

"Thank you, Karen. You've been a great help, really."

At last, she managed a smile.

"I don't quite see how this all joins together," Jordan said to Terry as they walked back across the car park, "but it's beginning to make a tiny bit more sense." His phone rang.

"Carr."

"You need to get here, quick."

"Gary?"

"Yes, get here as soon as you can."

"What's happened?"

"It's Jakey. Little Jakey in a box."

Chapter 47

Eddie snatched the phone from Gary's fingers. "What the hell are you doing?"

"What do you think I'm doing? I'm calling that copper. He gave me his card. Give me my phone back."

"No, you pillock. What have you done that for?"

Gary pointed at the box he had carried in and placed on the sofa. "Well, what else am I supposed to do? Look!" As he spoke and pointed, the baby stirred underneath the soft blue blanket. "It's Jakey."

"Yeah, I get that. But why ring the bizzies? He's okay, isn't he? He's wrapped up and he's not crying or anything."

"Well, yes, but…" Gary reached into the carboard and lifted his nephew out. "Phew, he needs changing – but look at him, Eddie. He's groggy. He shouldn't be all droopy, it's odd. I might take him up the surgery."

"You bloody won't. There's nothing wrong with him."

"How would you know? You don't know him. You've only seen him on videos and pictures. You've never even held him. I have, I know him and he's not right. I'll take him up the ozzy."

"I said no and ring the copper back. Tell him not to come here. Tell him everything's alright."

"Don't be so bloody pathetic. How can I tell him that? He knows this little fella's been missing. Anyway, you're not getting the point in all of this. You're so focused on yourself you can't think of anybody else."

"What are you talking about?"

"Duh, where's Molly?"

There was a loaded silence. Eddie glanced back towards the door as if the absence of his sister had only just occurred to him. "Well…" He shook his head. "Well, I don't know, do I? Stupid bint. We know she was here though."

"How do we know she was here?" The baby was stirring and beginning to grizzle. Gary jiggled him up and down awkwardly.

"Well, it's obvious, isn't it? She must have been here to dump her baby on the doorstep. She's a selfish cow, isn't she? She's dumped him here and gone off. She'll be with some gobshite boyfriend and he's a pain to her now, so she's left him for other people to look after."

"No. You never saw her with him. She loves the very bones of him. She might have been a bit of a divvy in the past but once she had this little lad she changed. He hasn't been easy, a lot of crying and not sleeping but she's lovely with him. Mam complained about him, but Molly never did; she just got on with it. No way would she leave him."

"Absolutely bloody typical." Eddie rooted in the carton, shifting aside the towel laid in the bottom.

"What's that?" Gary pointed at his brother's clenched fist.

"It's nothing, just a bit of rubbish. She's dumped him like so much garbage in a litter box, don't you see. She's just the same as she always was, spoiled and selfish."

"No. Look, I'm going to change him, and we need to sort something for a bottle for him for when he wakens up properly. Molly was feeding him herself, you know?" He made a vague motion sweeping his hand back and forth across his chest. "But I think she had some baby milk for when he wouldn't sleep, top-up she called it."

"Oh, aren't you the proper little mother?"

"Eddie, don't. We need to look after Jakey and then we need to tell that copper what's happened. This scares me."

"How do you mean, it 'scares you'?" Eddie made his voice mocking and high pitched. He waggled his fingers in the air. "Jakey's back, and he's alright."

"It scares me because the only thing that would make Molly leave her kid would be if she had no choice. The only reason she would have no choice would be if someone made her do it. So, where is she and who has made her do this? Or who else has done it because she can't anymore. It scares me because I think Molly must be in real trouble. She hasn't just gone away off her own bat. I reckon she's been taken. It was already on the cards, let's be honest, and this proves it." Gary buried his head in the bundle of baby and blanket as he lost the battle against tears of fear and panic.

"I reckon I knew it all the time, when they said about the hotel in Southport and the bloke in the car. Why after all this time?" he murmured. "I thought they'd leave us alone. I thought with Dada gone and all the years past they'd leave us alone."

"You stupid sod. This has nothing to do with Dada," Eddie said.

"How do you mean?"

"All of that stuff is well in the past. All those people, they're either dead or so old they can't even stand up, never mind go round murdering people. This is nothing to do with Dada. You have to understand. We're not the Ryan family, not Padraig's kids from Dublin. We're just the McCardles from Wavertree."

"Well, what then? What else could it be about? We've never done anything else, just kept our heads down, not made waves. How could it be something else?" Gary paused. "What do you know, Eddie?" He stared across the room. "Shit, Eddie, what have you done?"

Chapter 48

Jordan had bitten off the question he wanted to ask. It was too harsh. He had been on the verge of demanding to know whether the baby was still alive. The words would have sounded cruel, and they would know soon enough.

"Nothing about Molly, though?" Terry Denn asked.

"No, just said the baby was back and in a box."

"Eeuw, that doesn't sound good, does it?"

"Let's not speculate, eh?"

As he spoke, Jordan had a mental image of his own little boy. What would he do if anything ever happened to Harry? It would finish him. Okay, the McCardle baby didn't have a full-time dad but he was loved. That had been clear from the start. The family had suffered for years because of decisions taken far beyond their control and yet they were still being made to pay for things they had nothing to do with. And Molly – what of the young woman? Despite his terse comment to the DC sitting beside him, Jordan's mind was racing with possibilities.

He headed back the way they had come, through the town centre and out onto the coast road, but the time for enjoying the driving had passed. He turned towards the

Formby Bypass and onto Dunnings Bridge Road, down the M57 to the Tarbock roundabout with its confusing lanes. A huge articulated lorry joining from the Knowsley Expressway blared a horn at him as he swerved in front of it to head onto the slip road for the M62. He was aware of Terry beside him flipping the bird at the driver. Not very professional, and he realised belatedly that he could have turned on the integral blue lights in the pool car. But it was over, and he weaved his way into the outside lane.

"Ring through for a paramedic. No matter what, we should have the baby checked over," he told Terry. Then a moment later, "Get me Vivienne Bailey."

"SOCO, boss?"

"Yes, but make sure it's Viv if at all possible. This child could effectively be a crime scene and I don't want to waste any time. No matter how he is, we need to process him for evidence. Of course, if he's... well, if he's no longer alive, it'll be Phil Grant's job." He knew it sounded cold but there was no choice. He was aware of Terry staring at him across the car. "Just do it, Detective Constable, we're nearly there."

The motorway was relatively quiet before the evening rush and in just over three quarters of an hour they were back in Wavertree and parking outside the McCardles' house.

The door opened as Jordan and Terry walked up the short front path. Gary stood inside the hallway cradling his nephew. Jordan felt the tension leave his shoulders. The man would surely not be cuddling a dead child. "Is he okay?" Terry got the question in first.

"I don't know. He seems a bit groggy, but I don't know much about kids."

"We've called for a paramedic. They'll have a look at him."

"Oh, right. Good. Thanks."

They heard the siren in the distance.

"I'll hang on here, flag them down," Terry said.

"Good man," Jordan said. "Now if you and I could just go inside, Mr McCardle."

Gary led the way into the house. "He was in there." He pointed to the box on the couch. "He was wrapped up and the lid was a bit closed, but he wasn't out there long. They rang the bell. What if we hadn't been in, though, eh? What if we'd not answered? They didn't think of that, did they? He could have been out there for hours. Poor little sod."

Jordan had noted the use of the plural pronoun but didn't comment. Gary moved forward to clear a seat. "I'd prefer you to leave the box where it is, Gary. Let's not touch it more than we need to, yeah? And the baby, what have you done with him?"

"Done with him, how do you mean?"

"Have you taken any of his clothes off? Did he have a snow suit on?"

"No, he was just wrapped in the blanket. I changed him, he was wet and stinky."

"Okay, but you haven't bathed him?"

"No. Give us a chance! I rang you as soon as we found him."

"Okay, well for now let's try not to disturb things but maybe let me have that blanket." He had brought a plastic evidence bag from the supply in the car. "We'll need his clothes as well, but let's just make sure he's okay first."

When they arrived, the paramedics were quiet and unruffled by the situation. Terry gave them a quick explanation as they grabbed their bags and left the car double-parked outside. "I need to have a listen to his chest, boss," the older of the two said as he held out his arms for Jakey.

They were gloved up before they even came into the house and they received the baby onto a plastic sheet.

"Tell you what, Gary. Why not go and get him something else to wear and then when they've had a look at him, we can bag up his clothes," Jordan said.

Gary screwed up his face. He didn't like being told what to do. But once he had handed over the baby he ran upstairs and they heard his footsteps as he moved into the back bedroom.

"Can you disturb the clothes as little as possible, mate?" Jordan said.

"Yeah, I'll do what I can." And true to his word the medic peeled Jakey's body suit back carefully. He folded it inside out, handing it over to be bagged and followed it with the little white vest.

"Don't bother about the nappy, he's been changed already," Jordan said. "Is he okay?"

"No wounds visible. He's warm and reacting to stimulus. He's a bit floppy. Could be something worrisome or it could be that he's been given something. Best thing would be for us to take him in. Just in case."

"Can you hold on until my colleague from the crime scene examination section has a chance to get here?"

"Nah, I think we should be heading off. You'll have to come to the hospital. Sorry, my main concern is this little chap and babies can go off really quickly."

"Of course. I understand. If possible, can you see that they don't bath him or anything."

"Hey, mate. I'm not telling the medical staff what to do. You best come with us."

"Come where?" Gary was in the doorway with his hands full of baby clothes.

"I'd be happier if a doctor had a look at your baby. Quickest way is to let us take him up to A&E."

"What and sit there for bloody hours with a load of sick people? I don't think so."

"No, don't worry. We'll make sure he's seen quickly, I promise you."

"Well, where are you going to take him – Broadgreen?"

"No, there's no A&E there anymore. D'ya know what – I think we'll take him straight to Alder Hay – what do you think, Stan?" The paramedic conferred with his colleague.

"Yeah, children's hospital is best, I reckon."

"Okay," Gary nodded and held out the things in his hand. "Can you do it?"

"Yeah, course I can." And in no time the medic had the baby re-dressed and wrapped in the shawl Gary had provided. "There we are. All ready."

"Thanks guys." Jordan reached out and touched the tiny downy head. "We'll be along in a while." He turned to Terry. "Can you let Viv know?"

"Already done it, boss. She's going to meet us there. She's on her way now."

"Off you go then."

"I need to lock up," Gary said.

"Tell you what. Leave it with me. I need to make sure this box is taken care of. Have you got a dead lock?" Jordan said.

"Yeah, course."

"Well, if you leave me the key. I'll make sure you're all secure here and then I guarantee I'll personally bring the key to you at the hospital. Okay. DC Denn will go with you now, will that work?"

They could tell he wasn't happy, but the paramedic lifted Jakey in one arm and hefting his medical bag in the other, he turned to the door. Gary had no option but to follow. "Don't go gegging into my private stuff," he said. "Just move that box and lock up. Don't be nosing round the rooms."

"No. Haven't got a warrant," Jordan said. "I'll just see about this" – he indicated the carton – "and then lock up."

With a final look around and a nervous glance at the stairs, Gary followed the others out to the waiting ambulance.

Chapter 49

The ambulance didn't use the siren and blue lights. Jordan took it to be a good sign, but he had asked Terry Denn to keep him updated from the hospital. The baby didn't appear to have been mistreated and he was clean and warm but had barely opened his eyes. When Gary held him, he lolled loosely in his uncle's arms. Jordan knew that when babies slept, they took it seriously, but in the middle of all the fuss and disturbance by strangers it was worrying he hadn't cried.

He stood for a moment in the silence, listening. He didn't have a warrant and so anything he did now would be inadmissible in a legal sense. He could even have screwed up if ever they brought charges against Gary. But then, he didn't believe the young man had done anything more than be related to a 'problem' family. He walked around the living room rooting among the growing detritus. Jordan wasn't sexist in any way but he had to admit the loss of the woman's touch in this place had become very apparent in the last few days. In the sideboard cupboards all he found were two old bottles of spirits, whisky that had been opened but not finished and gin with a peeling label and damaged cork. There was a dinner service, dusty and unused. There was only one bookshelf set in the alcove beside the chimney breast. On the lower shelves were a few romance paperbacks and a little collection of baby picture books. A couple of pregnancy and delivery pamphlets were pushed into the corner. There were a few gossipy magazines on the next shelf and then nothing above but more cheap ornaments like the ones that lined the window ledge. There was nothing to see.

He walked very quietly out into the hallway and stood at the bottom of the stairs. In the street outside there was the noise of the odd car passing and the shouts of children, the thud of a ball. The house began to click and creak as it settled. He reached out a hand to the radiator. It was cooling.

He walked down the hallway and peered into the kitchen. It was messy and there was a smell. The bins needed emptying and there was the fug of hot fat and fried meat. He used a pen to lift the lid of the bin. It was stuffed with pizza boxes, and cartons from the Chinese takeaway. There was more than he would have expected for just Gary. By the door a black bin bag bulged with more rubbish. A box full of empties, cans and bottles, stood alongside, quite a number, and a couple of empty vodka bottles. Either Gary had been knocking it back all day long, which surely would have shown in his behaviour, or he had company to help him polish this lot off in a couple of evenings.

Jordan's ears felt stretched by the silence. He waited, and then there it was. The quiet creak just above his head. He raised his chin, tensed.

It came again.

He had known all along that the house was not empty. It didn't have the dead feel of empty spaces. The footling around in the living room and the kitchen had simply been waiting for this – looking for the permissible reason to go upstairs without a warrant. He could call out, climb the steps or run up roaring and scare the shit out of whoever was there. Gary had told him the house was empty, patently it was not – cause for investigation. If asked he could say he thought someone had walked in while they were distracted with the sick child. It wasn't true but it might fly.

He stood quietly at the bottom of the steps. The sounds from upstairs were louder now, more confident. He heard the click of a lock, the creak of a door opening. Whoever was there had decided there was no longer any danger. They were moving around freely and all he had to do was wait.

The light had changed as evening drew in. It was chilly with a draft from the front door.

He could act and force the issue, or simply wait here in the hallway until whoever it was appeared on the landing. He waited. The toilet flushed.

As he put a foot on the bottom step, the phone in his pocket vibrated. Before there was any chance to stop it, the jolly burble of the ring tone tore through the silence.

"Shit." He dragged the handset out and glared at the screen. It was Rosalind Searle. He rejected the call and flew up the stairs. The figure on the landing was ready for him, forewarned by the noise. There was a moment of stillness as the two men stared at each other. Assessing distance and possibilities.

"Eddie?" Jordan asked.

The brief scurry of movement came fast and unexpectedly. Jordan was taken off guard and pushed aside easily. He grabbed out at the rushing figure, but momentum had its way and he rocked for a moment on the edge of the step. His balance was lost and the next moment saw him rolling and tumbling, legs up and over his head, arms flailing, as he fell and bounced from top to bottom of the narrow staircase. As he lay groaning and befuddled in the hallway, his legs were thrust aside. Heavy feet stomped across his ankles. There was a sharp pain in his back as he was kicked viciously then the door smashed against the wall as the other man broke for freedom. He paused to glance back into the house, highlighted for just a moment in the light from the streetlamp outside. Then he was gone.

Jordan pushed himself awkwardly into a sitting position on the bottom step and poked at the buttons on his phone. He cradled his head in one hand waiting for the response. He didn't think there were broken bones but his back screeched at him when he shifted his position.

"Despatch."

"I want an alert out immediately." He gave them the location. "IC1 male, ginger hair, approximately one seventy metres. Dressed in jeans and a dark jacket, no hat. He's on foot, get some cars here as quick as you can. This is possibly Eddie McCardle wanted in connection with the murder of Mary McCardle. I'm presently at the McCardle address and I'm going out to find this bastard."

Chapter 50

The car was only a few metres down the road but by the time he bent to drag open the door, Jordan knew he was in trouble. The pain in his back wasn't much more than an awkward stiffness, but the fire that speared from his buttock and down his leg all the way to his toes was eye-watering.

He lowered himself stiffly into the driving seat and tried to push aside the knowledge he was hurt. He was the only one close enough to have any chance of finding Eddie McCardle. By the time anyone else arrived he would either be long gone, if he had transport, or he'd be so well hidden they would have the devil's own job to find him. Eddie knew this area in a way they did not. He had spent his childhood here, playing in the streets and alleys, climbing over the walls into yards and now he was nowhere in sight.

Jordan pulled away from the kerb and set off for the junction, his head whipping left and right. There was a group of lads on the corner, smoking and larking about, pushing at each other and kicking a can around. He pulled over and shouted to them. "Hey, guys. Have you seen Eddie?"

"Who?"

"Eddie McCardle?"

"Never heard of him, mate." One of them began to swagger towards the car.

Jordan didn't have time for this. The back and forth of a conversation that was probably never going to lead anywhere. "Thanks." He pressed the button to close the window and the tyres gave a chirp as he drove off. One of the lads picked up the can and flung it after the car. It missed but he could hear them laughing and jeering behind him. He glanced into the rear-view mirror as one of them jumped into the road, legs bent and arms jerking up and down, hands flicking into his armpits. They all began to make monkey noises. He could turn back, arrest them for racial crimes, but he'd seen it all before and now was not the time.

Eddie had gone. Jordan heard the wail of sirens as backup arrived, but he knew they were too late. Unless they had a piece of unbelievable luck nobody would see him. He could try and get approval for a full-on search with officers on foot knocking on doors and peering into bin stores and sheds, but even before the thought was properly formed he dismissed it. They had no proof Eddie McCardle had killed his mother. He had disappeared from his home in Spain around the time of the murder, there were the flowers that Jordan was convinced were left by him, but it wasn't proof of anything and DCI Cross would never go for it. They needed a conversation with him, of course, and he could have him for assaulting a police officer but there were more important things going on right now.

His shoulder ached a bit but nothing to bother about too much. His back was another matter. It was as if he had a tight band around his lower body. Moving was painful and difficult and he dreaded trying to clamber out of the car.

He turned towards Picton Road. He'd go back to the station, take a paracetamol and regroup. His phone rang. As he pulled it out of his pocket, he winced with the pain caused by the slight twist on the seat.

"DCI Griffiths, hello. What's happening?" Jordan said.

"Call me Dave, please. How are things your end?"

"Pretty dire, to be honest."

"Oh, right. Well, I might be able to cheer you up a bit, or at least give you something else to think about. I've received some information. It could be important. Be best if we could talk face to face, it's complicated."

"Okay, shall I meet you somewhere?"

"I'm on my way home soon, leaving for Spain in the morning. I really need to speak to you immediately. Would it be a pain for you to come to me at St Anne Street?"

It was one of those questions with only one optional answer. He really liked David Griffiths but at the end of the day, when a DCI suggested you went to him, there was no argument and all he was doing right now was driving around empty streets. He saw a couple of patrol cars doing the same thing.

"Yes, of course, no problem. I'll be there in about quarter of an hour."

"Great — I'll buy you a coffee and a bun in the canteen."

Jordan managed a laugh, but he really didn't need this right now. He was sore and frustrated and tired. He was worried about Jakey.

He had been tired before, but right now he felt exhausted to his bones. Molly was still missing. Her son was in hospital, and he didn't feel they were any nearer to finding who killed Mary McCardle. In fact, everything had become more complicated as time went on.

He shook his head and took a deep breath. The slight movement jarred his back and fire shot down his leg.

He couldn't be injured, there just wasn't time.

Chapter 51

"Bloody hell, mate, what happened to you?" DCI Griffiths was waiting in the foyer of the police station as Jordan walked stiffly from the car park.

"I fell down some stairs. It's okay really."

"Well, it doesn't look okay. It looks painful. You've got a bruise on your face as well, and your jacket's torn."

"Oh, sod it. Sorry, sir, I didn't know."

"Don't worry about that. Do you need me to get you to the hospital? Do you want to see our nurse?"

"No – really…" He paused for a minute. "Actually though, do you think she could give me some painkillers? I haven't got much time but a couple of paracetamols would be great."

Griffiths took out his phone. "I can ask her, but I doubt she'll agree without you having an examination."

"Oh, look, don't worry. I'll be fine. I've got a lot going on. The baby has turned up."

"How do you mean, turned up?"

"Left outside the McCardles' house in a cardboard box."

"Is he okay? Jesus, come and sit down before you fall down. You can tell me about it when I've got you a drink. Coffee?"

"Brilliant." It was harder sitting down than remaining standing up, but Jordan lowered himself slowly onto the chair. Every muscle in his back was tense and screaming.

"Here, coffee, and as promised, a bun." Griffiths put the mug and plate holding an iced pastry on the table. "And here, Shirley behind the counter always has a couple of these. You're not allergic or anything are you? I don't want a disciplinary because you've pegged out on the canteen floor." He handed over a sheet of white pills.

"Paracetamols?" Jordan asked.

"Yep. But honestly you should probably see somebody."

"I will, when I have time." He was trying to brush it off but every time he moved it was excruciating. He popped three of the pills from the blister pack and swallowed them with a gulp of coffee. "So, this news?"

"Yeah. We've been tracing the owner of the truck that brought in the guns. We have him now. No moves have actually been made against him, but we are watching him very closely. He's in a place called Malgrat de Mar on the coast of Spain. It's not very far from Barcelona, that's where I'll be flying to. It's a holiday resort, very popular. The transport company is based outside the town, of course. A medium-sized operation, a bit scruffy and low key. There is no doubt it's where the truck came from originally. As I've said earlier, he could have stopped somewhere on the way and interfered with the load. But with the customs seal on the trailer unbroken, chances are he didn't. We are yet to prove one way or the other whether the driver was in on it or just an innocent mule. He's playing dumb at the moment. Now we get to the interesting bits." Griffiths paused to take a gulp of his coffee.

"The trucking company is owned by a pretty influential businessman. Señor Neron Santos. He has quite a few strings to his bow. A hotel on the seafront. A little shopping mall. Some bars…" He paused now and waited.

Jordan shrugged his shoulders, and then the penny dropped. "You don't mean, Eddie McCardle's?"

"Bingo!" The DCI slapped the tabletop causing a couple of people to turn and look at them.

"Bloody hell. We were told he owned his own bar."

"Well, we are still rootling around in the details. However, it seems he rents it. Nominally anyway, but even that could be a cover for double dealing. Anyway, that's not the end of it. He is also on the books as the owner of an estate agency. It seems very unlikely, so we're looking into everything there as well."

"Oh right. That's never been mentioned. Although Molly did say he had rented a villa for the whole family when they visited. So, that makes sense if he had access to property. Probably the family didn't know."

"The agency is actually the more interesting side of things as far as we're concerned, and it may well begin to explain some of what is going on right now."

"How so?" Jordan leaned forward and winced as his back reminded him the problem was still very much there. He hissed through his teeth. "Bloody hell. This had better sort itself soon. I haven't got time for it."

"Are you okay to go on?"

"Yes, of course. Tell you what though, when I get my hands on bloody Eddie McCardle…" He gave a short laugh. "Well, let's just say he's not my favourite person right now."

"Sorry, I don't understand?"

"The stairs I fell down, they were at the McCardles' and… well, let's just say he has to take some of the blame."

"He's in the UK? You've seen him?"

"Yeah. We had an idea he was, didn't we?"

"Of course. But, are you sure?"

"Ninety percent."

"Hang on – take a look at this." Griffiths pulled out his phone and scrolled down a couple of pages of images. "Is this him?"

Jordan glanced at the thumbnail, obviously a passport photograph from the serious expression on McCardle's face, but there was no doubt it was the same man who had squared off against him at the top of the staircase. He nodded. "Yeah absolutely. I lost him but he was in the house. I was going to start a major search but didn't think Cross would go for it. Might be a bit different now. Can you forward the image on to my people? Mark it for the attention of Beverly Powell. I'll give her a heads-up."

Both men concentrated on their phones as Jordan messaged Bev telling her to expect the email and to ensure the image was printed out and distributed. He was itching to get on to Cross and start the major search but needed to know everything there was to know first.

As if he had read Jordan's mind, Griffiths clicked off his phone and continued the conversation. "I expect you want to move on that pretty quickly, so I'll cut this short. We very strongly believe that, apart from the illegal arms shipments, the businesses are being used for money laundering. Expensive property deals are ideal for that. We're arranging to access their bank accounts and what have you, but it all takes time. We have to move carefully until we're sure just who's involved and who we're dealing with. It's big this, Jordan. Very big."

Jordan whistled quietly. "Bloody hell. He's a heavy hitter then, Eddie?"

"Oh yes, we need him bringing in. I was going to suggest you coming over to Spain with me, but you just talked yourself out of a trip. I want you to get on with trying to find him. We'll help as much as we can."

"To be honest, right now sitting on a plane for a couple of hours and carrying baggage wouldn't be very pleasant. Shame though, I would have enjoyed some sunshine."

"Ah well, you win some, you lose some. Realistically, though, I doubt I'll see much sunshine. Not much outside at all probably," Griffiths said.

He began to gather his things together. "Look, I was on my way out but come on up to my office and I'll give you a quick precis of everything we've got. I'll introduce you to my sergeant and if you need any backup you can speak to him. We need to find this bloke."

"But Mary McCardle, Molly?"

"Collateral damage. We are assuming he has done something to upset some pretty nasty people. There's a reason he's run – has to be and you were right at the beginning of all this when you thought poor old Mary was just a warning. Not by the people we thought, though, as it turns out."

"After all this time hiding from the thugs in Ireland because of the father, they're being made to pay for things the golden boy of the family has done."

"I reckon that's about the size of it, yes. Bloody rotten when you think about it."

"Doesn't look too good for Molly."

"No – especially as the baby has been brought back."

Jordan tried to stand. His body wasn't very amenable to the movement and in the end, he had to push himself up with both hands flat on the table and straighten slowly before he could turn and follow Griffiths out of the canteen. He moved like an old man and the pain turned his stomach. He wished he hadn't eaten the pastry.

Chapter 52

The painkillers helped a little but Jordan was awkward and stiff when he moved. Driving didn't do him any favours and as he pulled into the car park at Wavertree and prepared to try and clamber out and stand, he wished deeply that he was at home in bed. He shook the self-pity aside. Time enough for that when he'd found Molly McCardle.

He had made phone calls all the way back from St Anne Street. The DCI had not been happy to be disturbed and less than pleased with the idea he was going to have to come into the station. Jordan had tried to dissuade him and rather had the idea he simply didn't want to pass up the chance of giving him a reaming.

"So, what you are telling me, DI Carr" – Cross stopped to take a slurp of coffee then wiped the back of his hand over his mouth – "is that you had this bloke. This bloke who we now know is a real arse – money laundering, arms smuggling, and God knows what else – you had him, and you let him go."

"I don't think that's fair, sir."

"Well, did you have him?"

"At the time I wasn't a hundred percent sure who he was. The situation was fluid. In the event, I admit he bested me and made a run for it. I did start a search immediately and I went out myself to try and find him. Unfortunately, it was unsuccessful. Either he was hiding, or he had a car. I can't say and I was called down to speak to DCI Griffiths who wanted me there urgently. I had to leave the search to officers on the ground. But we have more information now and most importantly we have an image of him. What we need to do, I think, is increase the parameters of the search, get some more troops out there looking for him."

"You do realise what that's going to do to the overtime, don't you? My budget is going to be shot to hell. I can't believe this. You had him and now this."

He would not apologise.

The DCI was being a complete asshole and Jordan was damned if he would apologise. He replayed the events in his mind. Yes, he could have acted differently, he could have dashed upstairs and hoped to catch Eddie off guard. He could have waited in the hallway for Eddie to come down. He could have done quite a number of different things. But he hadn't, he'd cocked up and this was all hindsight. He stood in silence and watched as Richard Cross collared another shortbread and stuffed it into his mouth, chewing furiously.

"If that's all, sir. I should go and get on with this. Are we going to put out an appeal for information in the media?"

"What is it with you and the bloody television, Carr? It's always the same, every damn thing and you want it on the box. Yes, okay – it might help to mitigate your screw up if we can find him quickly. I'll get on to the communications department myself. You can go."

It took all his reserves of strength for Jordan to turn and walk out of the office without limping or leaning on the chairs he passed. But he couldn't give Cross any excuse to take him off the case and the injury would be exactly what the DCI would use. The painkillers had taken the edge off and, provided he moved carefully and didn't jar his body, he could cope. He would cope because, in spite of the current situation, this was all starting to come together. He had to stick with it.

Rosalind Searle had taken over waiting with Gary at the hospital and Terry Denn was already back in the office co-ordinating the search and allocating tasks to the support workers. "Are we asking for the helicopter?"

Jordan hadn't mentioned air support specifically to DCI Cross, but he had the go-ahead to organise the search. "I reckon so. It's dark out there now, they will have the best chance of seeing him quickly with the infra-red if he's hiding somewhere. I'll get on to that."

"Okay. We've got a team out on foot and an alert out to the cars and any who are able have been diverted to the area."

"Okay, excellent work, Terry."

"May I speak freely, boss?"

"Of course."

"It's all a bit late, isn't it? I mean how long is it since you saw him? I know you got out searching right away but you couldn't see him. A couple of patrol cars were there within minutes as well, but they had no joy."

"What are you saying, Terry? Don't get me wrong, I agree, but it is what it is. We have to do something. There is an all ports alert out, that was sorted by Serious and Organised. I thought I'd go back to the house and work from there. Ros is at the hospital and aware, on the off chance he makes his way to his brother. We have requested the CCTV from the shops in Picton Road and any others in the area. That's ongoing now. We've contacted the bus and train companies and have people monitoring their cameras. If he's moving, we'll find him. We have to."

"He may have gone to ground, boss. I guess he could hide away for days. After all we didn't even know he was in the country. He knows how to stay below the radar."

"Yes, that's true. When she can, Ros is going to have a word with Gary and see if he has any idea where his brother might go. You know, from back when they were kids. But until we know the baby is okay, we have to be a bit sensitive about interviewing his uncle. I'm sick about this to be honest. I could have had him, and I didn't, so any ideas would be welcome."

"What about the port? The office in the warehouse?" Terry asked.

"Already covered by Serious and Organised."

"Right. So, it's just keep on looking until we find him."

"Basically."

Jordan's phone rang. "Carr."

"Hi Jordie. It's your favourite forensic expert."

"Hi there, Viv. What can I do for you?"

"Ask not what you can do for your forensic examiner and yadda."

In spite of it all Jordan had to laugh. "Okay, what can you do for me?"

"It's your cardboard box."

"Sorry?"

"Makeshift baby crib – come on – keep up."

"Oh right. Yeah, a lot has happened in the last couple of hours. Sorry."

"Well, I thought it might cheer you to know that in among the nappies and the blanket was a tissue with residue."

"Okay."

"Turns out to be breast milk."

"Oh – so…?"

"Yes, when they put the baby in the container, which can't have been long before he was dropped off, I reckon, given the condition of the box and the clothes we have. Your missing girl had fed him – ergo…"

"She's still alive."

"Well, as I say, she more than likely was when the baby was put in the box. Of course, there is always the possibility she had expressed milk but to be honest, in this situation, I would have thought it unlikely. If they had needed to feed the little fella without his mum around, they would have just given him some baby formula stuff. And really, low lifes like this… would they even bother?"

"That's the best news I've had all day. Thank you."

"Good luck, Jordie. This is turning into a real conundrum, isn't it?"

"Yeah, you could say that. Thanks, though, you've been a great help."

"Terry, you're with me, we'll go back to the house, have a word with the search team, and then I reckon we might as well go to the hospital and have a chat with Gary."

Chapter 53

There was a uniformed officer stationed at the front door to the McCardles' house. "Anything going on?" Jordan asked him.

"Nothing, sir. A couple of neighbours wanted to know how the baby was. They'd seen the ambulance. Apart from that it's all quiet."

"Have you had the picture of Eddie McCardle sent to you?"

"Aye, I have."

"Okay, so if you see him, let me know immediately. Don't try and detain him. I think you being here would scare him off anyway but keep your eyes open. It's important."

Jordan used the key he had been given by Gary McCardle.

"He was upstairs all the time we were here with the baby, wasn't he?"

"I reckon so. I wonder just how long he's been around," Terry said.

"Well, obviously that's one of the things we need to ask Gary, so we'll get off to Alder Hay as soon as I've had a quick gander at the bedroom."

"Are you okay, sir, you're limping?"

"I'm fine. Just jarred my back." Jordan had to drag himself upstairs using the banister rail but there was no doubt the pain was being held at bay by the pills. He glanced at his watch and calculated how long he'd have to wait before he could safely take more. It was a couple of hours yet.

The bedrooms looked the same as they had on his last visit except for the small one overlooking the back yard. The narrow single bed had been made up and obviously slept in, and there were clothes in a pile in the corner. Jordan pulled on a pair of nitrile gloves and took a pen from his pocket to separate the dirty socks and boxers. There was one pair of jeans and he pushed his fingers into the pocket. He dragged out crumpled tissues and a few coins. They were mixed British and European but there was nothing more.

Jordan went back to where Terry was in the kitchen peering into the bin and the bags by the door. "Well, boss, unless Gary has spent the last few days doing nothing more than eating and boozing, he's had someone here."

"Yes, I'd thought the very same thing. The bedroom upstairs has been used. So, Gary has been keeping secrets, hasn't he? I reckon the best thing we can do now is go and have a word. Give Ros a call at the hospital, let her know we're on the way, find out where they are. We can't do anything else here and I hate to say it, but I don't think Eddie McCardle will still be in this area. We have to look, of course, I guess we have to start somewhere. But there's no real point in us hanging about. There are plenty of bods out there."

* * *

"It's bloody impressive this place, isn't it?" Terry said as they parked outside the hospital. "I remember the old Alder Hay, it was really grim. A big old house converted into one of those workhouse buildings, I think, and then used for soldiers in the wars. It was really scary. Our Paul was in for a bit when he had his appendix out. But this is lovely. I reckon if you're a kid it's bad enough being in hospital without being in a dark old building. But yeah. This is good."

There were signs showing them the way from the short stay car park to the emergency department. "You stay here, Terry. Have a natter with the staff, show them the picture of Eddie McCardle. He might have been hanging around to find out what was going on. I'm going to have a word with Gary. I'm diverting my phone to you but if there's anything urgent you'll have to come up and find me."

Jordan was delighted to see the baby wide awake and smiling at his uncle who jiggled a blue teddy up and down in front of him.

Rosalind Searle was on a chair by the door. "He's doing okay," she said. "They took blood and gave him a real good going over but they reckon he can go home in the morning. He was probably given something. They haven't been able to decide what it was yet. One of the doctors said he reckoned it was possibly something pretty simple like an antihistamine. Not a nice thing to do with a little kid but, you know, better than some of the alternatives. They're keeping him in to just make sure there are no side effects, keep taking urine and what have you."

"That's good news. I bet Gary's chuffed."

"You'd think, wouldn't you? He was okay for a while, quite friendly, really. I think the shock of it all just made him glad he had somebody to talk to. But then…"

"Yeah?"

"Well, he took a phone call. Got down the banks from the medical staff for having his phone on. Since then, he's been sullen with me. Wouldn't say who phoned him, wouldn't talk about it. Got quite stroppy, to be honest. He is nice with the baby I have to give him that. But he's really narky with everyone else."

"Okay," Jordan said. "I have some news about Molly that might be a bit of a bright spot, so I'll have a word. You can take a break if you want. Get a cuppa or whatever."

"Brilliant, thanks, boss."

Jordan put a friendly hand on Gary McCardle's shoulder, but it was shrugged away.

"What do you want now?"

"Just a few words. I have some news for you about your sister."

Gary pushed the chair back from the cot side and stood to look directly at Jordan. "What? What's happened? Have you found her?"

"I'm afraid not, not yet. We do believe, though, that she fed Jakey, not long before he was brought to your house. I suppose it's even possible it was her who left him there. So—"

"No, she didn't leave him. She wouldn't have done. She wouldn't have drugged her baby either. What do you think she is? It wasn't her."

"Okay, so if you're so sure it wasn't your sister, Gary, who do you think it was? Have you any idea at all?"

The pause was just a few seconds too long. The glance to the side spoke volumes and now Gary wouldn't meet Jordan's eyes. He looked down at the cot where Jakey was drifting off to sleep with his little fist stuck into his mouth.

"We need to have a talk, Gary. The baby's okay. When my colleague comes back, she can sit with him and you and I are going to have an honest conversation."

Chapter 54

"Okay, come on, Gary. DC Searle will sit with Jakey and I promise you she'll let you know immediately if there is any change or any need at all for you to come back. Let's go to the coffee bar. You could probably do with a break and we really need to talk, somewhere quiet."

There was no service in the Costa and they were forced to buy drinks from a machine, but it wasn't important. "You had a phone call?" Jordan said.

"So?"

"My DC said it seemed to upset you."

"What would she know? Stuck up cow."

"Okay, let's not get off on the wrong foot here. I'm trying to help you. Surely you can meet me halfway. The main thing now is to find your sister and bring her home safely, yes?"

Gary shrugged his shoulders and mumbled. "Yeah, 'course."

"Okay. I've been back to your house. How long was he there?"

"Who? Jakey? You know I called you as soon as he was brought back."

"No, not Jakey. Your Eddie. How long has he been here?"

"I told you Eddie—"

Jordan held up a hand. "Don't – we know he's back in the country. What we need to find out is why and where he is now. Was the phone call from him?"

"No."

"No? Well, who then?"

Gary sipped at the paper cup and sighed. His shoulders slumped as he let go of the bravado and denial. "It was from Spain. From one of the waiters in the bar. I know him from when we were over there."

"Okay. So?"

"He was looking for Eddie. But not only that. He said he was closing up the bar. They're running out of stuff and they can't do the ordering – so that's one thing."

"Yes, and?"

"He was scared. He said he's going back home to his own village until Eddie comes back to sort things out. He'd had visits from some blokes who threatened him. He said he likes Eddie but he's not staying around to deal with these people. To be honest, I didn't really understand all he was going on about and he was gabbling. The guy was definitely scared."

There was a pause. Jordan knew there was more, and he waited in silence, giving Gary time.

"Okay, they'd given him a message. Said to tell Eddie if he didn't sort things, then more of his family would pay. Shit, that sounds so bloody ridiculous when I say it, like something out of a movie but it's what he said. Our Eddie already told me it wasn't the old stuff this was all about. He said this was nothing to do with Ireland and Dada. I reckon whoever they are he's got trouble with, they've got Molly and they killed Mam, drugged Jakey. They're bloody monsters. You have to find her. You have to find my sister and get us away. You have to make us safe."

By now Gary's hands were shaking and his leg jiggled up and down under the table. "We haven't done anything. I don't know what our Eddie is mixed up in, I don't want to know – but we haven't done anything, not me and Molly, not Sandy neither."

Jordan leaned across the narrow table and patted Gary's hand. "I'm going to do what I can. Anything you can tell me that might help, now is the time. I'll be honest, although it's great that the baby is back, I'm not sure it's altogether a good thing."

"How do you mean?"

"I just think it's an elevation of the situation and time is running short. Can you get in touch with Eddie? Tell me honestly."

"No. I can't. I've tried his phone but it just rings and rings."

"Okay – so have you any idea where he might have gone? Any place you can remember he might be using as a bolt hole to hide up? Maybe somewhere you went when you were kids."

Gary picked at the edge of the cup, pulling bits from the rim and dropping them into the cold coffee. Eventually he looked up. "It's so long ago since Eddie was here. But there was a place; when we were lads. You know where we used to go for a fag and to drink cider."

"Okay. It's a start. You need to tell me where."

"Will she stay with our Jakey, that woman? If I come with you. Will she stay and make sure he's okay? I don't want anything to happen to him and I don't want anyone to think I'm just leaving him."

"Yes, she will."

"Okay. I'll show you."

Chapter 55

It was breaking dawn as they left the hospital. Gary had picked up Jakey to give him a cuddle. "Don't let them think I've left him. Make sure they know I'm coming back," he told Ros Searle. "I don't want bloody social services poking their noses in. He's mine, my family and we're just waiting for his mam to come home. You make sure."

Jordan stopped off in the main reception to have a quick word with Terry Denn who was snoozing on an uncomfortable seat in a corner of the space, which was relatively calm at this early hour. "Nobody has seen him, boss. I gave a copy of the picture to the security blokes and they're keeping an eye out. I've had a walk around every half hour or so but it's all quiet. The local search was stepped down around the McCardles' at about two o'clock. They'll go out again in the morning if there's no change in instructions. The chopper is heading back to Hawarden, but they said they'll go up again tomorrow if you want them to."

"Okay, thanks for that. I think it might be best for you to hang on here. He still might show up. I'll keep you informed and if this doesn't lead anywhere, which I think might well be the case, we'll be back."

"I could go if you like, boss. Your limp is worse. Shame you can't see someone here."

Jordan glanced around at the bright colours and kid-friendly decorations and grinned. "Hmm, I might be a bit bigger than they are used to. No, it's fine – I've taken some more painkillers and to be honest, walking about eases it a bit." The bit about the painkillers was true, the rest of it was mostly wishful thinking. But he didn't want to hand this over to anyone else.

He sent a text to Penny: "Sorry love. Probably won't be home until much later. Give Harry a cuddle from me. Love you." She'd already played host to Nana Gloria. Taking her around Liverpool, showing her the Pier Head and the Beatles trail. He'd barely seen his grandmother but she'd been understanding in the way she always was. He'd need to make this up to both of them at some stage.

Out on the quiet early morning roads, Gary directed them back towards the McCardles'. "Head towards the Technology Park station, and then cross the railway and I'll tell you where to go. Mind you, I'm not sure this place'll still be there. It's years since I went down. Me and Eddie were together a lot when we were kids, even later when we were teenagers. There was always the secret at home. Always the worry about who you were mixing with. I don't know how much of it was real. Maybe Dada was too careful. He'd taken a big risk to get us out of Ireland. I think maybe it made him worry all the time, made him paranoid. Poor old bugger I'm only just now beginning to see what it must have cost him. Anyway, me and Eddie used to get our bikes and come here. Once we found the hut, we reckoned we had some big secret of our own. We had a little gas stove, torches, old sleeping bags. We never stayed overnight – we wouldn't have got away with it. But we came when it was cold and it was nice, sitting there all wrapped up drinking cider and saying what we'd do later, when we could get away. Ha, Eddie actually made it as well. Me? Well, look at me now, working in bloody Argos and living in a one room flat. Anyway, this place was far enough away so we wouldn't be seen by the neighbours and nobody looked twice at us because there were people around even quite late in the evening in the summer. There. Park in that gateway. Don't expect you have to worry about parking – you being a copper and that."

They were beside the railway where it ran along the backs of semidetached houses.

"You might have to shin over the gate. Can you do that?"

Jordan knew he shouldn't, and with his back stiff and painful he didn't even know whether he could. But if Eddie was in this hiding place he might not be there for very long and the risk of missing him grew as the light increased.

The gate was constructed of upright metal bars over a metre and a half tall. "Shit, that didn't used to be there." Gary pointed to the bar above, which had been fixed between the posts. Spaced along its length were sharp steel teeth.

"You really aren't supposed to get in here, are you?" said Jordan. "What the hell is it?"

"It's just allotments. That's how we found it. Mam knew somebody who used to sell tomatoes and we came with her one time."

"Well, there's no way we're going to be able to get over there. Damn it, I'm going to have to call for backup. Unless…"

The house next to the entrance was mostly in darkness but there was a faint light visible, shining out over the back garden.

Jordan marched up the short driveway and knocked on the door. A dog barked inside. He knocked again and pulled out his warrant card.

The old man who answered the door was wearing a thick woollen dressing gown and hung onto the collar of a growling Alsatian with one hand and hefted a heavy stick in the other. "What is it, what do you want knocking on doors at this time in the morning? You'll have the wife awake and there'll be hell to pay."

"I'm sorry, sir. We need to access the allotments urgently. Could we climb over your back wall?"

"Here, let me see that properly." He leaned the stick against the door frame and took the warrant card in his hand to hold it up to the motion sensor light that had illuminated the porch. "Right, well, DI Carr, no, you can't go climbing over my back wall. God knows what damage you'll do and don't bother to mention compensation, I know how that'd go. Anyway, you don't need to. I hold a key to the gate. I'm secretary to the allotment society. You'll have to sign a disclaimer, mind. I don't want you breaking your bloody leg and trying to claim off us. You'll have to wait as well. I'm not handing my key over to you, card or no card." He handed back Jordan's ID. "You could have nicked that – you just never know these days. Wait till I get my kecks on and I'll let you in."

He didn't take very long. The ends of his pyjama trousers poked out beneath the legs of his jeans and frilled over furry tartan slippers. Jordan bit back a grin and stood aside to allow him access to the padlock and chain. He had a clipboard and pen with him and a printed form.

"We use these when people come looking to take on one of the plots, so it'll have to do. Both of you – come on, lad." He thrust the paperwork towards Gary who glanced once at Jordan and then scribbled a signature.

"I'm locking this gate behind you."

"I'd rather you didn't, sir," Jordan said.

"I don't give a monkey's what you'd rather. I leave this open and by the time I've had my porridge half the bloody stuff in there will have been lifted. How will I explain that to my members? No, you'll have to ring me when you want to get out – here." He held out a scrap of paper with a phone number scribbled on it.

As they stepped off along the dirt path, they heard the rattle of the chain and lock behind them.

"Is it far?" Jordan asked.

"Down at the end there. It's past the very last one." Gary pointed into the distance where sunlight was just beginning to shine onto low shrubs and glint on the windows of the greenhouses and sheds.

They walked in silence beside the railway with the sunrise in front of them. Another day beginning and still no Molly, no Eddie and no solutions.

Chapter 56

The small wooden hut was beyond the fence of the last allotment in an open area surrounded by trees and shrubs. Beyond them were the back gardens of a short row of houses. There was a bank of bins. A tap attached to a water pipe dripped into an old bath filled with grey water. On the railway side of the space there was a storage unit which appeared to have been fashioned out of a shipping container painted green. A heavy chain and padlock secured the door. In contrast, the hut under the tree looked as though a strong gust of wind would destroy it. The roof sagged, there had been rainwater drainage at some time but all that remained now were the metal gutter hangers and a broken length of drainpipe leaning out from the wall. The small window still had glass or Perspex in the frame, but it was so filthy it was almost opaque.

Gary stepped in front and Jordan reached out and grabbed his arm. "Wait."

"How do you mean, wait? That's my brother. You'd better not be planning anything dodgy now I've brought you here."

"No, that's not it. We don't know if he's there and more importantly, if he is, we don't know whether he's on his own. He could be scared, and he could be armed."

"Don't be so bloody daft. Armed! Have you heard yourself? Who do you think you are, bloody Bruce Willis?"

"Listen, just give me a minute. Stay here." Jordan turned his phone to silent and slid it back into his pocket. He wasn't risking a repeat of the cock-up on the staircase.

The ground underfoot was boggy and uneven. Jordan was wearing leather shoes. He slipped several times and each time pain shot through his lower back and down his leg. When he was a metre away from the ramshackle building, he stopped and took a deep breath, gathered himself. Behind him Gary waited, fists clenched by his side, his body leaning forward braced to move.

The rickety door was pulled closed but there was no lock or handle, just the hole where a knob had been attached before the rotten wood had let it go. A flagstone had been used as a shallow step and it was covered with dirt. Tendrils of ivy crawled across it. But the growth had been pushed aside and scrapes in the muck showed where the door had been opened recently.

Jordan moved to the window and rubbed at the grime with the side of his fist. It hardly made any difference, but he lifted his hands to cut out the small glare of the rising sun and peered into the dark interior.

The hut was almost empty. There were a few things piled on the floor near to the walls and a plastic garden chair was pushed into the corner. In the middle of the space was a dark mound; it could be a body, a person, or just a heap of discarded tarpaulins. It was impossible to tell.

He would need to go in, but he didn't need the complication of Gary McCardle with him. He walked back to where the younger man waited. "I can't see whether he's in there or not, to be honest. I'm going to have to go in but for now I want you to stay here. Okay."

"No, I'll come in with you. Like I said, it's my brother."

"Yes, but we don't know how he might react. I don't want you in my way and it'll be my arse on the line if you get hurt." As he spoke, Jordan felt the flicker of his phone vibrating in his jacket pocket. "Just a minute." He moved back along the pathway. "Terry, what's happening?"

"Just wanted to let you know, boss, the search for McCardle resumed at first light. A team is going door to door in the area, looking in sheds and outhouses again, and the helicopter is ready to go up. Do you want them to concentrate around the house? It seems a bit pointless, doesn't it? I mean, surely, he'll be long gone by now. What do you want them to do?"

"Are they up already?"

"Just about to deploy. They tried to call you."

"Okay. Phone was on silent and I guess I missed them. Listen, I'm going to give you some co-ordinates. Ask them to fly over this way and see if there is any sign of life in the small hut at the end of the line of allotments. We're waiting nearby, but we can't tell whether or not he's in there."

"Okay, on it, boss. I'll wait for the location."

Jordan googled the address and forwarded the longitude and latitude of the place. "Okay, let's just wait a minute, Gary. If this works, it'll cut down on the risk to us all."

It wasn't long before they heard the sound of the helicopter and saw the dot in the distance grow quickly as it approached them.

Chapter 57

The helicopter flew directly towards them through the grey dawn. The brilliant beam of its spot swept the ground. It wheeled and circled to where Jordan and Gary waited. The idea was that the pilot would contact Terry via the Airwaves set and let him know if they had picked up the heat imprint of someone hiding in the hut. It was an efficient and proven way to seek out fugitives. Jordan held his phone ready, waiting for Terry to ring. His other hand was on Gary's arm, holding the man back.

The call came in quickly. "They've picked up a heat source in the building, boss. Looks as though there is someone in there. I'll get on to despatch and send backup. The chopper will hang around."

Jordan walked towards the dilapidated little hut, his arm outstretched holding Gary back. The roar of the helicopter was deafening, the trees and shrubs whipping in the downdraft. Suddenly the rickety old door was flung open and Eddie McCardle, dirty and dishevelled, half fell, half threw himself out onto the muddy ground.

"Stay where you are!"

Jordan's shout stayed him for a moment, and he looked back but recovered quickly, pushing himself to his feet and turning away and towards the stone wall at the end of one of the gardens.

"Police! Don't run, Eddie, stay there." As he shouted again, Jordan began to dash across the rough grass. The damaged muscles of his back had stiffened in the cold but he pushed through the pain, limping and lurching towards the wall. Gary was ahead of him by now and screaming out at his brother to 'just wait.'

It was no good, the noise and the lights had Eddie terrified and there was no stopping him. Now the Skyshout from the helicopter joined in the furore demanding Eddie stay where he was. He glanced up and flicked a V sign at the sky. He jumped onto the edge of the old bathtub of rainwater and launched himself at the top of the garden wall. Jordan almost had him, reaching up to grab at his feet but it was too late. In moments he had dropped from their sight. The aircraft hovering overhead moved with him as he ran through the garden, down a side passage and out into the road. It followed relentlessly as he tried to dodge between houses and down alleys.

Back in the allotments, Jordan and Gary tried to leave by the metal gate which was a repeat of the one at the start of the pathway. It was locked and bolted the same as its twin. The aircraft was wheeling and turning overhead as it followed Eddie in his panicked flight. Grimacing with the pain, Jordan clambered onto the old bath and dragged himself onto the top of the wall but the fugitive was long gone and they would never catch him now on foot. The best option was to make their way back through the gardens to where the car was parked. They called the allotment secretary to allow them to leave. Jordan was furious and disappointed with himself.

North then west. Eddie was running, possibly heading for home, or making for the station at the Technology Park. The area was a warren of houses and flats. It was crowded and busy with mothers and toddlers heading to the local schools and workers heading to the offices of the Technology Park on foot and in cars.

Jordan used the integral blue lights and leaned on the horn. He threw his phone to Gary McCardle. "Speed-dial DC Denn – find out what's happening."

They heard the scream of sirens from all directions as backup arrived but still the airborne pursuit was underway.

"Bloody hell, call 'em off," Gary yelled. "That's my brother, you don't even know if he's done anything. Call 'em off – he must be scared stupid."

"Sorry, Gary. He shouldn't have run. If he's done nothing he wouldn't have."

"Wouldn't have? What the hell do you think you would have done? A bloody helicopter with its lights on – the noise and then everyone yelling at him. Anybody would have run. I would have."

The tirade was interrupted by the chime of Jordan's phone. It had linked to the Bluetooth so they both heard Terry Denn. "They've got him, boss. The chopper drove him into a cul-de-sac and the lads on the ground have him. He's in custody."

Jordan breathed a huge gust of a sigh and pulled into the kerb, yellow lines be damned. "Okay, I want him back in Wavertree station by the time I get there. I'll bring Gary back to the hospital and pick you up. Update DC Searle and ask her to stay there with Gary and the baby."

They pulled back into the traffic. "If they let Jakey go home today, just ask my detective constable to let me know and I'll arrange some transport for you. She had best stay with you for now. She's not really family liaison but you know her. Is that okay?"

"I suppose. What's going to happen to Eddie?"

"I can't answer that until I've had a word with him. He's in this up to his neck though. There're other people waiting to speak with him. I don't reckon he'll be coming home soon. However, don't forget, in all of this the main thing right now is to find Molly and with luck Eddie will be able to help us do that."

Chapter 58

The police station in Wavertree was in full swing by the time they arrived. Terry had driven and Jordan popped three more painkillers then perched on the edge of the seat and tried to brace himself against the small jolts and turns. He was tired, in pain and frustrated but they had moved on a little more and he focused on that one brightness. When he tried to clamber out of the car he felt like an old man, pushing himself into a standing position with his hands on the bodywork.

"You really need to get that seen to, boss. Why don't you ask to see the nurse or take a couple of hours and go and see your own quack?"

"Nah. It eases off, sitting down doesn't do me any good. I'll be fine. Anyway, chances of getting an appointment anywhere today are pretty much nil, aren't they?"

"I guess. You could always see a chiropractor, my mam saw one when she had the sciatica. He was great."

"Thanks, I might even do that." Now he felt worse, likened to an old lady with sciatica. He straightened as much as he could and set off down the corridor.

"DI Carr. A word." Richard Cross didn't look happy, but then that was nothing new. He spun on his heels and marched back towards his office. Jordan followed him, giving instructions as he left.

"Update the boards, Terry. We'll have a briefing in half an hour."

In his office, DCI Cross threw himself into his desk chair. It lurched backwards as his not inconsiderable weight hit it and he grabbed at the desk to brake before it flew in reverse and hit the wall. Jordan pressed his fingernails into his palms to keep the laugh tamped down. He wasn't offered a seat, for which he was actually grateful.

"Right, what the hell do you think you're up to, Carr?"

"Up to, sir?"

"Don't come the innocent with me. You know what I'm talking about. I gave you permission to launch a search for this McCardle low life. I didn't tell you to create the debacle we have seen."

"Sir, I don't think debacle—"

"Don't argue with me. We've had troops all over the bloody place, cars, and then – to cap it all – the helicopter up. Have you any idea how much this is costing? Well, do you? And all this for someone who you should have had under arrest yesterday in his own house."

"Yes, sir. I felt that, for the search to have the best chance of success we needed the air support. McCardle had gone to ground and I needed to move quickly before he was able to leave the country or at least this area. Today it seemed even more important."

"Today! Don't tell me you mobilised it again today. What on earth did you think was the use of it today? He's gone man, fled and you have that money-eating machine buzzing all over Merseyside."

"No, sir. It wasn't like that. I had reason to believe I knew where he was. The helicopter was available, and it made sense to me, at the time."

He was spared any further explanation by the phone on Cross's desk.

The conversation was one-sided. Several times, DCI Cross glanced up at Jordan, anger in his eyes but something else. Not just the anger about the search but something bitter and peevish. "Right, well – thank you for that. Yes, I'll convey your comments to DI Carr, of course. We'll have him ready for you."

Cross clicked the phone off and took a deep breath. His fingers clutched at the edge of the desk – knuckles white.

"Everything okay, sir?" Jordan asked.

"That was your chum from St Anne Street."

"Sorry, my chum?"

"Yes, Griffiths, ringing from Spain. Apparently, his subordinates keep him informed about what's happening. As opposed to myself. Carr, I don't appreciate being made to look a fool. I don't appreciate being kept in the dark."

Jordan didn't speak. He hadn't a clue what he was supposed to have done and judged it best to wait.

"You didn't tell me you had, this morning, collared this McCardle."

"I haven't had time, sir. We have only just got back. I had to take Gary McCardle to Alder Hay to his nephew. Eddie is in an interview room waiting. When you met us in the corridor we had only just arrived."

"Get out. Get out and go and do your job. Go and speak to Mr McCardle and tell him Serious and Organised crime are on their way from Liverpool to take him back there. Absolutely brilliant. My bloody budget paying for all this overtime and the air support and S and O are going to swan in now and take the credit and you didn't even have the decency to inform me that we had him. Get out, Carr. Go and sort things out and find the girl. Find that girl and find out who murdered the old woman and leave Serious and Organised crime to deal with their end. That's all."

"Yes, sir. Thank you, sir."

Chapter 59

There was an excited buzz in the incident room. Terry Denn was the centre of attention as he filled everyone in on the events of the night. Jordan joined them and the fuss quieted. Jordan went to the coffee machine and poured himself a mug. It had been brewing a while and had a bitter stewed taste, but it was strong and hot and would give him the boost he needed to get through the next few hours at least. He was still annoyed and frustrated by his own performance, hampered as he was by his injury but in the end they had found Eddie.

"Okay. This is a breakthrough, of sorts." He walked to the whiteboard as he spoke. "We've got Eddie here in the interview room, but only for a short while. They want to take him down to St Anne Street in connection with the arms smuggling and quite a bit of other stuff, money laundering for instance. So, I am going to have to leave you and have a word with him now before our colleagues arrive. In the meantime, we are still looking for Molly McCardle. I don't know at this point whether Eddie knows where his sister is. My instinct is no, to be honest. So, we are still looking for the blue left-hand drive hatchback; or any sightings of the girl herself, of course. I'll leave you to get on with it. Go through the CCTV again and anything new that has come in from the media appeals. DC Denn is here for anything you think is urgent. My feeling is we still need to concentrate on the area around Southport, though in truth she could be anywhere in the country. It's important you remember that the baby was returned yesterday. So, organise between yourselves for the footage. Scour everything we have – bear in mind they could have other transport, it could have been Molly herself on foot or whatever else you might imagine. Don't discount anything and share your thoughts. Bev…" Jordan turned to Beverly Powell. "Will you keep the board updated, anything and everything? We have to crack this today."

"Yes, sir. What about the port and airports?"

"We have the all ports alert out for her. Everyone down at Bootle docks is on the lookout and there are posters of her everywhere there. So, Southport and surrounding as a start and we'll get together again as soon as I've interviewed Eddie McCardle. Get to it – we are losing the impetus on this. I know it's become much more complicated, but we need to focus on the young woman."

"What about Mary McCardle though, sir?" Beverly Powell had raised her hand before she spoke again and blushed now as everyone turned to her.

Jordan nodded. "My feeling is that this conversation I'm about to have will shed some light on everything. Eddie McCardle has made comments to his brother and I think, again, it is vital we find this blue car. The whole thing is connected from start to finish and that bloody car is the kingpin. Constable Howarth, come with me, would you?" Jordan had spotted the officer who he'd first met on the rain-soaked evening with Mary McCardle's body newly discovered. He'd obviously blagged himself yet more extra shifts. The young constable beamed at him as he crossed the room to walk down the corridor to the interview room.

They hadn't handcuffed McCardle and he still had his belt and shoes. Jordan knew it would all change when they took him to the city centre station, but for now he wasn't actually under arrest. Once that was done, the clock began ticking.

* * *

"We want to interview you under caution, Mr McCardle. I just want to talk to you about your sister." He went through the procedure. "I also have to tell you that there are officers coming from another police station and they have questions for you regarding your time in Spain and your activities there. But, right now I just want to know anything at all about your sister. We want to find her. I am going to record our conversation and you are entitled to have a legal representative if you want to."

They went through the rigmarole with the recording apparatus. Eddie hadn't spoken except for a gruff 'no' when Jordan asked him again if he wanted a solicitor present. He sat with his arms on the table in front of him and now and again he rubbed at his face. He was unshaven and grubby.

"Have you been offered a drink – something to eat?" Jordan asked.

"I don't want anything – oh no, I want a Coke – just a can of Coke, that's all."

Jordan turned to the constable standing by the door and nodded. "Okay. Do you need anything else?"

"I just want you to find our Molly." As he spoke the tough exterior crumbled in front of them. His hands began to shake and he gulped loudly. For a moment it seemed he might be about to throw up.

"Are you alright?" Jordan asked.

"No. I'm not bloody alright. I'm in the shit, good and proper, and there's no way out for me. But find our Molly. I'll help you as much as I can. Find our Molly and that bloody thug Mariano and the bitch Lili. You do that and

I'll tell you and your mates anything. I'll tell you everything but first you have to get my sister home safe."

Chapter 60

They brought him his Coke and Eddie swigged it back in big gulps. He took in a deep breath and blew it out noisily. "I never intended this. All I ever wanted to do was get on a bit and have a better life than Dada. But I'm a prat and it's all gone to cock and now my family are dead or in danger. I'm sorry. After all the effort my parents took to keep us safe, I've screwed it up. We're cursed. Our family."

Jordan didn't speak, he sat quietly and waited, and Eddie told them all of it. He told them about his problems with Señor Santos. "He's a thug. He owns the building my bar is in," he said. "I rented it on the understanding that I could buy it after two years. Then after two years the price went up and then up again. In the end it was clear he was never going to let it be mine. So, I called him out on it and we came to an agreement. At least that's what I told myself. He was playing me; God, I am an idiot. I agreed to do some stuff for him, and he promised to let me buy the bar. I knew a lot of what I was doing was sailing a bit close to the wind, but it was only small stuff and everybody's at it, aren't they? I bet half the people in this place are on the make one way or another, more than half. How else can you get anywhere? You have to be ready to play. At first it was just a bit of fiddling the books, messing about with the ordering and yes, okay, I let his blokes do a bit of drug trading out the back. I didn't do it though."

Eddie stopped, looked across the table at Jordan, waited for an approval that never came. He shook his head and then carried on. "Anyway, it got to be more and more and then the stuff with the guns started. He knew about Dada. God knows how he found out. I never told him, but people like him, they're connected. They can find out anything if it's going to get them what they want and, as I say, there's always some bugger on the make, someone with an eye to the money." He shrugged again. "He's been doing it for ages. It's huge, well organised and there're people everywhere making money off it. I never liked it. People were dying, I knew that and a couple of times I told him I'd had enough, I didn't want to do it anymore. That was when he threatened my family. Told me that if I didn't help him with all of it then everything Dada had done, and Mam, all those years of looking over their shoulders would have been for nothing.

"So, you just carried on? Breaking the law, helping terrorists," Jordan said.

"What else could I do? Look, it was nothing much at first. Just storing stuff for him. Guns, chemicals. Arranging to have things collected and then the property business. He got me to go into that with him. I didn't do anything, it was just in my name, so it didn't lead back to him. He never even paid me for any of that. We cleaned the money up through the books there. I didn't really understand what it was about. I just signed papers when he told me to, and I got deeper and deeper in so in the end I couldn't get out."

"And your mother?" Jordan asked.

Eddie paused for a minute, coughed and wiped a finger under the corner of his eye. "Poor Mam. It was my fault. I wanted to get out from under. I just wanted it all to stop. I wanted to live quietly without all the worry. That was why I went to Spain in the first place. To get away from the constant stress. I wanted to go back to the old country eventually and buy a bar there, but all of this was making it impossible. I'd thought I could do it, maybe in another couple of years. All the people who had a beef with Dada are ancient now. The new lot aren't bothered about the things he did. Okay, if they'd come across him, they'd probably have seen him off. But they weren't really bothered anymore. He was old news. So, I told him I was moving on; said I was leaving, I'd had enough. Santos told me what he'd do but I didn't believe him. I never thought he'd do it, not to an old woman."

"So, who was it killed your mum? Do you know?"

"It was Mariano. It must have been. When I heard about Mam, I was scared shitless. I came across from France in the back of a van – paid some bloke at the port and then hitched up from Dover. I never thought he'd turn my mam over to that nutter Mariano and Lili, his girl. She's just as bad. I bet they used to torture kittens. Honestly, they're out of their heads. Some of the stuff I've seen them do, well, it'd turn your stomach. And he did, he just had my mam killed as if she didn't count for anything."

"And they have your sister?"

The power of speech left him, and Eddie just nodded and buried his head in his hands. He muttered quietly, "I reckon so. There's no other explanation."

"So, you're going to help us to find her?" Jordan said.

He looked up and nodded. "If I can. I rang her. I told her to hide herself somewhere. I gave her money. I thought she'd go somewhere – not Southport. For Christ sakes. Why didn't she go far away? I meant her to get further away, go somewhere they wouldn't look and what does she do. She goes to the seaside an hour away. Stupid bitch. They must have already been watching her. She made it easy for them, didn't she? And, well, now they've got her." He thumped at the table top with his clenched fist. The empty Coke can bounced and rolled to the floor with a clatter. The uniformed officer moved from the door into the room. Jordan shook his head.

"But they brought the baby back. That's good, yeah?" Constable Howarth had been silent until now but obviously thought his comment might calm Eddie. It didn't work.

Eddie turned to look at him and sneered. "Don't be so bloody daft. Of course it's not good. It's the worst possible thing. The only reason they'd bring Jakey and leave him would be because they don't want to have to look after him, or... you know?"

"No, you tell us," Jordan said.

"Well, they love kids, don't they, the Spanish? They wouldn't want to hurt him."

"But they might well hurt Molly?"

"If she was no use to them, yes."

"How could she be of use to them?"

"If they used her to get to me. If you lot hadn't interfered and found me. You really don't know what you've done."

"Perhaps it's time you told us, Eddie," Jordan said.

Eddie pushed his hand into his pocket and pulled out a cheap mobile phone. He handed it over.

Jordan took it, turned it so he could see the screen. "Where did this come from?"

"The box," Eddie said.

"In with the baby?"

As Eddie nodded, Jordan fired up the device. On the home screen was a picture of Molly. Her terrified face captured as the dreadful wallpaper, her eyes filled with tears.

Chapter 61

Jordan opened the messages. There wasn't much. Just one small speech bubble.

"You've had nothing since this?"

"No. I was waiting in the hut."

Jordan made a short entry into his notebook. "Constable, take this down to the digital forensic department. Have a word with DC Denn first – he's got a mate down there. Tell them what's happening. Alert them to the fact there could be more messages or even a call. What we need urgently, though, is to know where the phone was when that message was sent. Do not leave until they've agreed to prioritise it. Don't take no for an answer and don't let the phone out of your sight."

"Do you want to divert the calls, boss?"

"What?"

"In case a call or a message comes in – we can have it diverted to your phone."

"Can they do that without it showing the caller?"

"I can ask?"

"Do it. You have my number?" DC Howarth nodded and waggled his own handset as evidence. "Don't hang about – we need this done now."

"Boss." He dragged open the door and they listened to the pound of his feet as he thudded down the corridor."

"What's going to happen now?" McCardle asked.

"You just stay here. I have a call to make." Jordan left the room and dialled the number for David Griffiths. He believed the DCI was still in Spain, but he needed his help.

"Jordan, hello there. Congratulations are in order, I hear. Everyone is rather pleased with you."

"Thanks. That's all probably a bit premature, to be honest. Are you still in Spain?"

"I am. Another couple of days, I reckon, and then I'll be heading back."

"I need a favour?"

"Another straw donkey – maybe a sombrero?"

"Ha! No. Listen, are they sending someone up to collect Eddie McCardle?"

"They are. Should be on the way already."

"Can you put them off for a bit?"

"What? Why would I do that? We need him under arrest and answering our questions. I need him answering questions. The quicker we get some names from him, the quicker we can set things in motion here to wind all this up. It may seem like a jolly to you but it's not. I'm in an almost empty hotel and spending most of the time in a back room in the local nick. I'm sick of fish and tomato sandwiches and, though the local bods are nice enough, you know what it's like when you're an outsider. No, we need him in custody at St Anne Street."

"But I need him here. Molly is still missing. She's out there in the hands of a couple of vicious killers. I need him just for another couple of hours. It'll benefit all of us, trust me."

"I understand, I do. But he's going to be in custody. Any help you need you can still get even if he's down in the city. What's the problem?"

"I need him physically, here." Jordan stopped. He couldn't explain his thinking to a senior officer. He knew what he was hoping to do would be vetoed even if he let his own DCI know. Letting David Griffiths know would guarantee he'd be told it wasn't on and to find another way. There might be another way. But given the length of time it would take to organise something else, he believed he needed Eddie McCardle. In the flesh.

"Sorry, Jordan. I am. But we have to take him off your hands. We have officers here raring to go and all we need are locations and names to formalise everything. My people should be with you in the next hour."

Jordan opened the interview room door. "Thank you, Constable. I'll look after him now. Mr McCardle, would you come with me?"

"Are you sure, sir?" The bobby on door duty looked puzzled and unsure.

"Yes, it's fine. I just need Eddie here to come and have a look at some images up in the incident room."

"I'm not sure, sir. I thought S and O were collecting him." Now he looked uncomfortable.

"Really. It's fine. I'll bring him back as soon as I can. You go and grab a cup of coffee and I'll give you a buzz."

Jordan had rank and spoke with confidence and, with a glance at McCardle, watching back and forth between them, the uniformed officer decided that making a decision was above his pay grade and he'd just do as he was told.

"Come with me, Eddie. Bring your coat." As he spoke, Jordan leaned out to scan the corridor and then set off for the car park. He spoke into his phone. "Terry, has PC Howarth spoken to you?"

"Aye. I sent him down to my mate."

"Okay, meet me outside. Quick as you can. Tell your mate to speak only to you or me by phone if he needs to."

"What's going on, boss?"

"I'll tell you in the car."

Chapter 62

Jordan plipped the key for his own car. Transporting a prisoner in anything other than an approved vehicle was just going to be another black mark. But he needed something inconspicuous, and his grey Peugeot was as vanilla as they come. He put Eddie McCardle in the back and drove around to the station door to wait for Terry Denn.

By the time the DC was in and belted up they were already out in Wavertree Road. Jordan handed a page from his notebook to Terry. "Put those co-ordinates into Google Maps and get directions."

A few minutes passed in silence as Denn poked at the screen on his phone.

"We haven't got very long. Those last figures are a time and date I reckon, and we have about" – Jordan glanced at his watch – "just over an hour."

"Shit, no pressure then," Terry said.

"I've already looked to see where it is," Eddie said, "while I was waiting in the shed. You're okay heading for Everton, I reckon. You need to head towards Ormskirk. I was going to get an Uber from the allotments. I'd planned part of it out."

"Do you know Ormskirk, Terry?"

"Not really. Well, no not at all. It's out in the sticks. My mam used to go for the market. It's all farms and fields out there. Not my thing at all, boss."

"Eddie, if you've already looked. What can you tell me?"

"I just looked up the location from the coordinates. Just what you saw on the phone. I don't even know whether it's where they're staying or just where they want me to go. Well, you saw. There was nothing just those numbers."

"The only thing we can do is go there, on time, and if she's there I'll get your sister back. I don't want you trying anything funny. You stay in the car unless I tell you otherwise."

"He might be armed."

"What?"

"Mariano. He was usually armed. I can't imagine him not being."

"He won't have been able to get a gun into the country," Terry said.

Eddie McCardle gave a sarcastic snort. "Oh yeah, because they don't know how to do that, do they?"

"Is there anything else we should know?" Jordan asked.

"Well, like what?"

"It just seems to me that they are very keen to find you. As far as I can see they could find plenty of people to run the bar – Terry's brother runs one in Spain, that's right isn't it, Detective Constable?"

"Yeah. Has done for years now. Hasn't done anything cockeyed though, far as I know."

"No, I wasn't suggesting he had. It's just that there is no shortage of people looking for that sort of work in a holiday place, I shouldn't think. Then there's the money laundering. You said yourself you didn't know much about it – 'Just signed the papers' I think you said – so they didn't really need you. I'm sure they're more than capable at forging the odd scribble. Now it's all set up."

There was silence from the back of the car.

"Nothing to say, Eddie?"

"I needed money. I needed to get out from under. I wanted to move to Ireland and be free."

"So, you've what – skimmed a bit off the top? But it was your bar, that wasn't necessary," Jordan said.

"I might have given you the wrong idea about the estate agency. I'm not stupid. It wasn't difficult to direct some of the money my way. He owed me. All I'd done. All those years when he said he'd let me buy my place and he kept taking rent. Way I see it, I only took what was mine."

"But it's not how he sees it, is it? Señor Santos."

"Oh great, so this has just got a bit more complicated," Terry said. "Not only have they got his sister, and guns probably, but they are very, very annoyed with him."

Jordan glanced across the car. "Do you want out, Constable? I'm committed now, there is nothing else I can think of to do if we're to try and get Molly. But if you want out, I'll drop you at the first opportunity."

Terry stared out of the windscreen in silence for a few moments. "I'm hoping you've got some sort of a plan here, boss. My mam's going to be bloody fuming if I turn up shot."

Jordan didn't answer because winging it didn't even come close to what he was doing. All he knew was that there was a young mum in danger, and he wanted to take her home to her son.

Chapter 63

It was late afternoon, and the traffic was becoming heavier. Jordan glanced at his watch. Apart from the co-ordinates on Eddie McCardle's phone there were the current date and the numbers "17:15" which could only mean a quarter past five. Why that particular time? Maybe it was simply arbitrary. It didn't matter, he had to be at the location before then and didn't have any idea what to expect. There were just so many unknowns and his stomach clenched at the thought of what he was doing. He knew it was wrong, he should have made proper arrangements. Once he found out there could be guns, or at least a gun, involved he should have gone to DCI Cross so they could mobilise armed response teams. They should have been liaising with the West Lancashire force and the Serious and Organised team. But that would have taken time they didn't have. Mariano was expecting Eddie to be there and, if he was as unstable as McCardle said, there was no telling what would happen to Molly if he didn't show up. Jordan knew he wouldn't be able to live with the knowledge he'd had the chance to help the girl and let it go. So, he drove on.

"Terry, look on Street View. I need an idea of what sort of place we're going to?"

Thank heavens the young constable was sticking with them even though they were bending the rules past breaking point. They were putting themselves and a civilian at risk. He had to know his career could well be on the line. "Terry. I really appreciate this. I'll take full responsibility if there's any crap afterwards," Jordan said.

"Oooh, get a room you two." The comment from McCardle in the back seat didn't help.

"It's fine, boss, don't sweat it. You need to turn onto the Dunnings Bridge Road at the next roundabout. And then head for Northway. The place is on the other side of Ormskirk. I think you have to go through the town centre. Head for Burscough."

"Okay, it's signposted here. Terry, what can you tell me?" Jordan said.

"It looks like a farmhouse with cottages. I've got it now. It's a place called Hurlston Moss Farm."

"Brilliant." Jordan glanced at his watch again. "How long before we get there, does it say on the sat nav?"

"Ten minutes if we don't hit any hold-ups. But it says there are roadworks in Ormskirk," Terry said.

"Do we have to go through there?"

"Well, it doesn't look as though there's much choice."

"Alright then." They were heading up a wide dual carriageway, flat fields on either side. The traffic was busy but free flowing.

"It's okay, boss," Terry said. "If you stay on this road then when we hit Ormskirk there's a roundabout, take the second exit onto County Road – it skirts the town proper which looks like a little place with narrow streets."

Jordan glanced at his watch again, they were going to cut it fine, but the traffic was moving well, and he'd slipped into the outside lane. The road began to incline slightly and there were more houses now, rows of shops and a couple of pubs.

"The roundabout is over the top of this rise, I reckon."

As Terry spoke the traffic began to slow, it didn't take long at all before both carriageways were moving at just above a crawl.

"Bloody hell." Jordan thumped the steering wheel. "Help me out here, Terry."

They moved slowly on over the brow and down towards the town. As they hit the roundabout, everything had come to a stop and there was traffic in all directions. The second exit was completely blocked.

"Boss, take the first exit, here, turn here. Cottage Lane and then on Asmall Lane."

"How small? We don't want to be on a farm track."

"No, not a small lane, that's what it's called, Asmall Lane."

"Bloody stupid name," Jordan hissed.

Eddie McCardle had been silent for the last few minutes and Jordan glanced into the rear-view mirror. His back-seat passenger was staring forward, worry turned to real fear on his face.

The other man caught his glance. "What are you going to do? I mean, have you any idea what you're going to do? He's a psychopath this bloke, he's got his lunatic girlfriend with him. You know what he did to my mam. I mean have you even got a tazer or something?"

They hadn't.

"You just do exactly what I tell you, right." Jordan hoped his voice sounded stronger and surer than he felt.

Terry glanced across at him and raised his eyebrows. It was too late to turn back now.

Chapter 64

As they drove away from Ormskirk it began to rain. Though it wasn't yet sunset, the sky darkened; thick grey cloud lowered over the flat fields. Lights began to pop on here and there in the houses they passed. The atmosphere was charged with threat as lightning flashed in the distance. Windscreen wipers struggled against the growing deluge and Jordan's shoulders tensed as the roads went from slick to awash in minutes.

"Bloody hell, that's sudden." As he spoke Terry Denn searched for the weather forecast on his tablet. "Right, well that's handy. There's a storm coming in and they're warning about high winds."

"Are we nearly there?" Jordan asked.

"Yeah. Just up here. Turn at the next junction towards Parbold and the farm is on the right. From the Google Street View it's a converted barn on the roadside. There's a gateway just a bit further on. You might be able to pull in there."

Peering through the water streaming across the windscreen, Jordan could see the imposing barn behind a low stone wall just a few more metres along the narrow road.

He drove on and turned into a gap in the low hedge. Heavy machinery had churned up the entry to the field and the ruts were filling with rain. "Terry, you stay here with Eddie, I'm going to have a quick look. We've got about ten minutes." As he spoke his phone chirped and vibrated. "Okay, this is a transferred call from your phone, McCardle."

"We are waiting. You come into yard. Your sister is here."

"Answer him," Eddie said. "Let him know we're here. I'm going in there."

McCardle pulled at the door handle but the child lock prevented him from leaping out into the road.

"No! I told you to stay here and do as I say. We don't want him to know what's happening. Not yet. He'll be puzzled and frustrated because you haven't responded. It'll mess with his head." Jordan swivelled in the seat to glare into the rear of the car. "I'm going to see what the situation is and then we'll decide what we're going to do."

"That's my sister. He wants me. That's why you brought me, isn't it?"

"Yes, and it's my job to get us all out of this in one piece. We didn't come to negotiate, we came to get Molly. Stay here."

"Do you want me to call for backup, boss? We're pretty sure now that this is where they are and it's all a bit dodgy. Be best if we know there's help on the way, yeah?"

"Give me a few minutes. If we can sort this without going in mob-handed it's going to be safer for everyone. If I'm not back in five minutes that'll make it ten past, then bring in the troops. I'm just going to have a look."

Jordan zipped up his jacket. The pain in his back had lessened and though he still felt stiff and awkward, he could move more easily. Whether it was the effect of all the painkillers or a genuine improvement, he didn't know. It could even be adrenalin. Whatever it was he was grateful for the ease. He fished a short spade out of the boot and then turned, lowered his head against the driving rain, and crossed the road. There were no lights on in the converted barn and no car on the paved area outside the door. A narrow path down the side of the big building led to a gravelled parking area. The blue car they had searched for countrywide was pulled into the corner against the garden wall. Only one cottage in the short row showed any lights and there were no other cars in the yard.

Wiping water from his face, Jordan sprinted across the open space and, crouching below the level of the windows, he approached the third little dwelling.

Peering through the glass, he could see a small, cosy room with a couple of easy chairs and a settee grouped in front of a wood burner. In the corner there was a dining table with four seats around it. Beyond a door at the back of the room he could make out a narrow kitchen. There were clothes piled on every chair and the table was littered with takeaway boxes and dirty dishes. He could see no one. In the corner opposite to the kitchen was another door, partly open, the light spilling out into the living room.

He backed away from the front of the cottages and ran around the corner of the block, splashing through the puddles and skidding on wet stones.

There was no need to crouch as he strode along the narrow pathway at the rear of the cottages. They had no windows but all five of them had heavy, wooden, stable type doors. All were closed apart from the third one where the top part was slightly ajar. As he watched, a cloud of cigarette smoke puffed out into the rain, disappearing as soon as it hit the saturated air. After a few moments, a glowing butt was flicked onto the stone walkway landing with a tiny shower of sparks. There was a short, shouted conversation in Spanish and the top of the door slammed shut. Jordan moved closer and stood beside the cottage, listening. He could feel the thud of his heart in his chest. He had to make a judgement call. Mariano didn't know they were there, yet. So, they could wait, call for backup and trust the thugs would do nothing to hurt Molly before they had the chance to storm the cottage. Or he could act now. Bring them out into the yard to Eddie. Then, unarmed except for this short spade and with only Terry to help, they could try to bring the girl to safety themselves. The second option was obviously ridiculous and ill-advised. He would go back to the car and wait.

As he splashed his way back down the side of the terrace of cottages, his phone which was on silent, vibrated again. He dragged it from his pocket to see another re-directed message.

> *Okay. You don't even answer. Now you will no longer have a sister. This is your fault.*

His throat dried and as he pushed the phone back into his pocket a scream of terror filled his ears.

They had run out of time.

Chapter 65

Jordan scurried back, retracing his steps to stand near the corner of the row of cottages where he was hidden from view. After the scream there was nothing except for the rumbling thunder in the distance and the pound of rain on the roofs. He should let Terry know what was happening. He typed a quick SMS and slid the phone back into his pocket.

Crouching low again, he moved along the front of the terrace until he was beside cottage number three. He peered through the window, resisting the urge to wipe away the raindrops racing down the dirty glass and dripping onto the soaking paving. Water ran from his hair and into his eyes, he blinked it away.

The man who must be Mariano stood in the middle of the room. One of the dining chairs had been pulled away from the table and Molly McCardle was huddled on the seat. She was dirty and dishevelled, hunched forward with her arms wrapped around her, hair falling in a tangle over her face. Behind her, gripping one of the girl's shoulders, was Lili, the woman Eddie McCardle had described as unstable. Jordan could see no guns and wondered if Eddie had been exaggerating the threat. But Lili raised a hand which held what looked like a large kitchen knife. So, even if there were no firearms in the little house, there were weapons.

Molly was still alive. That was a huge positive. She was in distinct and immediate danger. It would be legal for him to burst in and attempt to bring her out. Jordan looked down at the spade in his hand. It seemed feeble and ridiculous now. But it was all he had and if there were no guns then he at least had the element of surprise on his side. He couldn't crouch here and do nothing.

Another transferred text message came into his phone.

It is too late now. You were warned.

He turned the spade in his hand so he could hold it just below the blade and the heavy wooden handle became a ram. With a massive yell he drew back his arms and thrust at the window. The old single glazing shattered easily, sending shards flying into the room. Before either of the thugs inside had time to react, Jordan stepped along the pathway to the front door, where he didn't waste time with the doorknob. With all the strength of his shoulders, aided by surging adrenalin, he smashed at the lock and then kicked the door open into the room.

All three of the occupants turned towards him. Molly was terrified, her mouth a shocked oval, eyes wide with fear. Lili's face twisted into an ugly sneer and Mariano looked simply angry as he swivelled towards Jordan. Molly screamed yet again as the Spaniard raised the gun that had been hidden from view in front of his body. He pointed it first towards Jordan in the corner by the door and then swung back and aimed it directly at the sobbing woman. Lili reached out and gathered a handful of Molly's hair in her fist and dragged her head back. She reached around and placed the blade of the kitchen knife against Molly's throat and then stopped to look directly at her boyfriend.

The pause seemed endless, the main sound in the cottage was the gurgle of rain in the drains. If he didn't act, then it was all over for both of them. The spade in his hand seemed precious little against an evil-looking gun and a knife at Molly's throat.

Mariano was the first to move, taking a step towards Molly and brandishing the gun. With a great shout, Jordan leaped forward, sliding his hands down the wooden handle and turning the spade. There was a startling flash of white light and a roar. Jordan thought it was the retort of the gun as it was discharged, deafening in the small space. But there was no pain, and he was still moving, surging forward swinging his makeshift weapon from side to side. There was a second flash and crash and he realised it was the storm moving through. Mariano glanced at the broken window, at the flapping curtains, the rain blowing through the gaps, running down the walls and pooling on the floor. Jordan lashed out. The blade of the spade connected with Mariano's arm, knocking the gun from his grasp and across the room where it slid to a stop under the dining table.

Lili was yelling now, words that Jordan could not understand but the meaning of them was all too clear as she pulled back her arm and lunged with the blade at Molly, still screaming on the little wooden seat.

Jordan leapt towards Molly. He kicked out at the legs of the wooden chair, knocking it from under her. She toppled sideways throwing out her arms to save herself and the blade of the knife sliced into the muscle of her bicep. She screeched again but scuttled on her hands and knees across the floor. He stepped over her to where Lili still held the blood-stained blade. He lifted the spade high above his head and brought it down onto the hands holding the knife. He heard the crack as something broke in her arms or wrists and she bellowed in pain. The knife slid across the wooden floor towards where Molly knelt sobbing, her hand pressed against the gash in her arm, blood gushing through her fingers.

"Get out, Molly, run." Jordan's yell was lost in another crash of thunder and anyway the girl was too terrified to react, shocked into a stupor on the cottage floor.

"Molly, run. Eddie is outside waiting for you." He tried again and she raised her eyes to look at him.

Lili was curled into a ball in the corner groaning and rocking back and forth, broken hands curled in towards her chest.

Jordan turned to face Mariano. The big man had taken up a fighter's pose, legs bent, and fists clenched. He snorted through his nose and jinked from side to side. His quick glances to the space under the table told Jordan just what he had in mind. With the spade held across the front of his body he stepped forward. From the corner of his eye he could see Molly was crab walking towards the door, sobbing and gulping but still moving and at least heading in the right direction.

Mariano wanted the gun. Jordan very much didn't want him to have it. They faced off stepping side to side. If he could hold him long enough Molly would have a chance to get away. One problem removed.

Jordan heard Lili shifting in the corner, she was behind him. This wasn't good. He stepped backwards towards the centre of the room. He could see them both now, but he was further away from the table and the gun that lay beneath it.

Molly dragged herself up grabbing at the door frame and managing to stand. She half fell, half stepped out into the rain, crying out for her brother. Mariano turned quickly, she was his prize, he didn't want to lose her. It was only a moment of distraction, but it was enough. Jordan pulled back his arms stretched high and swung the spade, aiming it directly at the other man's head.

The noise was sickening – a cross between a thud and an odd squelch. Mariano crumpled to the floor. Lili screamed but quieted quickly when Jordan turned towards her. "Stay there. Just stay there," he said.

He reached his foot under the table and hooked the gun towards himself. He bent and retrieved the knife, juggling both weapons in one hand. He flung them out into the rain and staggered from the room pulling the door closed after him. Terry appeared around the corner. Molly was nowhere in sight.

"Boss, you alright, boss?"

"Molly?" Jordan managed to gasp.

"She's over in the car. Eddie is seeing to her. She's bleeding all over your seats."

"Okay, good." Jordan felt his knees begin to wobble. The adrenalin that had seen him through the last few long minutes ebbed and he leaned against the soaking wall of the little cottage. He took in a couple of deep breaths and then turned to peer inside through the broken window. Mariano was still in a heap on the floor, a worrying pool of blood spreading from under his head. Lili had crawled across and sat beside him keening.

"The troops are on the way, boss. Are you okay, are you actually hurt?"

"Yeah. I'm okay – I just need to sit down for a minute." As he spoke the world turned grey at the edges and Terry ran towards him his arms outstretched as Jordan slid down the wall to sit in a puddle of gritty, grey water on the step of the little cottage. He lowered his head towards his knees as much as his injured back would allow and listened to the scream of sirens growing in the distance.

Chapter 66

The road was closed off with crime scene tape. Blue and white cars were pulled across the junction and the place was thronged with first responders. Molly had been bandaged and stretchered to the back of a waiting ambulance. She had begged for Eddie to be allowed to go with her but there was no way it could happen. In fact, he was in the back of a squad car wearing handcuffs and a worried expression.

Jordan had repeated his rights and they were taking him directly to St Anne Street to be questioned by the Serious and Organised crime team. They were puzzled about the delay and diversion but just happy they would have him before the day was out. Yes, if he was being honest with himself Jordan felt bad, as if he'd misled McCardle. But he was a criminal when all was said and done and now, he would face the consequences of his actions. His mother was dead, and Jordan couldn't imagine how he would ever find peace with the idea that he had been to blame.

In the cottage, they were patching up Lili and her damaged hands and Mariano was hooked up to infusions, laid on a back board with a cervical collar protecting his neck. He was still unconscious and the doctor who had accompanied the ambulances had been non-committal about his condition. Jordan had looked for reassurance that the injuries were not life-threatening, but none had been forthcoming.

Jordan was bruised and battered. The pain in his back had returned but he didn't think it was quite as bad. Of course, it could all be relative, there were so many other aches and pains they were melding into one big whole.

"What do you want to do, boss?" Terry asked. "I can take you home if you like and then grab a taxi back to the station. Or I could take you down the ozzy, like."

"No, no hospital. I'm okay. I reckon I'll feel it in the morning, but I don't think there's anything too bad. I need to get back to the station anyway. There's a hell of a lot of clearing up to do. Then there's Gary and Jakey, we need to get them reunited with Molly."

"It's okay. I've sent a car for them. They'll go straight to The Royal, that's where they're taking her. I've been in touch with Ros and she's dealing with it all. She'll go with them and then I've organised some uniforms to take over so she can go off shift. They're taking these two losers to Aintree, though the doc thought the bloke will end up in Wizzy Ozzy."

"Where?" Jordan said.

"Sorry, boss. Whiston Hospital. With the head injuries specialists. We don't want them all in the same place, I don't reckon. Is that okay?"

"It's more than okay, Terry. You've done a great job. Well done. I'll see the people that need to know are aware."

"Oh, don't bother about that. The main thing is we're sorting this out."

"No, come on – you want to get your promotion, don't you?"

"Well yes. But…"

"It all helps. Anyway, it might take some of the heat out of the fact that you helped me to bring Eddie McCardle here. We both know that wasn't strictly kosher now, was it?"

"Well, when you put it like that."

"Okay let's get going. I have to ring David Griffiths in Spain and let him know what's happened. I reckon it'll make a difference to his actions over there and you know what, I could murder a cup of coffee and a bun."

"We'll stop on the way and get some Krispy Kremes. I reckon we could do with a treat."

"Okay. But don't tell the wife. She'll have me on lettuce for a fortnight."

The hammering on the car window was sharp and annoyed. An elderly man in a green waxed jacket and flat cap was leaning down thumping on the glass.

"Can I help you, sir?" Jordan asked.

"You DI Carr?"

"Yes, and, you are?"

"Brian Swettenham. This is my home." He waved a hand in the direction of the converted barn. "Just exactly what is going on here? I was told you're the chap in charge."

Jordan swung his legs painfully out into the drizzling rain. "Yes, that's right, sir." He pushed himself upright, biting back the gasp of pain as his back objected to the movement.

"Well, just what have you done? I go away for a few days and come back to this... mayhem. This absolute chaos."

"Your tenants, guests – whatever you want to call them. The people in the middle cottage. We have had to arrest them in connection with very serious crimes. I am sorry, sir."

"What guests? Which cottage? We're closed. We open in two days. What the hell are you talking about, man?"

"Ah. Well, in that case you may want to bring charges of breaking and entering. But I'll be honest, you might well have to wait for a while. As for opening, I think you may have to reschedule."

"This is not good enough. This is atrocious. I have never heard anything so ridiculous in all my life. Not open – what do you mean, not open? We have a living to earn here. No, I'm not having this. I'll have you know that DCI Cross is a close personal friend, and I shall be speaking to him in very short order. There had better be no damage to my property, Detective Inspector, or heads will roll. You can be sure of that."

Jordan sighed and closed his eyes, letting the cool rain wash across his face as Brian Swettenham ranted at him.

Chapter 67

Jordan tried to remember how many painkillers he'd taken and how long it was since the last dose. He couldn't. So, there were to be no more today. There was paperwork to do but in fairness a lot of that could wait. The incident room was lively, but it was mostly just high spirits. The staff in here hadn't been there at the end, but the job was done, and Molly was safe. The bad guys – at least a couple of them – were on their way to hospital and Eddie was on his way to St Anne Street and almost certainly a long time in prison.

Jordan was just tired. He ached all over and he was still processing the last few hours, trying to compartmentalise all that had happened. He had been here before and accepted it would take time. Writing up the reports, though it could be tedious, would help because they had to be factual and lacking in emotion.

Terry brought him a mug of coffee and one of the doughnuts from the huge boxes they'd bought. "You okay, boss? You look pretty done in, to be honest."

"I'm fine. It's late, you should get off home."

"Well, a few of us are going out for a bevvy, just to wind down, like. Are you coming?" It was clear by his expression that he knew the answer would be no.

"I think I'll just finish the essentials and head off home. We'll have a few drinks, though, maybe tomorrow; my shout." It was expected and he knew that when it happened, he'd enjoy it, but not right then with the images in his mind still so very fresh.

"Have you spoken to DCI Griffiths?"

"No, I've tried a few times, but his phone goes directly to voice mail. I'll call him from home. There's only an hour time difference so maybe he's out eating or something. Did Gary get to the hospital okay?"

"Yes, I facetimed Rosalind Searle. She said it was very emotional – 'lovely' was the term she used. Molly has to have some surgery on her arm but it's not too serious and they don't think there's permanent damage. Have you heard from DCI Cross, boss?"

"No, not yet. I had a message to say he was coming in. That's why I'm still here, to be honest. I could do most of this other stuff from home. Hopefully, it won't be too long."

As he spoke the internal phone rang and Terry raised his eyebrows. "Good luck, boss. That bloke, the nutter ranting afterwards, was well out of order. I don't see there'll be any repercussions because of that. Although his cottage was pretty bashed about."

"He was probably all bluster. If I had a pound for every pissed off punter who supposedly knew the Chief Constable, I'd be retired. Anyway, I'll go down and speak to DCI Cross and then I'm heading home. Have a good night. See you in the morning."

He hoped for recognition of what they'd accomplished. It would be nice to have congratulations and a pat on the back. What he didn't expect was anger.

He wasn't invited to sit down, and Cross paced back and forth behind his desk. "What the hell did you think you were doing, Carr?"

"Sorry, sir?"

"Rules, Carr, rules. They are there for a reason. They apply to everyone, including you, believe it or not. What possessed you to take a prisoner out to a potential crime scene? In what universe did you think that was acceptable? Why the bejesus did you think it was okay to go off, take a junior ranking officer with you and play bloody superheroes – smashing up people's property, destroying buildings?"

"Sir, I had to act quickly. I made a judgement call. I know I was sailing a bit close to the wind but... in the end..."

"No, let me stop you there. I have just had a very uncomfortable conversation with one of the senior members of my lodge. He is not happy, not happy at all. Thousands of pounds of damage to his holiday cottage, loss of revenue from cancelled rentals. There was no need. If you had stuck to the rules, if you had gone about this in a calm and orderly manner, we could have had these miscreants arrested calmly. Brought them in for questioning in the usual way."

"You do know, sir, that they were holding Molly McCardle captive? I had reason to believe she was in imminent danger. I had to go out there, I had to get her to safety."

"We do not negotiate with kidnappers. You know this, DI Carr, it is not the way we do things. There will be an enquiry. You will be suspended until further notice. You are not some TV action man able to go off on an unapproved jaunt just whenever you feel like it. We have to look at DC Denn's part in this as well."

"He was acting under orders, sir. I take full responsibility. DC Denn only did what I told him to do and he performed outstandingly in the event. I cannot commend him highly enough. I don't think what I did could be described as negotiating, sir."

"Are you trying to be clever?"

"No, sir. Of course not."

"Well, your commendation for DC Denn is pretty weak under the circumstances and this is not going to play well, not at all. Go home, DI Carr, and wait for further instructions."

Jordan turned and stomped from the office. He didn't close the door but walked the corridor towards the car park still tamping down the sense of unfairness, the anger at the narrow view taken by Cross. It would be okay. It had to be. Not the pat on the back he could have hoped for, but he knew he had done the right thing. The best thing for Molly and Jakey, and his conscience was clear.

"Brilliant, mate. Absolutely brilliant." Jordan had barely had time to press the answer button on his phone before David Griffiths' voiced yelled out, so loud that it was distorted by the tiny speaker.

"I've been trying to call you," Jordan said.

"Yes, yes I saw that. I was a bit tied up. Still am, actually, mopping up over here it's all a bit hectic but I wanted to call you to say well done and thanks. Once we got word that Molly was safe and the thug Mariano was in custody and Eddie in an interview room and spilling his guts about it all… well, it cleared the way for us to go in all guns blazing as it were. Not literally, but pretty heavy anyway."

"That was quick though. I mean it's only been a few hours."

"Yeah, well, we'd been working towards it of course, but the news about your work over there cleared the final hurdles for us. There're arrests being made on that side of the Channel as well. You'll see it on the news before the day's out, no doubt. Well done."

"Oh right. Thanks."

"I bet you're the golden boy right now, eh?"

"Well, I wouldn't say that exactly."

"Oh. Ah well, you are with my lot anyway. Listen, I'll be back in the UK in a day or two. You have to let me take you out, yeah. You and your lovely wife. This is excellent stuff, Jordan. Listen, pass on my thanks to your people as well, won't you? And, if ever I can do anything for you, just let me know. Got to go now, I've got banditos to interview."

"Right, well, thanks for the call."

And suddenly it was bright again. Okay, there were questions to answer and probably a couple of black marks on his record but, at the end of the day, the bad guys were caught, and the evil had been stopped. Only for a while, he acknowledged, and they would never win the war, but they had been victorious in another little battle and for now that was enough.

Chapter 68

Still smarting from the Cross interview but cheered by the other news, Jordan's nerves were jangling. He needed to calm down and soothe his spirits before he went home to Penny. He glanced at his watch. It was late but not too late for a hospital. They'd be quieter than during the day, but they never slept, and it would help to draw a line under it all.

It was only about ten minutes if he went straight there but he turned right and headed east along Wavertree Road. He drove along the quiet route to the building site where Mary McCardle had been found. He pulled in alongside the deserted bit of land. The little muddy pond in the corner had overflowed and the pathways were trails of mud. The patch of grass was completely indiscernible from the rest of it. All of the flowers and candles were gone, although there was a sad piece of sodden ribbon flapping on one of the railings. He could hear a train in the distance and cars swished by on the roads, but nobody stood in vigil and there was nothing now to witness what had been done there or what it had led to. He turned away and drove back to the main road and down into the city and the hospital.

There was a security guard on the door, but Jordan's warrant card cleared his way and the volunteer managing the reception desk was glad of something to do. "She's been moved to minor surgery." He gave Jordan directions and showed him on a plan. The walk along almost deserted corridors in the subdued night-time lighting was calming in itself and by the time he had arrived at the ward door he was in control again.

There was a uniformed officer, bored and tired on a straight chair outside the ward door.

"Is she alone?" Jordan asked.

"No, her brother is in there and the baby. They've never left. Well, apart from him going out for a fag break a couple of times. She's having an operation tomorrow and then they reckon she'll be able to be discharged."

"Excellent. I'll just pop in and say hello."

The baby was asleep on the side of the narrow hospital bed, but Molly's uninjured arm was wrapped around him holding him safe. Gary was asleep in a low easy chair but as Jordan walked in, Molly looked up and smiled.

"Hello. You're him, aren't you? You're the one who came to get me. Sorry, I should know your name, but I can't remember it, from before at the house. I was a bit of a cow, wasn't I? At first. Sorry."

"It's okay, you had a lot on your plate. How are you feeling?"

"I'm okay. A bit sore and I can't close my eyes. When I do, I'm back there, in that cottage, with those people." As she spoke her eyes filled with tears and she reached painfully for the tissues on her bedtable.

"Here, let me." Jordan pulled one out and handed it to her. "Don't get upset. You're safe now. It's over."

"I don't know how to thank you. I didn't think they'd let me go. I didn't think I'd ever see Jakey again. When they took him away I thought I'd die. I didn't want him, not when I first got pregnant. Mam was so angry and ashamed. I thought my life was pretty much over. No more parties, no more going out on the lash. But when I thought I'd never see him again – I couldn't bear it."

"Hey, come on. Don't do that. Don't torment yourself."

"No, you're right. He's okay and that's all that matters. What's happened to Eddie?"

Jordan pulled one of the plastic visitors chairs up beside the bed. "Well, he's in trouble, no point pretending. He's probably going to jail. I can't give you much information yet, they are still questioning him. We'll just have to wait and see."

"What has he done? I mean he wasn't anything to do with what happened to me, was he?"

Jordan didn't know how to tell her that her brother had not only been the reason for her own kidnapping but for the death of their mother as well. "Listen, you don't want to be worrying about that now. When you get home, someone will come and take a statement from you, maybe more than once and you will probably have to go to court. I'm sorry but it's just the way it is. There's plenty of time and it'll all make sense eventually."

"If Eddie was involved. If he was the reason for me and Jakey being in danger like that then I'll give evidence and you can lock him up and throw away the key. That's not what you do. You don't hurt your family. At the end of the day that's all we have. Each other. Now, there's just me and Jakey and Gary. Sandra's going off somewhere, she's marrying Brian – doesn't want to be a McCardle anymore. You can't blame her, can you? But it's okay, she's worked hard to get away."

"Will you be okay?"

"Yeah. Gary's going to move back to the house for now and then – later – when everything's all sorted, we're going to Australia. Well, I mean we're going to try. There might be problems with their rules. But, if that doesn't work, we'll go somewhere else, anywhere really. No point in staying here now. We'll go and start again. Properly. Not like Dada and Mam – new but not really new. Still tied to the old country, the old problems. No, we'll go right away and be something different. It'll be good."

Gary snorted in his sleep and Jordan and Molly smiled at each other.

"Come and see me again, won't you? I'd like that."

"I will. Yes, you and Jakey, when you're better."

"Cool."

As he left and wandered out into the deserted city streets, Jordan was perfectly happy with the way he had acted. Okay, they were going to investigate what he'd done. Maybe there'd be some sort of comeuppance, but it didn't matter. Molly was safe with the baby. Some bad guys were locked up and he could go home, take a long hot bath, and go to bed with his wife. He smiled as he walked back to the car.

Penny was asleep when Jordan arrived home. He undressed in the bathroom and settled for a long shower instead of the bath. He wasn't sure he'd be able to clamber out once he was in there and he didn't want to have to call for help.

The night light in Harry's room was the only illumination as he walked across the landing. He stepped into the nursery and tiptoed to his son's cot. He knew he shouldn't do it and might regret it, but he leaned down and gathered the sleeping baby in his arms.

He sat in the rocking chair and breathed in the warm, baby smell and felt the precious weight against his chest. Harry didn't waken, so Jordan sat quietly with him, watching the tick of a pulse in his neck. He was overwhelmed.

Penny was quiet until he was suddenly aware of her standing beside him. He felt the touch of her hand on his hair. "Are you alright? What's wrong?" she whispered.

"Nothing, it's okay. I just wanted to hold him." He adjusted his embrace on the baby so he could wrap a hand around his wife's waist.

"I'm sorry I haven't been here very much lately."

"It's alright, love. I understand."

"You are my life, you and Harry. You do know that, don't you?"

She leaned down and kissed him on the cheek. "Of course. But come to bed. You're exhausted and I see you have some bruises. You'll need to explain those in the morning. But for now, just put him back and come on with me."

The End

List of characters

Detective Inspector Jordan Carr – Jamaican heritage. Eldest son in a family of five children. Married to Penny. They have one baby, Harry, whom he dotes on.

Elizabeth (Lizzie) – Penny's sister.

Detective Chief Inspector Richard Cross – Late fifties. Impatient, overweight and short tempered.

Detective Constable Terry Denn – Mid-twenties. Red-haired Scouser.

Sergeant Vivienne Bailey – SOCO team. In a relationship with Rebecca.

Detective Constable Rosalind Searle – Newly passed the detective exam.

Beverly Powell – civilian collator.

Phyllis (Phil) Grant – medical examiner.

Constable Geoff Howarth

Gary McCardle

Molly McCardle

Mary McCardle (Mam)

Sandra McCardle

Eddie McCardle

Doug Crawley – crime scene manager.

David Griffiths – Inspector with Serious and Organised Crime.

Nana Gloria – Jordan's granny in London.

Señor Neron Santos – owner of trucking company and Mr Big.

Mariano – Spanish thug.

Liliano (Lili) – Spanish thug.

If you enjoyed this book, please let others know by leaving a quick review on Amazon. Also, if you spot anything untoward in the paperback, get in touch. We strive for the best quality and appreciate reader feedback.

editor@thebookfolks.com

www.thebookfolks.com

Also by Diane Dickson:

BODY ON THE SHORE (Book 1)
BODY OUT OF PLACE (Book 3)
BODY IN THE SQUAT (Book 4)
BODY IN THE CANAL (Book 5)
BODY ON THE ESTATE (Book 6)

BURNING GREED
BRUTAL PURSUIT
BRAZEN ESCAPE
BRUTAL PURSUIT
BLURRED LINES

TWIST OF TRUTH
TANGLED TRUTH
BONE BABY
LEAVING GEORGE
WHO FOLLOWS
THE GRAVE
PICTURES OF YOU
LAYERS OF LIES
DEPTHS OF DECEPTION
YOU'RE DEAD
SINGLE TO EDINBURGH
HOPELESS

The next book in this series:

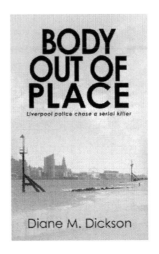

BODY
OUT OF
PLACE

Liverpool police chase a serial killer

Diane M. Dickson

Disturbed by wildlife, a body is discovered shallowly
buried in another person's grave. Initially dismissing a
murder, when a similar incident comes to light the police
realise they have a serious problem on their hands. One of
the serial killer variety. But with no clues, what hope does
DI Carr have of catching him?

Also of interest:

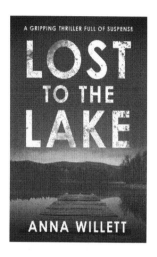

White Mist Lake Retreat is the perfect place for a couple's getaway. Yet Beth and Marty Jacobsen are grappling with more than marital problems. Having survived a home invasion, Beth is desperate to put their life back on track. Desperate enough to agree to do the unthinkable for the man she loves.

Printed in Great Britain
by Amazon

35136561R00157